Jam by the

L M Eason

Copyright © 2020 Lee M Eason

KINDLE Edition

All rights reserved, including the right to reproduce this book, or portions thereof in any form. No part of this text may be reproduced, transmitted, downloaded, decompiled, reverse engineered, or stored, in any form or introduced into any information storage and retrieval system, in any form or by any means, whether electronic or mechanical without the express written permission of the author.

This is a work of fiction. Names and characters are the product of the author's imagination and any resemblance to actual persons, living or dead, is entirely coincidental.

The views expressed in this work are solely those of the author and do not necessarily reflect the views of the publisher, and the publisher hereby disclaims any responsibility for them.

Lee M Eason

leemeason@icloud.com

Chapter 1

A Small Item…

A year ago, a walk home in the summer sun wouldn't have registered. Stress, guilt and too many other things would have been vying for her attention. How different she felt now, a work in progress, she had to admit, but getting there. Blue sky, sunshine and no dark clouds on any horizon, nothing and no one to spoil her thoughts. She took the long route back from the station, wanting to make the most of the light and the warmth. A quick stop at the local supermarket for milk and then down no railings avenue and on to long terrace. She passed the mixture of Victorian houses, cafes and shops and stopped at one.

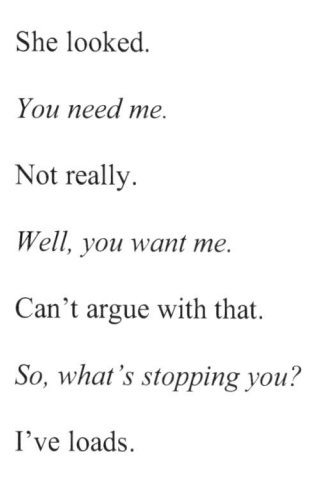

Hello.

She looked.

You need me.

Not really.

Well, you want me.

Can't argue with that.

So, what's stopping you?

I've loads.

Not like me.

True.

I'm red, they're not. I'm funky, they aren't. You need to be funkier.

I've never wanted to be funky.

Okay, okay, stylish in an individual sort of way.

She looked at the bag. It was nice, it was different.

I am.

It had caught her attention every day since its arrival in the window. Each time she'd talked herself out of it. If it was gone tomorrow, she knew she'd regret it.

Result.

She went in and bought it. A dark red leather handbag. Of course, at some point there would have to be shoes. What was it about a new purchase that made you feel this way? That little thrill. Endorphins?

With the new bag in a bag, she continued her way home. The cafes were busy, good weather bringing everyone out after work. Long terrace was alive and bright and cheerful. A glass of wine, a sit down and a good old gossip. The first two were at hand, the chat bit wasn't. Still Billy no Mates.

Ahead, she noticed the bin, only because it was odd to see one left out. It sat, waiting patiently, ready to be pulled back into its home. The inside was empty from the morning's collection. It was a bin lid, of all things, that had brought her here. It seemed as ridiculous as it sounded petty. But it had been the final straw that broke the camel's back, the last drop that makes the cup run over, a tipping point, but ultimately nothing more, or less, than an open bin lid. She gave it a wry smile as she passed.

She could walk this route without thought, in fact she'd been lost in her thoughts on several occasions only realising, once she'd climbed the flat's steps, that she was home and had no clear recollection of her getting there. If someone had asked for directions, she wouldn't have had a clue about street names. She knew them from the ones she'd given them. Becca passed grey tower church, continued along the side of the little green and then onto her road. It was a long one that ended at the park, tree lined and now dappled with shade. Her flat was one of six in a recently converted Edwardian villa, or was it Victorian? On reaching the top of the steps she even got the right key for the main door, opened it, noticed the flooring was done and checked her mailbox. There was a bundle of letters and junk; nothing exciting. Taking them, she closed the flap and jiggled her key out. She paused, no new smell of paint, they must have finally finished everything. Once in through her front door, she put down her bag, put her keys, the mail and new purchase on the hall table and checked her phone, no messages. The stillness was lovely. Not a sound, just her, that blissful moment of perfect peace, work done, journey home complete. She took off her coat and again walked past the small stack of pictures and the box. There were a lot of other boxes she'd not unpacked, but these hadn't made it any further into her flat than the hallway. They didn't belong, but she wasn't ready to throw them out.

She made tea and took it and two biscuits into the front room, if she took the packet, she'd be halfway through it before the tea was gone.

***

Great, the right key again, larger one for the front door, smaller one for her door. Why had it taken her so long to get that simple difference in her head? It was like her mobile number; she'd had it years, but only recently been able to remember it. She checked her mailbox, the simple action once again free from the feeling of unease. She glanced at the tall window that lit the communal entrance and stairs. Still no sign of the other inhabitants, other than...

There it was, it had been there yesterday and it was still there today. Becca looked at it with a mixture of intrigue and suspicion. Had a builder left it? Was it meant to be there? The windowsill was an odd place to put it. Maybe it was a prank, a joke, or simply forgotten. At least she hadn't started talking to it. Yet.

The next day it was still there...

The day after it was gone.

Chapter 2

Chewing...

It was all still a novelty, but looking about her at the other people on the train, she might have been the only one thinking the journey home was something new and exciting. No eye contact, no smiles, just focused on personal space or deep in thought. She wondered how long it would be before she was just the same and getting home was just another inconvenience. But for now, she wasn't going to close off the world with earplugs or hide behind a newspaper, or stare at her feet. To some extent she'd done all of that. A job she'd grown to hate, that along with everything else had made her miserable, made her shrink inside herself and put up barriers to keep people at arm's length. Odd looking back. It all seemed so distant now. She was loving a new job, living somewhere completely different and enjoying her own company. The people at work were nice, but she didn't socialise away from it. Talk would be about work and there was only so much time you could spend with the same people. Everyone seemed to get on and a small group often went out for drinks straight after work, which often led to a meal. She'd been asked, but made her excuses. She wanted to keep a good life-work balance, for a change. She kept the words in that new order after her boss had said it that way. She'd always talked about trying to keep a good work-life balance and been pretty good at it. He'd swapped the two words round and daft as it seemed, the phrase took on new meaning, emphasising the correct priority. So, away from work, it was just her and she was okay with that. She was still exploring, finding her way round and enjoying it. She'd always enjoyed her own company, and she didn't need anyone else right now, certainly not family. Right now, uncomplicated and simple was good.

Her face must have been doing that thing it did, because a man several seats down was looking. She had noticed him on the platform, he'd stood out in the crowds for obvious reasons. She'd stopped herself from staring, and now he was. Probably wondering just what on earth was on her mind. She could so easily get stuck chewing on the past, having a discussion with herself, so into the thoughts that her jaw or lips would start moving and her face would begin to reflect the emotions of that inner conversation. She hadn't known she did it until her sister had pointed it out, again and again and again,

You're chewing, Becca, do stop it.

She tried to keep a check on that, but sometimes she got so caught up in it all, that it happened. Here she was doing it again, so obviously that a stranger had noticed. The man smiled and then went back to his magazine. She felt foolish, but the smile hadn't been condescending. Whatever his thoughts, he was a stranger on the train, someone she wouldn't see again.

In the world beyond the train, the sun was shining; she'd been inside all day, it was nice to be out. Becca left the station and headed for the high street. She had two things to do on her way back. One was to buy jeans, the other was a food shop.

The jeans were available in her size, so that was a plus, normally there'd be any size but. The shop was quiet and the changing rooms empty, which she liked because she could have her pick of the cubicles. One with a mirror opposite. She could never get far enough away from the cubicle's mirror to get a proper view. With one outside she could fling back the curtain and check her front and back from a decent distance.

Curtain closed, she put down her bag and hung her coat. Was it only her that felt suddenly calm in a cubicle, so private after the busy streets and shops, a little box of breathing space? Work skirt off she clambered into the jeans, glad the curtain ensured no one saw that. God, they were tight, but would stretch with wear. Breath in, button fastened and then she looked in the mirror. Oh, god, what was it about changing room lights? There was obviously a reason why they had to be over head, but really? She called them saggy droop lights, because they lit everything from the worst angle. The one place where you'd think they'd want you to look great and you didn't. The bathroom mirror was much kinder, she looked fine in that. Even when she got out of the shower, everything looked okay, not fantastic, but okay. Bra and pants usually spoilt the look, even though they were the right fit, lifting and pushing up the bits she wanted, but gathering the bits she didn't, a mixture of lift and separate, divide and conquer, haul in and bulge out. Clothes over the top of all that, she was happy with herself. People would say, oh stop complaining, but in front of the mirror, in bra and pants she knew otherwise, it was all a matter of personal comfort and perspective. And from where she stood now, in front of this mirror and under that light, the perspective was off. She opened the curtain, backed up to the mirror and looked into the one on the opposite wall. Almost flat against the cubicle mirror, she was out from under the light and turned and stood in various positions to check everything fitted where it should. Normally they'd fit her bum, but not her thighs, or if that was okay, they were too short or too long. These looked okay, she pulled a semi-content face and decided they were a purchase and wondered if she should buy two pairs, because they actually fitted her well. Now all she had to do, was get out of them. An amount of gymnastic hopping followed, red faced from her effort and overheated from the light, she settled herself back into her work skirt and checked everything was tucked in and zipped up before heading to pay.

Leaving the shop, she made for the supermarket. She was going to try one big shop for the week, her flat wasn't too far away and she thought she could manage three carrier backs. She ambled round the aisles, picking this and that, trying to think of meals through the week. She resisted the urge to run off with a trolley left blocking the aisles, while its owner was focused on the intricacies of sausage buying. As she scanned her purchases, she felt pleased with how healthy they looked, of course when it came to it, she wouldn't fancy any of them and they'd sit in the freezer.

Her road was a nice one, it had a pleasant feel to it. Calm, welcoming, unbusy and turning the corner onto it always felt like she was on the last leg of the journey and had just entered the homeward straight. Passing the first of the trees felt like entering a gateway, a portal into a familiar, quiet and peaceful land. It still made her smile; knowing she was minutes away from the comfort and general niceness of her flat. She opened the front door into the communal area, put the carrier bags down and rubbed at her numb fingers before checking her mailbox, more junk. She was about to open her door and drag the shopping in when she noticed it was back. No, it wasn't the same one. It was a different one. She looked at it.

"Yep, jam."

The voice from behind made her jump. She spun round faster than she had intended. Oh, god it was the man from the train.

"It's a jar of jam, they keep appearing, I keep taking them," he explained pleasantly, with a slight incline of his head towards the object of her attention.

She knew what it was, had taken note of its comings and goings. She'd lost her tongue, typical. The first time she'd met someone from her flats and he'd seen her chewing on old thoughts. And here he was all pleasantness and easy confidence and with that hair, even when the wind had tugged at it, it still looked good. She wondered what hers was doing, but resisted the urge to pat it down.

"Nice to meet someone," he pushed his specs back up his nose. "I think I'm above you. Hopefully catch you again. I've got to run, or I'll be late."

"Okay, see you around," she attempted the same air of quiet confidence and casual something or other.

He was bounding up the stairs with his perfect hair, and his confidence and the jam. And here she was watching him, windblown, still wondering at the comings and goings of a preserve.

She shut the door behind her. So, the jam mystery was probably solved, it was the man with the hair, the man who'd seen her chewing. The stranger on the train she was never going to see again, lived right above her.

She dropped her bag, put her keys and post on the hall table, checked her phone, no messages, hung her coat, kicked off her shoes and headed for the kitchen. Noticing, yet again, the stack of pictures and the box. One of these days she'd get round to them. One of these days she'd decorate and unpack properly. In a practised ballet of moves, that started every evening, she made tea, let it brew while she took two biscuits and as always considered taking the whole pack and crunching and dunking and eating them all, but will power prevailed. She poured the tea into the first mug she came across and left the biscuits before she could change her mind. Flopping onto the sofa, she paused, nothing other than the tick of the clock, no loud noises, no one moving, just stillness and peace. It was the one moment in every day that was entirely hers. However, it was just that, a moment and as usual it passed all too quickly and the thoughts of the day seeped in and along with them the man with the hair and the jam. What would she say the next time they met? She had to redeem herself, the chewing had been an embarrassment. She didn't want to seem that interested, because then he might think she was coming onto him and that would be a real disaster. He was too good looking. She had to admit that, very good looking and probably arrogant. She found handsome men or beautiful women were often conceited. Used to getting their own way because it was easy to fall under the spell of their physical perfection. It happened, she'd done it herself and seen it in action. Stood in a queue in a card shop an average man had bought a card, he was polite, well dressed, but average looking and was all but ignored by the counter assistant. His polite custom earned him the privilege of paying for the card, no eye contact and a grunt. The next woman had received the same bland service. But the next man, the tanned god had been the recipient of very different treatment. Smiles, (showing every tooth), eye contact, coyness, you're welcome, leaning over the counter, what a good choice, smiles, eye contact, more smiles. He had treated it with indifference, he was apparently used to it and possibly quite oblivious to this special behaviour. Then it had been Becca's turn. No eye contact and a grunt.

Yes, hair man was good looking enough to be one of those, all they had to do was exist and the world swooned to their every need. She caught herself, probably chewing again. She was making assumptions, sorting this man into a box; that was another habit. She could hear her mother.

You never change. It's embarrassing.

She'd left all that behind and moved away, but somehow, the baggage had followed her. A colleague had said it once, I ran away, but I couldn't run away from myself. The woman had been right, new place, new life but the same Becca. Time for more tea. She went to the kitchen and reached into the fridge. No milk, she shook the bottle as if it would make some magically appear. As nice as it was outside, she didn't fancy venturing back to the supermarket, it was at that point she remembered the bags of shopping she'd left in the entrance hall.

***

She didn't bump into hair man the next day or the next, not on the train, or in the entrance hall, but the jam was back. Hair man's jam, or rather the jam he was taking. Not the same jam. The jar was different, because this time she'd picked it up. It was a little jar, the type of jam jar for single people. Wading your way to the bottom of the average jar of jam became a bore. It was cute and had a bit of brown paper covering the lid, held on with twine. It looked homemade and made her think of her aunty Irene. She was quite caught up in the moment and only just managed to put it down and scarper for her door when she heard keys in the front door. For the life of her she couldn't think why she'd scrambled, acting like a child caught nosing where it shouldn't. It made her laugh at the immature silliness of it. It was a nice feeling.

The next day, the jam was still there. It looked rustic, somehow authentic. It looked like a handcrafted thing should look. Certainly not a hair man thing, the suit he'd been wearing said as much. Brown paper and twine wasn't his style. He would be more brushed steel lid, designer jar, printed label in a trendy font. She put the jar down, checked her mailbox and stepped over to her flat. Just as she closed the door, she heard the one above open and footsteps descending the wooden stairs. Before she could stop herself, her eye was clamped to the spy hole. The shape passed. It was hair man, but she couldn't see if he'd helped himself to the jam. She watched him leave and then turned from the spy hole. So, it was official, she'd turned into the neighbourhood nosey parker. All she needed now were net curtains to twitch. She dropped her bag, checked her phone, hung her coat, kicked off her shoes and headed for the kitchen. Leaving the spy hole to keep an eye on the stairway. She shook her head, I need to get a life, I really do.

It was one of those nights when she couldn't settle to anything. She went through her film collection. No, maybe, no, no, maybe, no, no. She worked through two drawers and found nothing. Even the maybes failed in their attempt to get on screen. In the end she put on the TV and watched a film she'd seen before, complete with adverts that ranged from patronising to naff. She sat through it all, phone in her hand switching from it to the TV, neither sufficiently interesting to claim her full attention. Eventually, she put the phone down with a sigh of boredom. She should do something worthwhile, but frankly couldn't be pestered. So, she went to the kitchen and put the kettle on and stared at the treats cupboard. Most people, it seemed had a treat jar or a biscuit barrel. She had a cupboard, in her defence it was a half-cupboard, one of those slim ones next to the huge one tucked in a corner. The top shelf was full of mugs so it wasn't even a whole half-cupboard, but what space there was, was crammed with a jumble of things she'd bought and things she'd been given. She did have will power, a lot of it, but this was a dangerous moment. Boredom was easy to fill with eating, biscuits, cakes and chocolate, especially if you had a cup of tea or coffee. Things like that just seemed to disappear in her hand. Becca was generally good at keeping on top of what she ate, but she did enjoy food and when her jeans said,

hang on this is getting tight,

she spent the next few weeks being very careful until they stopped complaining. She did eat healthily, but her sweet tooth seemed to fill most of her mouth and when she was bored it made demands she was only too happy to meet. So, a trawl through the lower shelf of the half-cupboard provided chocolate biscuits, chews and a bar of something nutty. This small collection helped the rest of the evening pass. Angela at work did the same thing, but then stressed over it afterwards. She'd come into work the next day full of guilt and berating herself for being weak willed. Becca didn't do that, she enjoyed what she ate and then got on with the next day. The final sip of tea washed down the last of the treats and she luxuriated in the deliciousness of the moment. But she did need to start doing something more with her evenings, this was great once a week, but not every night and she could see how easy it would be to slip into that. Spying on her neighbours was a growing sign she needed to think about her social life and how to start one. An evening class maybe, join some sort of group. She knew she needed do to something, but they didn't grab her. There was that life-work balance thing again. It was another of the reasons she'd left her old job. Being called in to her bosses office and asked if she was committed to the job, after all the time she'd put into it, was the last straw. A life away from work wasn't the done-thing at that place. She would have liked to think she'd spoken her mind, walked out of her bosses office in flattering slow motion, her hair bobbing gloriously. Collected her things from her desk, flicked her coat stylishly over a shoulder, and walked out to the applause and admiration of her colleagues, who then watched, hands clasped, eyes wet with tears, as she walked off into the sunset with music playing and the credits rolling. The reality had been, stuff your job, or words to that effect, in an overly loud voice and silent stares from her colleagues as she left the office as quickly as she could, face burning at the embarrassment of her outburst. At least she hadn't tripped and gone cartwheeling through the door in a mass of arms, legs and exposed underwear.

As spontaneous as it seemed the outburst was the final push she'd needed. She'd packed her old flat in boxes and sent it ahead. Had three weeks holiday in India and returned in time to collect the keys to her new flat, move in, well move the boxes in, explore the area and start her new job. She'd been lucky, everything had gone well, dropped into place in a way she hadn't expected. So, it wouldn't be right to waste it spying through holes in doors, puzzling over jam and eating chocolate in front of films that had nothing new to say.

***

Friday evening, the gateway to the weekend, the thought of two whole days of free choice and no work. She checked her mail and walked to her door; someone was a floor or two up. She reached her flat and paused, funny how she now noticed the comings and goings of the other residents. She hadn't met any, or seen them, for that matter, apart from hair man and he didn't seem to be around much, but she now knew them by their footsteps, or the way they climbed the stairs and had labelled them as such. She let herself in, dropped her bag, put her keys and post on the hall table, checked her phone, no messages, hung her coat, kicked off her shoes and headed for the kitchen. Hair man tended to bound up and down the stairs. The person named high heels, pounded her way down the stairs at the same time every night and returned in the small hours of the morning. The third pair of feet, now named pauses in the entrance hall (pauses, for short), did just that in the entrance hall on the way out and seemed to keep a very structured timetable; coming and going three times in the day. Someone else also left very early, at about the same time every morning, including weekends and came back late, she'd called that one early bird. And that was it, including herself five residents, out of six, all new all settling in. Had any of them met each other and who would move into the empty flat? Of course, there were other footsteps, phone people sorting the internet, plumbers and fitters, all the things that went with people moving in and making a flat their home. There were visitors as well, in fact she could have been the only one who didn't get visitors, but despite all this coming and going there was the regular four sets of footsteps.

***

Saturday morning, she stretched in bed and enjoyed the warm soft space. It was nice to wake up without an alarm. She mulled over her plans for the day and eventually decided it was time to get up and do something about them. Saturday morning, always started with the bathroom scales, though after she'd been on the loo. Everything off she pulled them out and stepped on; her jeans had been feeling tight and she wanted to confirm what she suspected. There had been a lot of birthdays that week at work, yes, she'd put weight on. Just to be on the safe side she moved the scales to another spot. That spot said lower, okay, spot number three for an average. This one added about six kilos, how on earth? So, now she had to find another spot just to see where the truth lay. Why didn't her scales say the same thing no matter where she put them?

Showered, dressed and breakfasted. A slice of toast in case the six kilos were actually there somewhere. Shutting her front door, she noticed, no jam, but instead a candle. Had hair man taken the jam and was now leaving candles? She picked it up, it was in a little glass pot with a lid held on by two metal clips and was about the same size as the jam jar. She carefully popped the lid, the candle smelt of vanilla and reminded her of her Aunty Irene's kitchen table and creamy rice pudding, steaming in a blue and white striped bowl. She put the candle back in its place, now she wanted rice pudding. Talk about easily influenced. The front door closed, she paused at the top of the steps, it was warm already and the sun lifted every colour. Taking the long way to the high street she went through the park. It was a day for being outside and the only time she wished she had a garden, just a small one, some plants and somewhere to sit. The park was at the end of her road, but not the island of peace she was thinking. That said, it was nice to see so many people out enjoying the summer. Picnics, deck chairs, people lounging on the grass, feeding the ducks, sitting in dappled shade. It slowed everything down. People, including her, stopped focusing on getting from A to B and took their time. She wouldn't go as far to say communing with nature, but certainly something close to being in the moment. She almost walked past the ice cream man and instead left with a small tub of vanilla. It was thick, soft and made of the real thing. It was delicious and every mouthful tasted good. So good, she sat down to enjoy it and the sunshine.

As nice as it was, she couldn't help thinking a friend to share the morning with would have made it just that little bit better. The thought broke the spell and told her it was time to move on. The moment had passed and they were best allowed to do that.

Don't waste your time trying to recapture the past,

her mother had said.

It will always disappoint.

Becca didn't agree fully with that, she wasn't that cynical. But special moments shouldn't be re-enacted, it didn't work, better to wait for the next one and give it every opportunity to come along.

Leaving the park couldn't have been more of a contrast, relative calm turned into the noise of busy streets, a bustle of people and all the other things your senses were bombarded with. It was still exciting, even the suburbs of the city had a vibe to them. Again, she wondered how long that would last, until it just became background noise. The shops were varied and there were several she liked to go in. All food. Bread from that one, pastries from there, fruit from this one and meat from here. She bought the ingredients for rice pudding; the thought still hadn't gone away even on a hot summer day. Why she stopped and looked in the window, she couldn't say. Obviously, she'd walked right past it the other day. She looked at the lamp, something about it caught her eye.

If you had a small round table, I would look great on it.

No, there's enough in boxes without adding to them. She walked on, her subconscious lamp-buying-cells registering where the shop was so they could direct her eyes at some later point in the future. The sun and the thoughts of a garden made her buy flowers, she had a vase somewhere. It was a small attempt to bring a bit of the summer into her flat, they smelled lovely and the shop front had done the job of bringing her in, it always looked so nice, so full of colours and, well, nice things.

On her return she checked her mailbox. She flicked through the junk absently not expecting to recognise handwriting. The effect of seeing her address written in that hand was a shock. She'd written, but had no reply. She'd since given up any thoughts of receiving one and now, just as she'd got that right in her head, put it behind her, here one was. Not a welcome to your new home card, judging from the floppy envelope. She hesitated; do I really want to read what's in here. Wouldn't it just be better to leave it somewhere to forget about and open at some distant point in the future when its contents had become so distant, they wouldn't re-open old wounds. Open it, get it over and done. Her stomach was churning, it was a letter, just a letter. With a sudden flash of activity, she tore it open and pulled out the small folded piece of paper. It had been torn off the bottom of a note pad.

Rebecca, it's your mam,

If I don't hear from you by the 12th, I'll assume you no longer want to be in my will.

That was it, she looked at the back, nothing else. No Dear Rebecca, as if there would be, but it wasn't even signed. How did you respond to anything like that? As if she cared about money. Was this some clumsy attempt to make her contact her mother? It was the 14th now, the stamp was second class, was she meant to have missed the deadline? She read it again, part of her said rush to the phone explain that the letter arrived after the date enclosed, not because she wanted to be in the will, but if she was going to be dammed for not responding it was because she had chosen to, not because the letter arrived after the deadline. The other side of her said don't you dare, it's more of a threat than anything else. She read it again. No matter how she phrased it in her mind, it was an ultimatum and out of principle she wouldn't have responded to such a thing from anyone. Even if her mother had said something along the lines of, look this is ridiculous, we should talk, she would have tried yet again, written, rang, but this was her only contact in a year.

Chapter 3

Empties and Candles…

She woke on Sunday; thankful the initial surprise of the letter had faded through the night. She'd slept well, only waking with the sunlight now streaming through her bedroom window. She got up, stopping to admire her flowers, jammed in a drinking glass because the vase had refused to be found, poor things. The rice pudding bowl was still soaking in the sink, there was still a faint smell of nutmeg and baked cream. She felt flat, but if that was the worst of it, she'd count herself lucky. She didn't want to chew on it, she'd done enough of that last night and knew the best thing for this kind of morning was to get ready and get out into the sunshine.

As she left, she noticed the candle was gone, fast turn over she thought. She didn't pause, she wanted to be out, shake off any guilt that might attach itself. It had become her habit to go out for breakfast on a Sunday. She liked going out for breakfast more than any other meal because it became unrushed and was the gateway to a day of deciding what she wanted to do, not what she felt she had to do. During the week she always ate the same thing. Porridge, it was healthy and it gave her the feeling she was doing at least one good thing for her body before dashing off to work. Saturdays it was toast, tea and the radio before getting on with all the other stuff she'd not had time for during the week. Sundays were about taking time to enjoy a meal she normally rushed, a meal she hadn't cooked, well toasted or reheated in the microwave. Sundays were about taking time and treating herself to what she liked, it didn't even have to be healthy, the time to ignore that endlessly confusing search to find out just what she should, or shouldn't eat. She was still trying to find a safe route through fruit. Once it was all good, now some of it was a sugar trap. But on Sundays she gladly threw herself on the sugar trap, but only after she'd leapt off the fat cliff into the caffeine sea.

She'd found a small café just off the park, not many people seemed to bother with it, but enough came to give it life without spoiling the quiet atmosphere. She always went early, to get her usual seat; it got just the right amount of sun. The café itself had been owned by the same family for seventy years, passed down through the generations. It'd had its heyday in the seventies and hadn't been decorated since. Sometime in the two thousands the family line had run out and the cafe had closed. At that point Patricia, its current owner, had stumbled across it. She had said herself; she was the most unlikely of people to take it on. She came from a very well to do background, but had always been its wild card. She'd studied with distinction at one of the country's best universities, but had chosen to live an unorthodox, yet extravagant, life in Europe. Learning about food, wine and sex; she wasn't a prude and wasn't afraid to show it. But, as she'd told Becca, all that sort of stuff has to come to an end and at forty she'd toured the rest of the word, become a successful food critic in America and published several books. While visiting relatives the café had caught her eye and once again her life had set off in a new and typically eccentric direction. Becca liked its laid back, if aged, style. Today it would have been called period, the café and its owner were more stubborn than retro. It was clean, the coffee was good and Patricia loved food and had a talent for making something as simple as toast taste in a way the average human could never hope to achieve. Becca always ordered a fried egg and bacon in a soft bun that greeted the tongue with salty, runny lushness. And cake, there was always a second cup of coffee with a piece of cake. Patricia's impatience with anything mechanical was balanced by infinite serenity with flour, eggs, sugar and butter. She made cakes that hit every spot. Not those horrible mountainous things, that came in slices bigger than your head and tasted of nothing. These were real cakes, they looked homemade, they were homemade, but tasted like soul food. Becca had a theory about soul food, it might not have been the correct meaning, but this was her understanding of it. Soul food didn't just feed the eyes, the nose and the tongue, it fed the spirit. Soul food demanded your whole attention, you didn't talk while eating it, you focused entirely on the experience, it thrilled the senses and nourished some deep central part of you. It lifted you for the time you spent in its company. It was the reason why most dinner parties always fell silent when the pudding was being eaten. No other part, no matter how good, demanded such undivided attention. Patricia, for her part, maintained that a cake should be the best thing you ever put in your mouth, no exceptions.

"Morning Becca, my darling," the perfectly enunciated tones greeted her, a rich sensual voice that didn't match Patricia's appearance, in the least. Becca had first met her voice. Patricia had been in the café's little kitchen and not visible. They'd had a brief conversation and then she'd appeared. Patricia had confronted her, with "Yes, I sound like a sex kitten, well an aging one, but look like one of my cakes, dumpy and homemade." It wasn't an apology; Patricia didn't give a damn what anyone thought. What you saw was what you got and bugger you if you didn't like it.

"Morning."

"Coffee?" Patricia asked with a certain amount of weary resignation.

"And a bacon and egg bun."

"Are you alright my darling?" Patricia could be disarmingly observant.

"I'm fine," Becca smiled.

"Go and make yourself comfortable. While I tackle this cursed beast." Patricia rolled up her sleeves. Round one of the daily arm-wrestling was imminent. The coffee machine made a derogatory sound in response.

Becca was glad Patricia didn't delve further, she wasn't in the mood for swimming the depths of her personality or her past, she just wanted to leap off the fat cliff, she just wanted a bacon sandwich.

Becca took her seat and looked out of the window at the world passing by. People watching was a pastime she liked to pass the time with. Humanity was infinitely varied, perpetually surprising. And endlessly interesting. Man, in a hurry (no clock?), woman with bad hair (no mirror?), sandals man with socks (no hope?). She was so lost in her time passing that,

"'ucking hell," was all that reached her ears, it didn't take a great leap of imagination to fill in the rest of the sentence or guess the cause. It was interesting that even when Patricia swore, the words, no matter how rough, lost their edges, having been smoothed by her velvet tones and perfect diction.

"Coffee?" Patricia panted, spattered with grindings and looking decidedly frazzled.

"Great, thank you." She watched Patricia bustle away to make her breakfast and then looked at the coffee, steam curling into the sunshine and that smell, the smell of Sunday mornings. She sipped it and drifted with the steam, but thoughts of the letter and the life she'd left behind began to mingle with it. She was startled when breakfast appeared in front of her.

"You were away with the fairies then, my darling girl," Patricia pointed out. "Deep thoughts this morning?"

"Oh, just daydreaming."

"I would say you were chewing on something, but I shan't pry. You clearly don't want to talk about it. Let me just say, I have a good listening ear if you ever need it." Patricia gave her a knowing look, peering out from under a fringe of wild greying hair.

Again, Becca was left watching her leave, this time to greet customers. Patricia was right, she had been chewing. It was the quiet moments that allowed stuff to creep into her thoughts. Sometimes she'd catch herself before a negative cycle could begin and think of something positive. But that didn't always work and before she knew it, she could be chewing on some event from the past, caught up in the cycle of reliving it, sometimes altering it, saying or doing the right thing. The letter was a fresh straw on an already broken back. She knew she was still searching for closure, a way to settle the whole thing once and for all, but the only way to truly do that was to confront the two people involved, the two people she'd come here to get away from.

Becca looked back to the window; she should have known it was going to be one of those days; one haunted by the past. But, enough already. To break this particular cycle, she watched people now heading for the park. An intimidating man, covered in tattoos, once passed the hedge revealed he had another side, a proud dad pushing a pram. The removal of a few leaves completely altered her initial thoughts about him. Just behind, an older woman shuffling along to a park bench. She sat and started feeding birds, Becca felt sorry for her; she looked lonely. Then the woman looked up as someone called her name. She smiled and got to her feet as her friend arrived, the two were soon arm in arm chatting and laughing. What you saw wasn't necessarily what you got. What would people assume about her? Sat alone every Sunday. She looked down at her bacon and egg bun, maybe life wasn't that bad.

When she got back, there was a new jar of jam, a candle and some empty jars. If nothing more, this was a distraction, she'd chew on this little mystery instead.

***

The next week flew by, work was busy, the weekend had flashed past her and the whole candle, jam, empties thing had something new to offer. Monday night, she got in, dropped her bag, checked her phone, no messages, hung her coat, kicked off her shoes and headed for the kitchen. The pictures and the box were still there, they had been her weekend job, but she'd been tired and found plenty of other reasons to leave them be. Again, she'd let another weekend pass without doing anything to the flat. She put the kettle on, grabbed a mug, added milk and a tea bag and sat back against the countertop. Candle gone, empty jars gone, no jam, but a new jar of chutney. That was the highlight of the day. She turned as the kettle started to boil and poured steaming water into the mug. Being careful not to scold her fingers she bobbed the tea bap up and down by its corner, watching for the moment when the milkie water looked like a proper cup of tea. As she put the teabag in the bin, she noticed the pad, grabbing it, a pen and her tea, she made her way to the chair by the window. This time not even bothering to stop and enjoy that moment of peace she took a sip and then made herself comfortable. She thought for a moment, putting the thoughts in order and began making notes

Jam

Jam gone

New Jam

Jam gone

Candle

Candle gone

New jam (different flavour)

Jam gone

New jam, new candle and some empty jars

Chutney

Was there a pattern, was hair man and mystery person getting complex? Who was mystery person? Early bird, high heels, or pauses (chief suspect). Which of the footsteps was leaving jam and chutney? She wanted to put a face to it. She done some knocking on doors during the week, deciding to finally say hello, but no one was in. She had the coming weekend, she had nothing better to do and her window, this very window, offered the perfect view of the main door.

She added…

get a life

to the list.

She was still asleep when early bird's footsteps left. It was only after she'd listened to the main door close and the sound of shoes on pavement had faded that she remembered her plan. Daft idea, she mumbled and turned over. It was sometime before her eyes opened again and she lay there for a while before the urge to get up made her. She made tea and toast, watching the butter melt before she spooned on marmalade. Positioning the chair, her only chair, to give her the best view of the door and the street, she sat. God, this room needed stuff, but she wasn't sure what. Pulling a face, she turned back to the window. It was sunny already. The day was going to be a nice one.

She didn't have to wait long; hair man was out early. She heard him bound down the stairs and then there was a gap before she heard the front door. Was he leaving jam or candles or empty jars? He was a runner; she'd guessed that or gym. Looking at him now, it was clearly both. From the direction, he was probably heading to the park, apparently there was a run there every Saturday morning. All that energy, that early in the morning. She watched until he was out of sight. Toast and tea gone, her surveillance became dull, there was a few people out in the street going about their business. She liked a woman's coat and wondered where she'd got it, watched another and wondered what had made her buy it. Apart from them, nothing much happened. She could of course stop all this snooping rubbish and go and knock on doors again.

Hi, I'm Becca, I live here and wanted to say hello. Have you been leaving jam by the stairs?

Err, hi. Jam? Err, no.

Candles?

No.

Chutney, then?

Which apartment are you in? Riiiiight, Well, err, nice meeting you. Got to go.

Chapter 4

Hair Man...

A week later and another Sunday morning saw her about to head for Patricia's. The entrance hall offered an addition to her list. The Chutney had gone, but there was another candle and what looked like homemade biscuits. Becca picked up the small clear plastic bag, tied at the top with a ribbon. They looked oaty and golden and good for dunking. She considered taking them and putting something in their place, like a trade. That did seem to be what was going on here. If they were still there on the way back, she'd join in, see what happened. It was far less weird than sitting by the window spying on her neighbours. Though, in her defence, she'd only done it for half an hour.

Patricia greeted her as usual and they chatted while she made, no, battled coffee. Becca ordered her usual and flapjack, not that she'd been influenced by the biscuits. She carried her coffee, trying not to spill any and so the first thing she saw was someone's feet at her table. She looked up and there he was, hair man.

"Oh," was all she managed.

"Hi," he beamed. "Fancy seeing you here."

When she looked blankly. He added "It's me from the flat, we live in the same building." He was still smiling.

"Sorry, yes of course. I usually..." she was about to explain her surprise and then move to another table.

"Sit down, we should chat. We're neighbours."

He was on his feet in a flash and pulled out a chair for her.

She was going to say something about not wanting to invade his privacy, but instead she sat, not wanting to appear rude.

"The coffee's good here. I found this place shortly after I moved in," he was saying. "Patricia knows what she's doing."

"She does, I come here every Sunday."

"Saturday's normally my day, but I did the park run yesterday and was shattered. Too long a break since the last time and tried to do too much."

Becca had enough presence of mind not to say I know; I was spying on you. "Running and I definitely don't get on. Walking, hiking, yoga, even swimming, but trainers and stuff no."

"What else do you do when you're not running?"

"That's a good question," Becca had to think about that one. She considered concocting a story. "To be honest, not a lot. I've only moved in a few months ago. Work and coming to this place seem to be the only things I do."

Hair man shrugged. "It takes longer than a few months to find your feet in a new place. I'm guessing this is a new place?"

"Totally, a fresh start."

"There you go then. I must have moved in a few weeks after you, I knew someone else was in, but then I've been away. Have most of the flats been taken?"

"I think so. There's only six and I've heard five lots of feet."

Hair man was looking at her.

And then she heard her own words. She shook her head and felt her face flush. "There, I've said it, that sounded weird."

Hair man only smiled and gave her time to explain.

"Everyone has to pass my door. I can often hear them as they come down the stairs. I've not met anyone, present company accepted, so I made up names for them based on the sound of their feet." There, honesty was the best policy, it never worked if she pretended to be anything she wasn't, she forgot too easily and then, like now, let stuff slip.

He laughed. "I did that. My last holiday. The first day before I met anyone properly, I had names for them. The best was chicken boy."

"Chicken boy?"

"Yep, he looked like he had a frozen chicken stuffed down the front of his speedo's"

Becca had to laugh; the image was ridiculous. "You mean his…"

"Believe me, if you'd been there, it's not an exaggeration."

"Not that you were looking."

"Nope, but it was difficult to overlook. My brother pointed it out and he was definitely looking."

"From the image now burning in my head, I'd have to agree."

"So, come on. What names have you given us all." Hair man sat back.

"I'd hoped you'd forgot."

"Nope," he was grinning again. It was infectious.

What the heck, she thought. If they never spoke again, she didn't know him well enough to miss him. "Hair man, high heels, pauses and early bird."

His eyes had narrowed. "So, which one am I?"

"Hair man," Becca looked apologetic.

He laughed, perhaps a little embarrassed. "I suppose I could have been any of them."

"Possibly not high heels."

"Why not," he shrugged.

"No judgements here," Becca said. "Seen a sign of any of them yet?"

"Nope, this is my first weekend properly here. You?"

"None. I thought you might have. You seemed to know about the jam thing."

"It was there, looked like it was meant to be, when it remained, I thought take it, see what happens. It's developed since then."

"And you've no idea who."

"Other than it's not you, nope."

The more they talked, the more she relaxed, or he was the type of company that allowed her to do that. He was confident, but not overly. There was a big difference. He wasn't how she'd imagined him to be. That surprised her, not arrogant, not full of himself, but hair man still fitted. He did have perfect hair, her name for him still worked... What was his name? "I've just realised; I don't know your name."

"How did that happen?" he held out his hand. "Jack."

"Becca," she said shaking it.

"Pleased to meet you Becca, or should I call you jam girl." He smiled the smile that must have set a few hearts fluttering in his time. For the briefest of moments, she pictured him again in his running gear.

"So, what brings you here, or rather the flats?" Jack was asking.

Becca was almost caught out by the questions, turning her thoughts as quickly as possible from shorts to editing a life story. "I was ready for a change in more ways than one. It's been a fresh start. New job, flat, life in general."

"Family and friends?" he asked conversationally.

"New everything," she wasn't going into too much detail. Unravelling the last year into his ears was, to say the least, premature, though the idea of being able to talk to someone about it was appealing, letting some of the mess out of her head would be cathartic. "I don't know anyone."

"Well, now you know me, so that's a start."

He was being diplomatic, had he sensed her reluctance to give away too much about her past. "What about you?" She steered the conversation just in case he was forming any deeper questions.

"Pretty much the same. I had to move, new job here, or no job. So, new place in a new city. Girlfriend decided she didn't want a long-distance relationship and as for friends, I've none close enough to see without several hours drive and an overnight stay."

"Sorry to hear about your girlfriend." Was he announcing his availability or just being honest? It felt like the later.

"One of those things," he shrugged. "We'd not been going out for long, so I don't blame her. What about you, anyone special?"

Anyone, that was interesting, not any man in your life? That's more or less how it had been phrased at work.

He'd noticed her pause "Was that prying?"

"No, not at all. There's no boyfriend. It's just interesting you said anyone. Most people seem to assume it'll be a man. Is there a man in your life? Do you have a boyfriend, a bloke, a fella?"

"I've a brother who's gay, so I suppose he's educated me into not making assumptions."

Hair man was turning out to be nothing of what she'd assumed him to be. She'd labelled him, had expectations based on past experience and had employed an amount of stereotyping. Now, here he was giving her a lesson in not making assumptions. "Good for him."

"Yep, he's great. Working in London, good job, travels the world. Makes me look very boring." Jack talked with a sense of pride in his voice.

"You're close," she said.

"Talk every week. What about you, any brothers or sisters?"

"A sister, we're not close." Becca added quickly, a little too quickly.

***

It was mid-way through the following week when Becca and Jack's return from work coincided.

"Wow," he said, bursting in through the door and noticing the array of objects.

"It's become quite a collection," Becca looked at the now carefully arranged jars and made things.

"Yep, like some photo shoot for a magazine," he noted.

"It's all very hand-crafted, country living. I used to buy those magazines all the time. Never did me any good."

"What? Your place not a haven of style and comfort?" Jack asked.

Becca had no problem in admitting it wasn't. "Mine still looks like I moved in yesterday."

"Really, I'd have thought differently."

"Are you going to tell me yours is?"

"Come up for coffee, or tea and find out," he grinned enthusiastically.

It was difficult to say anything other than...

"Yes, great. I'll dump my stuff and come up in about ten minutes, if that's okay." Becca promised, thinking of the time it would take to make her kitchen look decent. The rest of the place was fine; it was all still in boxes.

She gave him fifteen minutes. It seemed long enough to do a quick run of clearing stuff and shoving things in cupboards, but not so long as to make him think she'd forgotten. The door was open, but she knocked anyway.

"Come in," he called.

She entered. Quality; less was more and just, well, really nice without trying, bugger it. She walked from the hallway, to the living room, each step revealing something else to touch or covet. He was clearly a sci-fi fan; posters dotted the walls. Stuff from the fifties, maybe sixties and stuff even she knew from the seventies and probably later. She'd made her way through the dining area and then the kitchen, she was glad the invite hadn't come from her. Compared to this, her place looked like storage. Again, she found herself thinking this was not what she's imagined. A huge TV, beer cans, old plates and scattered underwear. He'd not had time to clear that kind of mess away, maybe it was always like this.

Becca was still slightly dazed when she got back to her flat. It had been a nice hour. He'd made coffee, the proper way, produced chocolate biscuits from a tin, a nice tin. It had been comfortable and friendly and his flat felt like a home. He wasn't precious about it all. He'd told her to fling cushions on the floor if they were in the way. He'd flopped down in a chair and she'd ended up sprawled on the sofa. They'd laughed, joked and he'd been easy company. He'd given her a quick hug as she left.

His flat wasn't what she'd expected. She'd thought minimal, but it was smart and comfortable and filled with things from his travels or stuff that meant something to him. Now she was back in her flat and for the first time she noticed just how faceless it was, bare and heartless. It could be anyone's and no ones. She didn't know where to start and frankly needed a rocket to get her to do just that. Maybe she could ask Jack to give her a hand. He'd probably not mind, he seemed to be enthusiastic about everything. He was a good guy. The question suddenly came into her head. Did she fancy him? She pressed a finger to the gap between her brow to smooth out the furrow that had just gathered there. She searched inside for some hint that she did and found that, she liked him, he was good company and certainly easy on the eye, but a friend was what she needed, an uncomplicated friend. Her sister would say men and women couldn't be friends, sex always got in the way. She would maintain only gay men and women could be friends and then would shudder at the thought. Yet another reason why they didn't get on.

Becca had made enough assumptions that turned out to be wrong about Jack. Gay, straight, bi, fluid; a friend was a friend and that's what she wanted. She looked up from these deliberations and her eyes settled on her chair by the window. With a sudden flash of inspiration, she dashed into the bedroom and after some rummaging found the box she wanted. The box provided the two things she was looking for. A throw and a cushion. They didn't really match, but after a few attempts at draping and positioning, she stood back and admired her handy work. It was a start.

Chapter 5

High heels…

She dropped her bag, checked her phone, no messages, hung her coat, kicked off her shoes and headed for the kitchen. Walked past the box and pictures as if they weren't there, but caught sight of her chair-cushion-throw arrangement, it gave her a feeling of satisfaction. This weekend she was planning to do more. Then she could return the invite to Jack. He'd been away with his work again and not been around, but she'd not been able to return to her flat without thinking about his. It had occurred to her that the state of the flat reflected, or affected her mood. Tomorrow night she'd unpack properly. That would give her Saturday to get busy and buy any bits she needed and still go to Patricia's on Sunday.

***

It was Saturday before she knew it. Friday night had not been unpacking night, so now she was up early. She'd painted two walls in both bedrooms and had arranged some furniture before breakfast. Now she could get onto the huge number of boxes she taken out of both rooms. She'd bought a book on the way home and spent Friday night reading it. Now she had some ideas. Arrange in groups of three, match edges, lead the eye... She hammered nails, hung things, swapped them, took them down. Arranged this and that, stood back, swapped them and put them to one side in frustration. By lunchtime, the place looked like a small explosion had gone off.

The day progressed, but her efforts only went in circles. She was about to flop down into the chair of resignation when a knock at the door made her freeze in indecision. Look at the mess, if that was Jack, she couldn't let him see the place like this. She could pretend she was out. The knock came again, most insistent this time. Sounded like a knock that needed an answer. She waved an irritated hand at the disarray and headed for the door, ready to greet Jack and tell him to ignore the mess, which was his fault anyway.

"Oh, my, god," she faltered.

"No, Shirley Bassey, but you're not far wrong. Babes, is your electricity off?"

"Who? I mean, electricity?"

"Yeah, the stuff that makes hoovers work," said the huge eye lashes after a glance into the havoc behind Becca.

"Err," Becca's hand fumbled for the light switch.

"Hmm, that answers that then. I must have blown a fuse. Something exploded in here as well?" the eyes were suddenly distracted. "You do know who Shirley Bassey is, don't you?"

"Err, yes. Dame...."

"Babes, are you okay?" The eyes now looked concerned.

Their intensity was mesmerising, the lashes, the colours, the size. Before she knew it, she was being helped down her hallway to the chair by the window.

"Now, do what Tina tells you and sit down...The minute I walked into this joint, I thought something was up. What the hell happened here?"

Becca's wits finally kicked in. "Believe it or not this is interior design."

"Which version. Explosion, whirlwind or hysteria?"

"Bordering on the hysterical."

"It's a look, I'll give you that, babes." Hands on huge, yet perfect hips, the eyes surveyed the room like sequinned lasers. "You need some help." Then the eyes remembered something. "Shit. I've got to get my diamonds, I'll be late." With that, they departed. "I'll be back, and if you find a twelve-inch gold finger it's mine, and it's not a finger," the voice trailed back towards Becca. The sound of six-inch heels was unmistakable, high heels was leaving the building.

***

Becca had literally just got in from work, she was about to put her bag down when a knock made her start. She opened the door.

"Oh."

"Is that your usual greeting?" It was the voice that gave him away, it was deeper, but it was high heels.

"Sorry, not used to visitors."

"Given yesterday, I'm not surprised." High heels folded his arms. "I said I'd be back." He offered Becca his hand.

She wasn't sure if she should shake it, or kiss it.

"Just in case you haven't put two and two together, last night was Tina Meatballs, now it's me, Benjamin, Ben for short, pleased to meet you."

"Rebecca, Becca for short, same one as last night, pleased to meet you too."

"Is that Becca with a tidy flat, or Becca I went to bed and left it?"

"Bed."

"Come on," he gestured theatrically. "You need the help of a drag-godmother."

Ben swept past her; even out of heels he was tall.

"Come on, you can do this."

In about three hours, they had. Ben stood, hands on hips, admiring their handy work.

"Not bad," Becca smiled. "Not bad at all. We make a good team."

"You did most of it, babes. I only got you to click your heels. It's bare, but it's more like someone lives here, rather than passes through to bed."

"Have you eaten?" Becca asked. "I don't know about you, but I'm really hungry. I've enough in for two."

"Monday is my night off. Cook away," Ben shooed her into the kitchen and sat himself down.

"This has probably been said to you a lot, but I've never met a drag queen."

"That and a whole lot more. I could write an encyclopaedia." He drew his hand through the air as if fanning open a book a very thick book. "And now you have."

"How long have you been doing it?" Becca asked. She might be repeating a question he'd been asked too many times, but she was interested. Either way she had the feeling Ben would only answer if he wanted to.

"Tina," he made a gesture with his hand, Becca assumed was one of Tina's affectations, "has been with me for about fourteen years. She found me just before I turned twenty and we've been together since."

"What brough the two of you together?"

"Lilly Savage DVDs and then dressing up for a school play. I liked the attention. It let something out of me and made it okay."

"Where do you, or should I say Tina work?"

He laughed. "It's fine, babes. She's an alter ego not an identity disorder."

"Do you mind me quizzing you like this?"

"No, as long as you keep off the, where do you tuck it crap and the assumption, I automatically want to be a woman. Ask away. You're going to get the same from me, get ahead while you can."

"Okay, from the start then. You've told me when, what about where?"

"The where, is Leeds. The what, a chance to express another aspect of myself full time." Ben framed his face with a flourish. "She didn't have a name then, which is just as well because she was a mess, not the finely honed vision of splendour you saw last night."

"Does your family know?"

"Yeah, from the start. They were there for me. I was lucky, a lot of the queens I've worked with don't have that. It hasn't all been plain sailing though, I've taken my fair share of shit and learnt to dish it straight back. I worked hard, I listened, I watched, I learnt. I went from, Adora Borgia, to Tina Tuna, to Tina Meatballs and somewhere along the way got a lifelong friend and business partner, Miss Pasta Pesto, she's Italian and goes off like a cannon, but we've managed not to kill each other. Ten years ago, we moved here and eventually bought a club. It's small, we struggled, but we're good at it, it's paying for itself now, bought me a new flat here and we've been able to give regular work to some of the girls."

"How did you get to know them?"

"Babes, when you've done the rounds for as long as I have, you get to know everyone who's on the circuit. Good and bad."

"Who's good?"

"The ones we employ," he answered dryly. "There's Chocolate de Clar, Lady Tear and Share…"

"That's an odd one, why that name?"

"Everyone's had a piece."

Becca groaned.

"Mount Rushmore, she ain't just a two-faced bitch, Tonya Tickle Tongue and Lady Straight Up…"

"Explain that one?"

"She heard one of the local 'ladies' quoting prices on the phone to a prospective client. And I quote, twenty-five for a hand job, love and fifty if you want it straight up."

Becca laughed. "Straight up, what on earth?"

"The mind boggles, babes."

"They're a good bunch," Ben frowned. "Is there a collective noun for a bunch of drag queens."

"A fierce," Becca offered.

"A fierce of drag queens," Ben tested it, pulling a non-comital face. "A shade of drag queens. A pack of drag queens, hmm, too close for comfort that one."

"A house of drag queens?"

"Now," Ben snapped a finger and pointed it at her. "That's got legs, that's not bad at all. He spread his hands through the air as if illuminating the phrase in lights. "A house of drag queens. Quick copy write it. We could make millions."

"Do you all get on?"

"Like anyone, yes and no. We call each other something rotten, but let anyone else try and believe me that's a pack of wolves and a wasp's nest you don't want to go poking." He folded his arms. "We get on well enough for me to have them over once a week. It's good to let our hair down, talk, listen to each other, give support. We don't have time when we're doing a show, but it helps things to run smoother; we can be a touchy lot and understanding all our collective quirks helps keep the pot from boiling over."

"That makes sense," Becca thought about her own job, was she right to keep the people she worked with at arm's length, keep life and work separate?

"This looks good." Ben smelt the plate of pasta placed in front of him. "Speak of the devil."

Becca didn't catch on immediately. "Right, I get it, we're eating your business partner."

"Someone has to, poor cow."

They ate and Ben regaled Becca with some of his many stories. Tales from his early days, to ones of them getting the club started to some of their more recent dramas and escapades.

Ben put down his fork. "Thank you, that was good."

"There's pudding."

"Not a proper meal without one." Ben fixed Becca with those eyes, even without enhancement they held the attention. "I can see you look after your appearance," he gestured. "You know how to dress well, but strangely that doesn't extend to your flat, you have a good job, this stuff isn't cheap. You're easy on the eye, but single. How am I doing so far?"

"Keep going, I don't think I'm insulted yet."

He looked back down the hallway. "You're not close to your family."

Becca was surprised by the comment, it came out of nowhere, it was true, but still a bit too close for comfort.

Ben nodded slowly, at the same time confirming his insight and acknowledging her mild discomfort.

"What made you say that?" Becca now fixed Ben with a stare of her own.

"The box and pictures in the hallway. I looked at the pictures. They're the only things we didn't unpack. You don't have to explain." He held up a hand. "At this point I'm one step up from a stranger. All be it a fabulous one."

"It's fine, I didn't know you were a part time detective as well. Might make a good film, drag queen detective."

"I've seen worse on telly. Teena Meatballs on the Job."

"Shouldn't it be on the case."

"I know what I mean. But are we going back to the box, or is that a closed subject?"

"Not a lot to tell really. It's family pics. My father died sometime back. I don't get on with my sister and haven't spoken to my mother for about a year. We're estranged. Interesting there's a words for that, clearly happens a lot if it has its own label."

"Relatives, you're born with them. Doesn't mean you have to like them."

"You're the first person I've told that to, who hasn't tried to fix it. Or told me she's your mother, you should make an effort with your sister. They're family, blood is thicker than water."

"Not from me, babes. As I said, I was lucky, but I've heard enough to know family ties can cut the deepest. I can understand why you haven't opened the box, but I'm interested why it's sat there."

"Good questions."

Ben inclined his head in benevolent acknowledgement.

Becca thought for a while. "This isn't my best answer and I reserve the right to change it. There's still a bond there, a part of me, heritage, identify? Call it what you will. It wasn't all bad and for that reason I can't quite throw it away."

"And you don't have to, babes. I'm just nosey."

"No, you're…"

"Keep going, I'm not insulted yet."

"You're provocative."

"Oh yeah," the eyes had it. "And sooooo much more."

After Ben had gone Becca walked to the box and stood for some time looking at it. She reached down and pulled out the first picture, it was dusty. She flipped it over, two girls looked back at her, one six the other fourteen. The age gap alone had meant they were not destined to be bosom buddies. At six she was still into dolls and cartoons; her sister was into sulking and producing hormones. Becca had learnt from a much younger age that her sister wasn't interested and considered her an intruder. She looked at the two of them, this was the only time she actually remembered having her photo taken with her sister. Their expressions made it clear why. Becca looked like she'd been stood next to a dung heap and her sister looked like she'd been told to eat it.

***

Having not seen anything of Ben since she'd moved in, she now saw him the next day as she got in from work.

He turned to look at her. "You know anything about this?" he gestured expansively at the jars and candles.

"Someone in the flat's started it. Jack, in the one above me, takes the jam and leaves the candles."

Ben frowned, "Is he the one who goes running?"

"When he's here," Becca replied.

"I've seen him, too much energy for that time of the morning. Well it looks like others are getting in on the act." He smelt one of the candles and picked up a packet of biscuits, testing the bow they were sealed with. "My place, these and tea?"

"Great, sounds like a plan. Do you need tidy time?"

"Babes, take it as it is, or don't come again," he smiled with lots of teeth and headed for the stairs.

Becca looked at the growing collection. She still hadn't got involved. Becca picked up the jam, she didn't know what she could make to put in its place.

She dropped her bag through the door and shut it before heading up to Ben's. She had a definite image of what his place would look like and when he opened the door, she couldn't have been more wrong. Everywhere was minimal, neat, tasteful, perhaps a little staged, but that at least seemed to go with the job. She's expected a lot more colour and well, stuff. She had to admit it, tacky stuff.

"You look surprised," Ben was peering at her.

"I expected a more flamboyant style." She worded her answer with better care than her thoughts.

"If it was Tina's it would be, take a look in there." He gestured to one of the doors. "She's in there," he said dramatically.

Becca hesitated. "Can I look?"

"Yeah, she doesn't bite."

Becca stood trying to take it all in. Aladdin's cave would have been close if he'd worn more frocks.

"I call it the drag cave."

Small wigs, big wigs, huge wigs, frocks, costumes, gowns, dresses, photos, posters, feathers, sequins, false boobs, padding, makeup, shoes, more makeup, shoes, even more makeup, more shoes, several things she couldn't name and a huge…

"Vibrator. A fan sent it."

Becca closed her mouth. "Impressive."

"Yeah, but not solid gold. I use it in the act."

"Right, Dame Shirley." Becca continued her eye tour of the pictures. Some portraits and cartoon drawings of Tina, posters for shows and photos of other people. "This is a nice one, you look really happy."

"That's an old one, back when I was young and beautiful."

"Was he a friend?"

"Yes, and more. It wasn't straight forward."

Becca looked at Ben expectantly. "It's a tale worth telling then?"

He waved the idea away with a hand. "No point dwelling on the past. Come on tea'll be brewed."

Becca followed. "This guy," she began tentatively. "He was special, wasn't he? You wouldn't keep a photo for that long if he wasn't."

Ben pointed at a worktop in front of the window and two tall stools. "Sit, I'll be mother."

The biscuits were open and he'd taken the ribbon and tied it to a hand full of hair on top of his head. If she'd done it, it would have looked daft, on him it looked quirky. She didn't pursue her last question.

Ben sat down. "Brian would have been special." Clearly, he was going to answer anyway. "Well, he was and would have been more so. If we'd had a chance."

"You don't have to…"

"It's fine," Ben said.

Becca watched him take a drink and then absently pull the ribbon out of his hair, it seemed somehow connected; a veil removed, a drawing back of a curtain to something more serious.

"We were part of a group, all got on. Brian and I had a thing for each other, but timing was always off. He was with someone when I wasn't and vice the versa. We flirted, but always made it clear we were just friends. Played jokes, threw shade. This went on for a year, will they, won't they? There was a club we all went to, centre of town. We used to get groups of lads, drunk morons who'd come specially to heckle. I was about sixteen, we are talking a while ago here. It was very different then to be gay and, in my case, gay and black gave the twats more ammo. It wasn't worth arguing, you can't with that low level of brain cells and the names they threw said far more about them."

"That's usually the case," Becca agreed. "Their insecurities."

"We always arrived in a group and it was a rule no one left alone. If someone had to go early, two of us would escort them out, walk them far enough away and then go back in. This night, Brian left early, he'd split with this guy who showed up with his new boyfriend and was rubbing his face in it. Apparently, Brian had left and got into a slanging match with a group of lads outside. They followed him and beat him up. As soon as we noticed he'd gone, we went looking, couldn't find him and assumed he'd gone home, so we returned to the club. I get woken up the next morning, by a friend who'd found out what had happened and we rushed to the hospital." Ben paused briefly and shook his head. "You know I can still see him as if it was yesterday. We walked down the ward and I glanced in a room, it was a split second and I thought poor sod, what happened to him? Didn't give it another thought until we got to the desk and the nurse took us back up the corridor." He looked at Becca.

"And took you to the poor sod's room," Becca's hand went to her mouth. "Oh god, that must have been awful."

"Babes, you have no idea, my friend took a minute outside to talk to the nurse. I walked in; there he was lying there. Eyes puffed up so much they were closed. Nose broken, more bruises cuts and bandages than him on show. The only place I could find was his right hand. Poking out of the cast. I kissed it. We talked and when our friend left, we talked more. It took a long time for him to get well and we realised what everyone else had seen. The months that followed were great, but then he started getting flashbacks of the attack and started to go downhill. Eventually his family decided they wanted him home. And it was the best place for him, but there wasn't a place there for me. We phoned, but his family made it difficult, mobile phones weren't the thing they are now, this was the early two thousands. He needed peace and quiet not me rubbing his parents the wrong way. So, I stepped back and told myself it was the right thing to do. I was young, had no money."

"And at the time it was the right thing to do." Becca wanted to assure him. "Someone once said to me, you make the best decision you can at the time. I think it's a well-known quote."

"It was the best decision. At the time." Ben inhaled suddenly and straightened. "Que Sera, Sera."

"Where did his parents live?"

Ben half laughed, "Ireland."

"So, no popping down the M1."

"Not quite. Anyway, there you have it, true drag queen torch song material."

He sounded blasé about it, but it was obvious, even after all this time, that Brian still meant something to him.

"Your turn," Ben was looking at her. "Come on, you've sampled some of my beans, spill 'em."

"Really," Becca groaned.

Ben suddenly looked upset. "B-but I shared my pain, a piece of me, my hurt laid open…"

Becca was mortified. It had been personal, but she'd no idea the casual telling had been that difficult, that painful. "I-I'm… sod, you absolute sodding sod."

"She swears. Sorry babes, couldn't resist."

"That was too convincing, you should be on the stage," Becca leaned forward. "I thought you were really upset."

"What can I say, it's all in the performance."

"Okay, okay. No torch song, but maybe good enough for a sub plot on one of the lesser soaps. We met in a night club, I noticed him from across the room and he was looking at me. He was sort of handsome, black shirt and jeans. For once I went over and we started talking. It should have registered with me then that there was going to be a problem. The pint in his hand often seemed more interesting than me. I stayed over."

"Well, well," Ben gave her a knowing look.

"Girls do it too."

"They do," he agreed. "Just learning things about this girl. Never judge a book by its cover."

"I do that too much," Becca confessed.

"We all do that. Now, stop diverting and get on with the story."

"We started seeing each other. He was kind, interesting, took me to meet his friends, we went on holiday. He had a good job and, at the risk of sounding lame, had an enviable lifestyle, a very jet setting international life. It was dazzling. But, despite the glamour of it, after six months it was going nowhere and through it all there was one common thing."

"Drink," Ben guessed.

"Exactly, not drunken slob stuff, not aggressive, but always there like it was blotting something out. He'd ring and cancel a lot; I could tell from his voice he'd been drinking. Might have been someone else, might have been any number of reasons. He wouldn't talk about it; I wouldn't force him, that's not me. I began to get that mind set where I felt we'd gone as far as we could. He was okay with things the way they were, but at that time I was looking for more. We carried on for a while, but I'd lost the ability to invest in it, not sure what there was in return."

"Emotionally bankrupt," Ben was nodding slowly. "You invest more of yourself than you get back. Relationships, jobs blah, blah. Continue."

"Good phrase, I'll remember that." Becca paused. "That really is a good phrase." She looked at him, he inclined his head in benevolent acknowledgement, a now familiar gesture. "Anyway, you keep interrupting. I went up one night to break it off. I worded it well, I'll give myself that. He sat there, and just accepted it. A part of me expected him to at least argue the point, make some effort. I stood waiting for something. I could see his eyes were filling up. But no words. In the end I felt stupid standing there. I said something corny like, I hope you'll be happy someday, turned and headed down the stairs. A few days later it still felt like the right thing. I felt very flat, I did have feelings for him and they were going to take some time to shut down. But I was okay with it and then he rang and said could we be friends. Like a fool I said yes. I should have said ring me back in four months, if you still feel that way. All it did was drag things out for me. It was more about his needs, whatever they were. In the end I just stopped answering the calls and eventually moved on. Though like Brian he's still there in the back of my mind, for reasons I can't explain."

Ben raised his glass and Becca followed suit. "Babes, here's to us and the ones that got away."

Chapter 6

"Hi, I'm Ben, I'm a gay drag queen…"

"Okay, so, I'm Jack, a straight graphic designer and I don't like carrots."

Ben's introduction had been defensive, Becca could see it and it looked like Jack could too. Ben had said to her, he felt he had little in common with straight men. For a start, what could he talk to them about and were they all so insecure that they assumed the gay guy was always trying to get into their pants? She assumed this kind of introduction normally left his opponent at a loss. But Jack came right back at him and smiled too.

"You're hair man, and I don't like carrots either," Ben recovered quickly.

"And you're high heels, we have something in common," Jack grinned.

"I'm breaking them in," Ben looked down at his feet and clicked his heels together.

"I get the reference, but your only a friend of Dorothy, not the real deal."

"Oo," Ben's voice lifted into the upper atmosphere where Tina's voice resided. "He speaks gay."

"Yep, always good to have a second language."

They both turned to look at Becca. "Jam girl," they echoed.

Becca held up her hands. "Guilty as charged, but I know you both now." She wondered if they'd get on and for the briefest of moments it looked as if they wouldn't, but now Ben had linked arms with Jack and was leading him away from the door to Becca's kitchen.

"You can close the door, babes," Ben called back. "I like this one, we're keeping him."

They sat and talked. Easy conversation about work, the news, the collection in the entrance hall and Becca's now fully unpacked flat, fully, but not including the box and pictures in her hallway.

"So, you've both added to the collection in the entrance hall," Jack asked as Becca made more tea and got out biscuits.

"Well, you've cornered the market in candles," Becca began to explain. "I put a little vase of flowers out there."

"Nice," Ben picked up a biscuit. "I made the gingham cloth its now sat on. I was going to add sequins, but they're not rustic enough and everything on that table looks like it's come from a craft centre. Sequins don't say country."

"You sew?"

"Made to measure, in my size and with my shoulders, doesn't grow on trees. And when I first started, I couldn't afford someone else to make my frocks. I went to a night class and I learned."

Jack shrugged, which Becca now knew was his shorthand for, yes, I agree, it's okay, I understand… and a host of other things. "You've both made things, I bought the candles. They don't fit the theme."

Ben rolled his eyes and spread his hands, this time shorthand for its obvious. "You said you're a graphic designer, draw something, put it in a frame."

"What we should be doing right now," Jack said. "Is the three of us to going and saying 'Hi' to the neighbours."

"I've tried and I know it sounds daft," Becca replied, "but I quite like the mystery." She left the tea pot to brew and sat down. "Where are all the biscuits?"

"Oops," Ben paused briefly, before putting the last one in his mouth. "They just disappeared."

"They are, or were my favourite digestives."

"You're gluten free?" Jack looked at the packet.

"No, I eat anything and everything. Amy, who is free, brought some into work. I tried one. They're oats, nothing magical. I liked the texture and the layer of chocolate is really thick. I could eat them until they come out of my ears, they're so nice." She looked at Ben. "When you get the chance."

"What can I say, babes. I'm a hedonist. I'm all about pleasure."

"Hmm, I usually buy a pack on the way home on a Monday, sort of makes the start of the working week tolerable."

"Good idea," Jack said. "Even if you like your job, Mondays can be a real downer."

"You're not usually around on a Monday," Becca noted.

"Nope, but now we've a big project for a city firm, so I'll be around a lot more for the foreseeable future."

"Well, in that case we need to do something next weekend. Pasta owes me."

"I'm in," Jack said with his usual enthusiasm.

"Great, how about a road trip," Becca suggested. "Leave the city behind."

"I'm happy to drive," Jack offered.

"You're coming in useful. Any chance it's a convertible," Ben asked.

"Yep, I can wangle that."

"Then I've a head scarf and Jackie O' sunglasses I've been dying to wear."

***

Anyone driving the Coast Road might have been left with a Kennedy flash back as the open car passed them by. Ben sat in the back-seat, arms spread wide in luxuriant comfort, chin high, huge dark sunglasses catching the light and head scarf fluttering in the wind. Jack had promised them breakfast with a difference. After driving through a seaside town with an abbey, they continued further north past a large bay, guest houses and hotels, ice cream parlours and fish and chip shops. Becca had the feeling they were passing through different villages or towns. Places that had now been swallowed up in a continuous urban sprawl.

They parked easily; Becca had insisted on leaving early to avoid the crowds and so when they walked towards the sea front, their only company were runners and dog walkers. The sun glinted off the sea and the air was warm already.

"You ditched the head scarf," Jack noted.

"Babes, as stylish as it might be, I'm not baiting anyone this morning. I'm not in the mood for battles. Though I'm keeping the sunglasses. One has to have a hint of the unique."

"I wouldn't have thought you'd care what anyone thought."

"Sometimes I don't, but I've also learnt to pick my battles and I'm out with you two. My fight isn't yours."

"We're your friends, I'd say it goes with the territory."

Becca watched this short exchange, she was going to add her two-penneth, but Jack's use of the word friends was unexpectedly touching, it made her smile and she caught herself watching Ben to see his reaction. Oddly there was no witty retort. Was he caught out by the statement? No, she thought, it was quiet acceptance of support.

"What's so special about this place then?" Becca asked.

"To borrow Ben's term, it has a hint of the unique," Jack grinned.

"Hallelujah."

"So, I suppose it has the feel of somewhere that's managed to avoid being completely altered by the passage of time." Jack explained. "If you want an Americano and a biscotti, you can get one. But, before all of that there was milky coffee and a three pack of bourbons. It feels like the nineteen fifties are still alive and kicking in this place. You'll see."

They went through a kind of short tunnel to the sea front and into an open area that was once something else, but had succumbed to the passing trends of time, just to their left was a picture straight out of a bygone age. They stepped into it.

"I have a red and white polka dot circle skirt that would be perfect for this place," Ben enthused. "It's fabulous. I love it before we've even sat down."

As they walked to the long counter, Becca had to agree with Jack's brief description. He hadn't needed to say anymore. She had an image in in her mind of a nineteen fifty's seaside café and this was it, not in black and white on a post card or an old BBC documentary. It was a bit like walking onto a film set, but one built with impossible insight for a future film project decades in the future. It had the sense of time about it that couldn't be reproduced. Like Patricia's it was spotless and simple and a bit frayed around the edges. She wondered if Patricia knew about this place.

Ben was delighted and looking into the glass-fronted shelves at things that had once been commonplace and unfortunately now seemed dated and basic. He pointed it all out to Jack, who had obviously seen it all before, but indulged a friend seeing it for the first time, enjoying it through his eyes. He turned to Becca.

"Like it?" Jack asked.

"It's great. It feels like a breath of fresh air."

"How so?"

"There's no pretence, no trendy, no in thing, no passing fad. Just stuff that has been around for decades. Things you thought had gone, but apparently are still there quietly getting on with it in the background."

In honour of the place, they bought milky coffee, bacon butties (had to be on white bread), custard creams, bourbon creams and those round shortbread biscuits with the bits in, which Becca only now realised were currents. They sat by the window and Jack ask the woman on the next table to take a photo. He tweaked the end product and showed them it.

"Black and white, how totally appropriate," Becca passed it to Ben. "I'll be back in a mo' just off to the loo."

"That way," Jack pointed as she stood looking about her for a sign.

"I look like Pearl Bailey," Ben enthused.

"Carmen Jones," Jack said, not totally sure if that was the right film.

Ben looked at him.

"What?" Jack asked.

"If someone had told me last week, I, a gay man, sometimes drag queen, would be sat here having an actual real, proper conversation about Carmen Jones with a hettie man, I'd have laughed them out of the room."

Jack laughed. "You know, if I'd have said that, someone would accuse me of stereotyping."

"Babes, you're right. I shouldn't have said it, but old habits die hard."

Jack shrugged. "I wasn't having a go, it's just something I've noticed. I'm tired of being lumped in with the Neanderthals who's views haven't lifted out of the seventies."

"It's a messed-up world. Some people won't change, some can't change, some don't realise they need to change and others are trying to," he pointed at himself.

"Me too," Jack readily acknowledged.

"It's difficult to keep up with it all. One minute it's okay to say one thing, the next minute it's not and habit can be a difficult thing to stop."

"Yep, it's like new stereotypes are being created in the process of trying to get rid of the old ones?"

Becca returned. "What are we talking about?"

"Stereotypes," Jack explained.

Becca pulled a guilty face. "It's no good, I'm going to have to confess."

Jack looked at Ben. Ben looked at Jack. They both looked confused.

Becca took the look for something else and grabbed the wrong end of the stick. "I'm going to apologise for labelling the two of you."

Jack frowned. "What, hair man and high heels, you're joking?"

"We weren't talking about you, babes."

"Well there's more to it than that." She looked at Jack. "I assumed you'd be conceited, entitled, self-obsessed and a narcissist." She didn't give him time to answer before turning to Ben. "I thought you were an aggressive female prostitute."

Jack was laughing. "All that from footsteps."

"And a quick view of you on the train, oh and leaving the flats," Becca added.

Ben's mouth stretched open in comic outrage. He looked about himself, as if to say, she couldn't possibly mean me.

"Babes, people have assumed a lot more."

Jack looked at Ben. "I pulled you up about it and it turns out I do it too." He looked at Becca. "You remember chicken boy."

"How could I forget him?"

"Chicken boy?" Ben asked. "If this is anything to do with stuffing, I'm all ears."

Food finished, the sun and the sea beckoned and they headed up the coast. Chatting as they walked the time passed quickly, the sun rose higher into the sky and its heat brought more and more people to the beach. Wind breakers, mini tents, towels, laughter, buckets and spades. With the sea a brilliant blue, and the beach drying quickly to golden sand they took off shoes and walked back. They ambled along with kids running in and out of the gentle waves and wagging tailed dogs criss-crossing about them. Ben wandered down to the water and was soon chatting to a lady, who tottered about hanging onto the hem of her frock as the water managed to reach her toes.

Becca and Jack sat and watched as the two began splashing about in the water, both shrieking at the childish pleasure, one thirty-something the other eighty, but both remembering what it was like to be kids.

"Did you and Ben manage to sort the world's problems," Becca asked.

"Nope, we got as far as stereotypes and neither of us had the answer for the tiny bit we scratched. It turns out we've all done it and been on the receiving end of it. What about you?"

"Well, I've made it very clear I do it," she rolled her eyes. "But as for on the receiving end, I've been pretty lucky on that front. I know a lot of women haven't, but generally I've worked with, and for people where it's not been an issue, at least not to my face anyway. I've done well at work and I get paid properly for it." She stopped to think. "I have been lucky, especially when you hear so much in the news and social media, though some of that is about selling their product, making a headline to capture interest and make money. Public interest or profit? You?" Jack seemed to be considering his answer, or possibly if he should answer. When he finally did, there was a definite note of reluctance in his voice.

"There's been times when I've really liked the person, but they were only interested in a trophy shag and that was it. And I get it, people would say, if that's your only worry, get on with your life and stop whinging. And don't get me wrong," he added with a self-effacing look, "there are times when I'm only too happy to be nothing more than a one nighter. But, not every time and the more it happens, the more I stop and think, is looks all they're interested in and am I that boring? That could sound conceited," he apologised. "It's complicated."

"It is complicated and you don't sound arrogant. I'll admit I'm not sure I've ever thought of it that way, but of course, it would get to anyone, no matter how confident they might appear. Once you start questioning yourself, it can be a downhill ride all the way."

"Your mother and sister, did they shake your confidence, or were you able to keep it in perspective?"

Becca laughed. "I'd say annihilated my confidence and it's taken me a long time to pull it back together. I keep saying I'm a work in progress."

"You generally come across as confident," Jack said.

"If I do, it's the swan thing."

"Right, I get you, serene on the surface paddling like mad underneath."

"You as well?" Becca asked.

"And then some."

People are never what they seem, or are infinitely complex, Becca thought to herself. You get to know something new every time and sometimes you never truly know a person. That's when you make assumptions to cover the gaps, back to stereotypes. Was it a survival technique? Label someone in an attempt to understand them? Or was it plain and simple insecurity? She glanced at Jack, he was watching Ben and the woman as they danced in the waves.

"Speaking of paddling," Jack gave a nod toward the sea. "You coming in?"

"No, I'm too comfortable here. You go and play."

Jack whipped off his trainers and jogged down the beach to where Ben and Agnes were now back in conversation; Becca had decided she looked like an Agnes, was that labelling? The sky was now a perfect blue and the colour of the sea had lifted to match it. The sand felt warm, the air smelt of baked seaweed and vinegar. She watched as a dad and older brother strode down the beach to the rest of their family, who were waiting for the sweating parcels they carried. The waft of vinegar and hot fish was unmistakable, so much a part of days by the sea. Becca moved her attention away from thoughts of chips and tomato sauce and cast her gaze around the beach. Colours, sights and sounds, a sea of people as far as the eye could wander. Towel family, the wind break camp, sand mountains and sandcastles. Lobster legs, big hat lady and tattoo man; a kaleidoscope of people, all seemingly content with sun, sea and sand, all individuals, all complex.

She could people watch all day and then she noticed the little group. At first, she wasn't sure who they were watching, but when

Ben headed off with Agnes, the looks and asides continued, they were watching Jack. The object of their attention was looking out to sea. She scanned the beach again. There were some attractive men scattered about and a few who were slim or toned as well as good looking, but the group were definitely watching Jack, sizing him up. At work Amy rated all the men and women who walked past. Becca could be on the phone, but Amy would still catch her eye and mouth a four, or a three with a disgruntled look, or an eight or nine with flared eyes and an insistent nod in the direction of the lucky passer-by. She looked back at the group, they were watching and talking about him. One of the women got up at the encouragement of her friends and walked over. It was a walk of intent. There was a casual greeting as she approached. He must have been deep it thought because it seemed to catch him off guard. But soon the smile was there, and it worked its usual charm. They chatted away, the woman brushing fingers through her hair, touching her neck, smiling a lot. There was a lot of eye contact. Lots of small and not so small signs that spelt out she found him attractive. Becca wondered if she would still have the confidence to walk up to a stranger, she fancied and start chatting them up. She also wondered how easily she would find the conversation if she was the object of such attention. Like the hugs he regularly dished out, Jack managed it with ease, an ease that to a casual onlooker, with a habit of labelling people, would consider to be over-assured, an air of entitlement, but she knew him to be better than that. The woman, beach phone girl, had her phone out. Numbers were being exchanged. It all seemed so easy.

"It looks so easy," Ben's voice broke her reverie.

"Doesn't it though."

Ben flopped down beside her. "I could do a lot with looks like that and the inner confidence to make the best use of them."

"You're attractive," Becca looked at him, she hadn't considered that Ben lacked any kind of confidence.

"Babes, in a gown and a wig, I'm a goddess. Out of them it's different. I go back to being me, don't get me wrong, I'm okay looking and I'm no shrinking violet. But Tina's confidence would be a ten and I'm about a seven, maybe an eight on a good day."

"Funny, I was just having a similar conversation with Jack. Outward appearance not always matching the inside. You were chatting away with Agnes like you were old friends."

"Agnes? Oh, you mean Joan. That's nothing. I just talk."

"It's not you know," Becca thought back on her own efforts. At work, she could do the whole introductory line and maintain a conversation, with anyone, but she had to work at it. "And you're funny with it. There's something magnetic about you. I can't quite put a finger on it, just a certain something."

"Well, let me know when you have and I'll put it to good use on the next adonis that stumbles past me."

"Wouldn't you get sick of it?"

"I'd like the opportunity to."

"Don't you get a lot of attention? I mean you're up on stage, a celebrity."

"That word rubs me up the wrong way, it used to mean something, now it's anything that's been on the telly for five minutes and has the mouth to match an over inflated ego. What they see on the stage isn't me. Some guys want Tina and once I'm done performing, Tina goes back in the box and jars she comes out of. Her gone; they quickly lose interest. Others think, even out of costume, we're the same person and are disappointed to find I'm quieter, different. I'm not a Jack out of drag, but I ain't bad looking. I don't shave my eyebrows and I keep my sideburns."

"What is it with the eyebrows and sideburns. Why do drags queens shave them off?"

"Easier when you're putting the slap on, a better finish, less messing with glue sticks and hair lines and too many other reasons to list."

"Why don't you. You're in drag most nights."

"Babes, I want a shag every now and then, having no eyebrows freaks out the ones that are interested."

Becca laughed and they both looked back to the enfolding saga. "Numbers swapped," Becca watched as the woman made her move.

"Double D number; date or dump," Ben explained.

"Or trophy shag," Becca spoke, half to herself.

"You're not jealous, are you babes?" His question wasn't provocative, more surprised that she might be, or astonished he'd missed the signs.

"No," she replied casually, "but he said something earlier about being liked for him and not for what he looks like."

Ben pulled a face. "Babes, it's hard to feel sorry for someone who looks like that."

"Jack said as much himself."

"And as for that smile. I'd pay a lot, correction, I have paid a lot for a smile like that and it doesn't pack the same punch," he grinned.

"Dazzling."

"Maybe, but not captivating. So, he's insecure, just like the rest of us. Or should I say like me?"

"Stick with us. Honestly I don't know anyone who isn't."

"And your insecurities?"

"You have to ask?"

"Babes from where I'm sat, you've everything going for you."

"Oh god, where do I begin? Let me just say I'm working on them and at the moment they seem unimportant." She shielded her eyes and looked up at the blue sky. "The sun is shining, I'm out with friends, I've a good job and a great flat. I've had milky coffee, biscuits and a bacon sandwich. And I'm about to have chips. What more could I want?"

***

The summer rolled on to those final weeks when even the best of gardens looked tired, exhausted from their show of glory. The heights of the season had passed and began to move into the darker nights of September. The collection of handmade, homemade things in the entrance hall continued to change, each of the residents, known and other wise, contributed and took from it. Caught up in their work, Becca, Ben and Jack hadn't seen as much of each other as they would have liked, quick coffees at Patricia's or tea when they caught each other. This might have continued had life work balance not tapped Becca firmly on the shoulder and looked at her expectantly in the mirror. With that timely reminder she caught the other two and suggested they make a point of doing something that weekend. Somehow, they all managed to wangle the time and somehow, they managed to coincide their plans with summer's final weekend performance. All woke to sunshine streaming in through their windows and heat more expected, and rarely found, in August. They loaded themselves into the car and headed south, picking up the moors road that took them through the national park, a patch work of heather, dales and rough grass grazed by sheep. They crossed a high-level bridge with dramatic views down a river to a harbour watched over by a ruined abbey and then climbed back onto the moors. They passed forests and villages until the road once again descended to the coast with a view of a castle, proof they'd reached their destination. It was still early when they parked and walked the length of marine drive, Becca excited to introduce them to, what she considered, the only way to eat breakfast by the sea.

"Ice cream, for breakfast?" Jack said without conviction, as they crossed the road from the harbour.

"Maybe they do bacon flavour," Ben said.

"Wait 'till you've tried it," Becca said, grabbing both their arms and dragging them across the road. They sat on stools at the bar, in what Becca called nineteen fifties heaven. Their order was taken and they all sat in eager anticipation as three tall glasses were taken from the yellow Formica shelves and expertly filled with layers of ice cream, fruit and sauces that could only be topped with cream and a wafer. They were works of art and photos were taken before conversation stopped and they communed with sweet creamy goodness. Even the pictures on the wall attested to the benefits of ice cream, so it had to be true.

From there they walked along the busy sea front, ducking into arcades and craning their necks to look up at the vast hotel that dominated the south bay, before making their way past the spa and further to a café that again had changed little since the bygone days of seaside holidays. They sat outside in the sun, the sea below them and the valley gardens above and behind them.

Becca breathed a deep contented sigh, allowing the moment to sink into her soul. "This is bliss."

"Yep, I didn't think we'd get a seat, it's popular," Jack looked about them and at the queue now forming from the interior of the old wooden building.

"It's another of our F.B.T. places," Becca said.

"F.B.T?" Jack turned back to look at her.

"Forgotten by time, like your milky coffee café."

"I get it. Then yep, I'd say it is. Ben, have you got one of these places in mind? We might as well complete the set."

"Ben pushed the brim of his hat up and pulled the top of his sunglasses down. "Hmm, I'll have to think about that one."

"How do you know about this place?" Jack asked.

"Childhood holidays, we often came here and my nanna always insisted we came to the 'old café', she'd been coming since its hey days. She'd sit there, national health sunglasses, hospital neck support, which she didn't need, flowery dress and cardigan, no matter what the temperature. This was her holiday treat and I guess I liked it too, my mother hated it, but condescended to come.

Even my sister liked it, which was a novelty, in that we agreed on something."

"What about your dad?" Ben asked. "You hardly mention him."

"Don't I?" Becca frowned. "I suppose not, he always seemed to be at work. He was on shifts, so often slept during the day. It was almost as if he was a bystander to the family saga. The show revolved around my mother; my dad made appearances when work allowed. He was quiet and unassuming, anything for a quiet life. I was more like him than my mother or sister, so maybe I sat more on the outside of that family like him."

"So, you weren't a close a family, even when you were young?" Jack asked.

"I don't think we were. Not a united one. Coexisted; I think might be a better choice." Becca paused again; she hadn't thought about this really. "We weren't a huggy family, that's for sure. They argued a lot I remember. Were they happy together? You know, I'm not sure they were. But it was never talked about openly. We were kept out of it, or at least I was. My sister is older, by a big gap. Maybe she saw and heard more."

"Did you get on with your dad?" Jack asked.

"Yes, I did. When he wasn't at work it was usually me and him that did things. He died shortly after I got back from university. I have wondered, had he lived, if we'd have become closer, got to know each other as adults. You have a different relationship with a parent when you're a child. I'm not sure I really knew him."

Jack nodded; she could almost see his thoughts playing across his face. Something she'd said had struck a chord.

Jack turned to Ben. "What about your dad?"

"My dad is Tina's biggest fan and more importantly mine too. He's the most sorted man I know. When I came out, he did exactly what I needed. He hugged me, told me he loved me and was proud of me. Mum hugged us both, it's a moment that glows inside me, even now. I was lucky, no I am lucky. They didn't judge, just accepted me, supported me, and still do. I love them both to bits."

Becca smiled, all his bigger than life gestures and expressions stopped. For that moment it wasn't Ben, his semi persona, sat there, not Tina, just Benjamin the son of two proud parents.

"And your dad, Jack, did you two get on? Becca wondered if she already knew the answer, something was on his mind.

Jack shook his head. "Like you said, it turned out I didn't know him. We haven't spoken since my brother came out. He told me when he was fifteen and swore me to secrecy. He suspected dad wouldn't take it well and didn't want to be dependent on him in case he was right. Anthony said he waited until he'd moved out before telling my parents. And as it turned out, he was right. Mum was totally fine, he told her first. She said she would tell dad."

"And how did your dad react?" Ben asked.

"We went round the following Sunday for lunch. Dad wouldn't come down. Mum said he'd come round, I was surprised. Anthony wasn't. We were laughing about something and then dad was in the kitchen shouting at Anthony, telling him to get out. Anthony tried to reason with him. Dad grabbed him. I jumped in and pulled them apart. Why does that always look easy in films? Not the best idea, it turned out because I was right in the middle of them. Dad was angry, trying to get passed me. Anthony said he'd expected this and then dad tried to hit him. I blocked it and then dad was on the floor. Mum was shouting, I was shouting, Anthony was shouting. It was a mess. Anthony left. Dad shouted after him not to come back and then started on me. I can remember the look he gave me. I thought I don't recognise you. He got up, right into my face shouting, Did I know about it? Was I a poof too? I laughed at him, told him he was pathetic, that if Anthony wasn't welcome, I wouldn't be coming back either."

"Did he back down, come round. Apologise for god's sake?"

"Nope, we haven't spoken since." Jack shrugged. "Looking back, I realised he'd always been a jerk. Funny that. Things he'd said, comments he'd made about all kinds of things. They don't really register at the time, or you make excuses for them."

"You're close to your brother," Becca said. "I remember you saying."

"Very," Jack smiled.

"How long ago was this?" Ben asked. "How's your brother taken it?"

Jack thought, "Five, or so years. Anthony's fine. As I said he suspected it wouldn't go down well. He was prepared for that. Had his own place and job by the time he was twenty-three and then told them."

"Do you see your mother?" Becca asked.

"Yep, she and dad split. I think the incident with Anthony was the last straw."

That phrase again, Becca knew all about that. "How are things now?"

"Anthony and mum are good. We talk regularly, she often goes to stay with him. I don't see him as much as I'd like, but that's only because of work and distance."

"And what about you?" Becca asked.

"Me?" Jack was genuinely surprised by the question. "My brother's happy, mum's fine. It was never about me and as long as they're fine, I am too. I had it easy. I had a lot of girlfriends and that was okay as far as dad was concerned. I'm older than Anthony, so I suppose that gave him a bit of space to decide who he was, he went away to university and that gave him the real space he needed. He didn't move back afterwards."

"Do you miss your dad?" Ben asked.

Jack considered the idea. "I miss the idea of a dad, but not the reality. What about you Becca? Do you miss your mum and sister?"

"I think you gave the perfect answer. I miss the idea of a mother and a sister. The roles you think they should play in your life but don't. The pictures and the box in the hallway probably go back to a time when things were okay, or I was too young to know better. They're a reminder of better times and are difficult to let go of."

"Babes, who says you have to?"

"That bit you said about the last straw and things not registering," Becca went back to Jack's words. "It was like that with my mother."

"How so?"

"Putting up with things, making excuses, thinking things would get better. The older I got, the more I realised how different we were and had nothing in common beyond being related. She would say all sorts, and eventually I just couldn't agree. It was then a case of argue or me keeping my mouth shut. The final straw was a bin lid. It was a Sunday," she looked at Jack. "Why is it always a Sunday? She wanted to go to town, so I went round to collect her. She'd fallen out with all her neighbours, but particularly disliked the one she shared a drive with. She'd often complain about their leaves coming onto her drive," Becca shook her head and smiled. "They had no trees; it was just leaves and their side sloped onto hers. This Sunday their bin was out and the lid was up. As we left, my mother stopped to look at it.

That's why we've got rats, it's them leaving their bin lid up that does it.

I didn't answer, I was thinking about work and we got in the car. We were well on our way before I realised, she'd gone quiet. Normally I'd get the latest update on who she'd fallen out with and why it was their fault. I asked her what was wrong.

Nothing.

It was a very blunt reply, so I knew something was up. I gave her time to calm down and when we were almost there, I asked her where she wanted to go for lunch.

I'm not bothered, anywhere.

Right, I thought, this isn't going away, why I was surprised about that I really don't know. I think my mother had discovered perpetual motion; she could keep a grudge going indefinitely. We got to the car park, it was really full and I said I was surprised. And she went Bang.

You should have known it would be like this.

She ranted, and I mean full on red face, arms folded, huffing and puffing the works. It was almost comic, like a sulky teenager and an old boiler about to explode. What on earth is this about? I asked her.

You never support me.

And it all went on from there, but I'd had enough. I turned the car round and started to drive back. She demanded to know what I was doing. I told her I was taking her home and then I was going."

"And her reaction?" Jack asked.

"It took her back a bit, because she was used to dealing it out and me putting up with it. We had this big argument in the car which finally gave me the chance to say my piece, explain how her behaviour made me feel. I actually thought we'd got somewhere at last. We ended up going back to town, with me feeling things would be different, but she was just brooding on what I'd said. Within half an hour she had started again. That's when I knew it was never going to change. It would always be like this. And I had a choice, accept it or walk away."

"Wow," Ben said. "What a number."

Therapy session over they got up to leave, Becca linked arms with Jack and Ben followed behind.

"You two," Ben called.

They turned, "What?"

"I've just realised something. You've both got a shit-load more baggage than I have."

Determined to work off some of the calories they'd eaten Becca took them back along the sea front and then up into the jumble of houses that climbed the hill to the castle. They explored the keep and crossed the huge expanse of rough grass enclosed by the castle walls. Vantage points offered views out to sea, across the north bay and back over the town and the south bay. The sun shone and a breeze made it pleasant. Becca thought about their conversation. I miss the thought of a mother, but not the reality, she tested out the words. It was true. All the thinking she'd done trying to figure out her feelings and a sentence from someone else made sense of it all. This is why people talk to each other, she reminded herself.

After that Becca took them to the north bay. There they watched a mock naval battle in the park, Becca's father had watched it as a child and so it had been a part of her holidays. It could be called typically British, in the same way that pantomime is. They cheered the goodies and booed the baddies and enjoyed the whole display. They sat for some time after because it was pleasant to. Becca's final childhood memory had them on a model railway that steamed its way along, whistling through tunnels as its passengers waved back at children and those adults still young enough to join in the fun.

Delivered to the farthest tip of the north bay, the three ambled back along the front, past beach huts and scatterings of families still enjoying the beach and making the best of the late summer sun. Just as the heat of the day began to wane, they ate fish and chips, the sound of the sea before them and the lights and sound of the arcades behind. The day couldn't have been better, for Becca it was a brief reminder of the good part of her childhood, a chance to revisit old memories, but more importantly make new ones. It was almost tempting to stay over and do it all again the next day, but she knew this sort of day, one where everything fell into place and was just as it should be, couldn't be repeated. They drifted back to the car, legs aching and faces tingling from the sun.

Chapter 7

Handy, homely, woolly, woody, cakey, cosy…

The nights were pulling in fast, but she'd only just got out her bigger coat; it had been mild. The trees had turned, the air was chill, it finally felt like autumn. The collection in the entrance way had continued, its turnover regular. Back from work, Becca stood looking at it. She knew two of the other contributors, but two remained a mystery. She'd tried knocking on doors again and either they didn't want to answer, or her timing was out. She'd not expected to catch early bird; those footsteps were out well before she was up and returned late, but by now she thought she'd have caught pauses. It was as if the thought had triggered something and above a door shut and she heard footsteps coming down the stairs, she listened. Not early bird, or pauses. Had she missed something, of course it could be someone like a plumber, or had someone moved into flat six. Surely, she couldn't have missed that. She waited, interested to see who the footsteps belonged to. They were neither slow nor fast, heavy nor light. It was difficult to form any picture of who owned them. They reached the last flight and she saw the shoes first. They belonged to a woman, somewhere in her fifties, possibly. It was difficult to tell.

"Hello," the woman greeted with a warm smile and a slight accent Becca couldn't place. She offered Becca her hand, even before she'd taken the last step. "I think we are neighbours."

"I think you might be right," Becca took her hand and found herself smiling. "It's been several months."

"It has. I'm Ann."

"Becca."

Ann looked at the collection. "This is good. Julia said it had become something."

She went over and began to examine everything with simple delight. Becca wondered how she had not seen any of it before. It was difficult to miss even when it was just a single solitary jar of jam. She wanted to ask why and she wanted to know who Julia was. Daughter, partner, they had obviously been one of the other sets of footsteps.

"Have you just moved in. I haven't heard- I mean seen you."

"Broken leg. I've been holed up in my flat since early summer, the time has dragged, but I kept my forehead lifted. My leg has taken quite a while to mend an' Julia has been looking after me. Shopping, popping in three times a day to help. She has been wonderful, but now I'm sorted, eager to be out an' about."

'And' shortened to 'an'; that could be easily missed, but the accent, subtle as it was, was there. Dutch? Swedish? Danish maybe, upbeat, relaxed. "I didn't know. I knocked several times, but didn't like to pester. If I'd known I'd have offered to help."

"I gave up on daytime telly very quickly an' there is only so much you can stream before your head implodes. I started listening to audio books, with my headphones on, they could have demolished the building an' I wouldn't have heard. I'm just heading out. First time, I'm actually excited; shopping," she explained. "In Denmark they would say, really up on the liquorice.

Anyway, small things bring the easiest joy. Come in for some tea, say about seven thirty?"

"Err, yes. That would be great."

Ann had noticed the slight hesitation. "You don't have to of course; I'll not take offence an' of course you may have plans."

"It's not that," Becca was quick to reply. "For a second I lost track of the days, we have a regular video night, but it's not tonight."

"That's easy, especially when you're retired. I used to teach, wrote the date on a board of one type or another for over thirty years. Always knew what day it was, what time it was an' exactly what I would be doing. Now I often cannot tell if it's the weekend or a Wednesday. I love it. Seven thirty then?"

"Definitely."

"Enjoy."

With that Ann pulled on her gloves and headed for the door. Becca made for hers. The helper, Julia, must have been pauses. That only left early bird.

By tea Becca had assumed just that, water in a cup with milk and a tea bag. Ann's idea of tea was something else again. Becca knocked on the door, the fourth floor flat, below was Ben, then Jack and then her. She wondered at the view from here, would it reach over the houses on the other side of the road? The door opened and from that moment she was transported into a magazine. She smelt cinnamon and something else, it announced the warmth and comfort beyond. Everything was simple, or rather looked effortless. Handmade and crafted, wood, ceramics, pictures, furniture, throws, cushions, candles. It was light and airy, and at the same time warm and comforting. Warm matt colours in sage, teal, pale blue and soft greys flowed past her eyes as Ann led her through to the dining area. The rooms embraced her and she felt instantly welcome. How did things do that, or how had Ann made things do that? Candles flickered, the lighting was soft and picked out items and pictures. If this hadn't been enough, the table was set. Freshly baked bread, (the smell was unmistakable) homemade chutney, (familiar because it had appeared in the entrance hall) fruit, (which Becca would have said Ann had grown herself, if it had been possible to fit an orchard into a flat) and other dishes with interesting things in them. For god's sake even the cups and plates looked like they'd come straight off a potter's wheel.

"Sit down, make yourself comfortable an' don't stand on ceremony. Eat what you want an' as much as you want. It's there to be enjoyed an' not politely nibbled at." Ann stopped and smiled to herself. "That is unless you've already eaten?"

"No, nothing since lunch. I'm starving and even if I wasn't, I'd make room, this looks amazing. Do you normally eat like this?"

"No, but food is so important to me an' I love to bake." It was clearly a passion. Becca could see the way Ann's face lit up when she talked about it. "I'm a feeder, I love to feed people. I think food is a doorway to friendship. Its preparation, takes time an' time is a great gift."

"My world revolves around food, I live to eat, not eat to live."

"Wise words. Go on tuck in."

And so, they ate and talked and ate and talked. Ann, it turned out, was a real home baker and very good at it. Everything tasted good, smelt good, did her good. Becca learned that Ann was newly retired from teaching, had moved to the city because she wanted a complete change and had broken her leg badly just after moving in. Becca assumed she had moved in just after Ann and told her of her new job, her need for change and about Jack and Ben. Tea finished, Ann suggested they sit by the fire and brought a fresh pot of tea and some cake. A rich fruit cake that Becca could do nothing other than devour.

"My parents met in Vedbæk, my mother's hometown. A chance meeting as my father was exploring one weekend, he was English and working in Copenhagen. They courted, got engaged, married an' travelled, eventually settling in England, shortly after which I was born. Family was very important to them an' so I have two sisters an' a brother. My mother taught us all Danish, she very much wanted to keep our heritage alive. She in fact kept her accent all her life an' as you can hear, it rubbed off on me. We visited Denmark often to see relatives an' they visited us. It was always a busy house as well as family, friendship also played a key part in their lives an' entertaining was a passion."

"It had an impact on you." Becca looked about her. "All of this, it's so welcoming."

"Thank you. If you visited my brother's house or either of my sisters it would be the same."

"Do you see your family much?"

"We keep in touch through the computer, most weeks we talk together. My oldest sister is in Edinburgh, the second settled in America an' my brother returned to Denmark. My son, James, lives in the Lake district. Each year we rent a big house there an' get together for a month and we stay with my brother in Denmark near Christmas. Everyone under one roof, it's always a great time. Lots of board games, walks an' lots of food."

"Speaking of which, that was all delicious, I was expecting a cuppa. That was a feast."

"That, I would say, comes from my mother's Danish heritage of which hygge is a key element."

"Hoo?"

"It's spelt h-y-g-g-e an' pronounced hooga, well it can be pronounced in a variety of ways, that's; possibly the easiest, but is still difficult to translate to one word in English. You would have to use several." Ann got up and went to a bookcase. Returning with a small book. "Take this with you an' have a read, it will become clock-clear."

Becca looked at the cover, that, in itself was appealing and did what all good covers should do- make you want to open it. She flicked through briefly, a picture of homemade preserves jumping out at her. "Was it you who put the jam in the entrance hall?"

"Julia put it there for me. Legs working, I would have done it myself. It was meant to be a way of sticking my finger in the soil." Ann noticed Becca's puzzled expression again. "The sayings; Danish expressions. They sneak in especially if I have been talking to my brother. In English it would be, testing the water. Connect with my neighbours, until I was on my feet again. It was bait to reel in likeminded people. Friendship is very important to hygge an' of course me. My leg took longer to heal than expected, so the hygge took on a life of its own. I'm happy to see it thriving."

"It's certainly been a talking point, we ended up calling it the collection. Jack was the first to get involved and then Ben and I got sort of sucked in. You could say it started our friendship, so it's worked some form of magic. They will want to meet you. I'll arrange something," then Becca got a mental flash of her flat, a grey lifeless place compared to this. "As soon as I'm properly settled in."

"That would be very good."

"Perhaps you could give me a bit of advice on how to add a bit more, what was it, hooger to my flat."

"Hoo-ga," Ann corrected. "An' you would make your flat more hyggelig, pronounced hooglig. Anyways, enough of the Danish. Have a read of the book an' then, if I can help, I will be very glad to."

***

Jack came in and greeted them both with his usual hug and sat down. "So, Ben tells me you've added one more to the list of graduates?" Jack kept his expression even.

"Graduates?" Becca returned a suspicious look; he was being facetious.

"Yep, I graduated from hair man to having a name, as did Ben. Now another of your label people has too."

"I'm not that bad"

Ben cleared his throat. "Did I not sit with you in town, did we not have coffee and cake and did you not name everyone who passed that window." He was unblinking in his accusation.

"Not everyone."

He cleared his throat again.

"Just the interesting ones," Becca picked up the book and showed it to them. "Ann gave me this."

"Higge?"

"Hyg?"

"It's pronounced, or can be pronounced, hooga."

"So, what's that about when it's at home?"

"It's about friendship and being cosy. It's about food and good company. It's about cushions and throws and woolly jumpers. Real log fires and the right lighting. It's candles and handmade furniture and so much more. It's cake and coffee, a favourite mug, being in the moment, making small things special."

"All that in one word," Ben passed the book to Jack.

"We've got the food bit right," Becca continued. "And the good company."

"Babes, I'm always good company when there's food."

"So, what's on your list next then?" Jack asked, having skimmed through the introduction.

"I need to make this place cosy, special. Erm, more handmade. I'm hoping Ann is going to give me a bit of advice."

"Why don't you take her shopping. She must know some places where you can get what you're after," Jack suggested.

"That's what I thought I'd do and then, I'll cook a meal and have you all round in my new flat."

"Babes, not just any flat, your new, handy, homely, woolly, woody, cakey, cosy flat."

***

It seemed silly to be excited about shopping, but Becca woke early and couldn't get back to sleep, so she got up and got ready. Having unpacked her flat with Ben, she'd spent the last week going through it all and had taken a lot to charity shops and the recycling. It now looked almost as bare, as it had, before she'd unpacked. Ben had watched, nails drying, with an air of doubt in the wisdom of such a clear out.

He'd sat on the only thing that was safe, the chair with the cushion and throw she'd first assembled after being in Jack's flat. An island of hygge in a sea of scarcity and cold utility. She'd told him, that without the clear out, she would be tempted to keep stuff, stuff she didn't really like. If she got rid of it, she would have to buy something to replace it. Ben's only contribution, and it had been typically provocative, was to stand, arms folded over the box and pictures set apart in the hallway.

"And this?" he'd said expectantly. "Anything happening here yet? Babes, these have squatted here for months, they glower at me, so the gay gods only know what they do to you. Why not put them in a cupboard. It's not getting rid, just clearing a trip hazard."

She looked at them, oddly the box and the pictures had become something like invisible, an all too familiar feature that had faded into the walls. She'd acted on impulse and told him to take them with him. Before she could change her mind, he'd swept them up and left, dressing gown flapping, hip padding on show.

Had she made a mistake? She pondered for only a while until there was a gentle knock on the door. She grabbed her coat and bag and opening the door greeted Ann with…

"I've a list,"

"Good. We'll look through it over coffee an' cake. This is going to be good; can't wait to see what you buy."

"You and me both."

They paused in the entrance hall.

"And this is what started everything," Becca gestured to the collection. "A little pot of your jam."

"Indeed, jam, chutney, Jack's candles. You said Ben's cloth and your flowers."

"And your biscuits," Becca picked up a fresh pack. "These really are very good."

"They are not mine. We must have five people contributing."

"I still haven't managed to say hello to early bird. I've kept calling, but they never seem to be in."

Ann looked at her. "Early bird? There is a story here."

Becca rolled her eyes, feeling a little foolish. "Oh, I haven't told you about the names. There's always a story, and usually it's embarrassing."

Ann took Becca to parts of town she'd never been, never considered visiting. But each new place offered a small shop, some of which must have survived online, judging from their out of the way location. Ann had searched them out long before she moved to the city and was a regular enough customer, in some, to be known by name. Each shop was a pleasure to be in, let alone the trove of treasures they contained. It was a reminder to Becca that while endlessly convenient, online shopping didn't have the atmosphere of a real shop. These weren't just browse and click pages. These were browse, and touch and smell and feel places. The objects and the shops that sold them, offered a level of participation the computer couldn't. Places like these were quite possibly the last outposts of the high street and with any luck its future. Becca had an idea of what she wanted, and Ann offered suggestions that drew it together into a unified assault on her plastic. Ann's instinct was to touch, to pick up and gain a sense of the thing they were looking at, appearance alone wasn't enough. The object had to be special, and have some link to the other things she'd bought, through colour, or style. Being able to put them together physically gave her a palette she would never have thought of. She went with ochre, pale pink, a strong blue, light grey and blonde wood. Ann encouraged her to trust her own taste, and if in doubt, do nowt.

There was something about striding about town with her hands full of shopping bags, it was deeply satisfying and by the end of it she was thoroughly retail therapied out. It took two trips for both to empty Ann's car of all the stuff Becca had bought, and more was being delivered. The mountain of bags was put in the spare bedroom, Becca wanted to wait until she had everything before trying to place it all.

They sat in her kitchen, kettle on, carefully chosen mugs out because Ann was there. Becca had also arranged the biscuits onto a plate. She couldn't put a packet out in front of Ann.

"I hope you've noticed I've made an effort," Becca spread her hand across the arrangement of biscuits, in a very Ben like fashion she realised.

"I certainly have. Even the seemingly smallest of gestures can help make something special, more hooglig." Ann reached over to the tiny vase of flowers and placed it next to the plate of biscuits. "Pleasure in small things an' the difference they make."

"My sister could learn a lesson from that," Becca quipped and got up to make the tea.

"Are you an' your sister close?"

"Close," Becca's scoffed, "is not a word I would use in the same sentence as my sister and I, or my mother and I for that matter. My mother and I had an odd relationship. It's only now that I've come to realise it. As a child I thought it was normal, as an adult I thought of it as something to endure and that all families were like that."

"How did your opinion change?"

"At university, talking to friends. I began to realise just how unlike their relationships with their mothers mine was." Becca poured the tea and got milk out of the fridge. "In a jug," she said proudly.

"Very Hyggelig," Ann congratulated. "It's interesting that people who have a good relationship with their parents can't understand how someone might not. An', why shouldn't they, a good relationship with your parents is a natural thing."

"After we'd fallen out people told me, I should make it up to her, repair the bond and all that sort of thing."

"And did you?"

"The first few times we really argued, I would always be the one to ring and meet her more than halfway. The final time, we had a big argument, over something ridiculous. I'd forgotten to agree with her, because I was distracted. I thought it might be sorted, but within half an hour she was back to normal and back to her old tricks."

"Tricks?"

"She was right, I was wrong and then went onto how things were going to change, mainly on my part. She liked to be in control of the situation, she spoke, you listened, she was right, you weren't. She expressed her opinion and you had to accept it without question or offence. And I did for too long."

"It began to affect you," Ann was nodding, perhaps on a familiar page herself.

"After our final argument, we had one last conversation which ended with her putting the phone down. In the past I always rang her back. This time I didn't. The weeks passed and I began to realize just how much her moods affected me, coloured my whole week. I would dread calling her, or visiting because I never knew what I was going to get. Conversation, or accusations, based on her ability to put two and two together and come up with five."

"When did you last speak, or hear from her?"

"She sent a letter, written in capitals, with a deadline. The letter had been posted a day before the deadline. I didn't get it until three days after."

"Would you have answered it, if it had arrived in time."

"No because it was a threat."

"Do you think you will ever talk to your mother again?"

"If I did, it would be entirely on her terms and I've no doubt things wouldn't change and I would be back to feeling miserable. I know it sounds heartless but it's such a weight off my shoulders."

"It does not sound heartless. At the end of the day if someone can't change, or is unwilling to, it's not your fault. You can try to negotiate, but I think you can end up giving away too much of yourself. The best thing to do is to walk away. She is an adult an' should have more experience, emotional maturity. She knows where you are. The letter could have been more reasonable, offered a solution a way forward, but age does not guarantee wisdom."

"My mother wasn't one for offering solutions. I could never go to her with a problem, or rather I learnt not to, as it would ultimately come round to how my problem was now her burden. I quickly learnt that sharing a problem made things worse and so I learnt to keep them to myself. Not that you'd know from that outpouring. That's the second time I've done that lately. I'm sorry Ann, that's a bit much over tea and biscuits."

"Do not apologise. A comfortable situation encourages talk, heartfelt or vacuous, it's all talk an' communication is a good thing. I'm glad you felt you could share it with me. Sometimes there is no time to stick a finger in the soil, you just have to jump in." Ann took her hand and gave it a little squeeze. "I would like to think we are becoming friends an' that is what friends are for."

"Absolutely," Jack and Ben had first made her realise talking was good, she might have forgotten that lesson if Ann's timely questions hadn't reinforced the idea. It was odd to think how ingrained some of her habits were.

***

There was a hurried knocking at the door, great, Becca thought, just as the delivery van arrives.

She opened the door and Ben marched in. "Someone's got deliveries?" he rubbed his hands together.

"The van's just arrived."

He sat himself down. "Don't mind me. I'm just here to be nosey, see what you've bought and decide if it would look better in my flat."

Becca shook her head. "You're incorrigible."

"First I was provocative and now I'm incorrigible."

Becca answered the intercom and buzzed them in. She was expecting a sofa and side tables, coffee table and bookshelves. When the delivery men, or rather when delivery man number two appeared Ben stopped being interested in the delivery and directed his attention to the method of transport.

They left to collect the next of Becca's things.

"Why sir," Ben drawled in his best southern belle accent. "You're more than I expected."

"Stop it, they'll hear you," Becca hissed.

"And you're not vaguely interested," Ben asked.

"I didn't say that, but I'm not going to announce it."

"I can be subtle." Ben picked up a magazine, opened another button on his shirt and positioned himself carefully. "There, I'm doing nothing more than reading."

They seemed to be taking a long time to come back. Becca went to the window; they were struggling with the sofa. "He is good looking," she admitted. "Though, not quite on a par with Jack."

"Don't bring him into this. It makes it feel like lusting after your brother." The mutual shudder couldn't have been better timed, or more over the top, they both laughed.

"He is still seeing Laura, isn't he?" Becca asked, still looking out of the window.

"You mean beach phone girl. As far as I know, yes. You heard differently?"

"No. It seems to be going okay. He doesn't really mention her. I just wondered if he'd said something to you. All I get is, it's fine."

"Same here," Ben looked up from the magazine he wasn't looking at. "But on to more pressing and immediate matters. How's things outside. They on their way back yet. Pity it's not a hotter day. Warm work, all that carrying, makes a guy want to take his shirt off?"

Becca pulled the cushion out from behind him. "Don't put images into my head. I'll go red, it'll be embarrassing. You really are outrageous."

He recovered quickly. "What is it you say? Think of me as a work in progress, fundamentally flawed, but with a heart of pure salt. Shh, they're coming back. Is it getting hot in here?"

"You're a piece of work alright."

Why was she now feeling so self-conscious? Was she going red? Becca put her brain in gear enough to show them where she wanted things. She did feel hot, Ben was humming an Olivia Newton John song, she purposefully stood in front of him. She could feel his eyes boring right through her and he kept prodding her in the back. She shooed him away with a discrete, but increasingly insistent hand.

Finally, the sofa was manoeuvred in. Becca got out of the way and stood by the chair Ben occupied, or rather, was now draped in. She tried to look casual, not to stare at delivery man number two. Delivery man number one asked for a signature and with a certain amount of relief, Becca showed them both out.

She closed the door and marched back into the lounge. "Oh my god. Remind me next time to get things delivered when you're out."

Ben showed no signs of guilt. "Babes, those arms and the eyes, did you see those blues eyes. I could dive in and swim there for hours."

"I wasn't thinking about swimming," Becca felt her face flush.

"Why Rebecca, you do have a slutty side. I approve."

"Right, you need to go. I'm going to mop up this pool of drool and then get sorted."

"I've been thrown out of better places. Enjoy."

***

She stepped back from the dinner table and admired her handy work. It all looked very nice, candles, plates, the room all cosy with lamps and stuff. Hygge, she said to herself and turned back to the kitchen. It was decidedly less hygge. She wasn't a cook, and seemed able to use every pot, pan and spoon in the place. She'd relied on the few dishes she knew she could cook. All shown to her by friends at university. Palmiers were the only thing she could bake and even then, she'd bought the puff pastry. After that it was simply a case of unrolling it spreading it with pesto and cheese, rolling it into a sausage, slicing it and putting the heart shapes onto a baking tray. She'd forgot to chill it before cutting so the hearts looked a little more like deformed butterflies. Main course was tuna surprise. It was made from tuna and there was no surprise. But once she'd learnt to cook it, it had become a staple at university and she did it well. Onion and bacon fried in the oil from a can of tuna. Sliced courgette and mushrooms added. Then she made a white sauce, her second culinary skill, to which she added the tinned tuna and some herbs. Then it was a case of mixing it all together and serving it with rice. Her other university dish was savoury mince made with tomato sauce, but the less said about that the better. Pudding was a bought pastry case; pastry was not a third culinary skill. She chopped bananas, made a toffee sauce using condensed milk butter and sugar, maybe that was her third skill. Poured it over the bananas and then whipped cream with a bit of sugar and vanilla. This was her best stuff, more assembled than properly cooked, or baked. Now to clear the wreckage she'd amassed creating it all. Becca looked at it, there was so much and she still needed to get showered and changed, she smelt of onions and time wasn't on her side. The kitchen would have to wait. So, she closed the door firmly and headed for the bathroom.

One by one her guests arrived and introductions were made. Becca proudly gave a tour of her living room and the dining area, all offered suitable compliments and Ann gave it the official stamp of approval. While they chatted, she boiled the rice, hoping she'd get the light flaky rice she saw on the telly and not the usual porridge she managed. In the end it came somewhere between the two. The meal went well, everyone made the appropriate noises and were still alive at the end of it. The banoffee pie had all gone, which she was disappointed about, it would have been breakfast the next morning, or a midnight trip to the fridge in her silk dressing gown.

They'd been talking about the food of their childhood. Becca, Ben and Jack had talked about food of the nineties.

"Babes, orange food. Cheese string and Sunny D."

"The start of yoghurt drinks, pop tarts you put in the toaster and Fuse bars," Becca said.

"Yep, I really liked those bars." Jack said. "What about weekday teas. Did you used to have potato waffles and those smiley faced potato shapes?"

"Babes, weekday teas were those with baked beans or spaghetti hoops. Turkey Twizzlers and those pancakes with a savoury filling. Oh, and Vienetta on special occasions."

"I loved that," Becca said, recalling it for the first time in ages. "It was so posh looking. I liked the mint one."

"Yep, me too, there were a lot of flavours I think."

"We used to have something called Ice Magic," Ann said. "You might remember it. I think it's still around in some form, or another."

"It sounds familiar," Jack said. "What is it?"

"Back in the day," Ann began, "it was hugely popular. It was a chocolate sauce that you put on ice cream an' it set the minute it touched anything cold. It was like magic. There were different flavours, the bottles were brown with a funny lid that looked like it had melted. Mint, orange, plain chocolate an' one with a yellowish lid."

"What else was big in the eighties?" Becca asked.

"I overlap two decades. I'd probably have to say I was a child of the seventies an' eighties, as well as two countries. From my mother I remember rye bread an' sliced sausage, we ate lots of pickles an' smoked fish. But mother had to make those, they were not readily available in England back then. The food I really remember was typically English. Weekends stick in my mind, always the same things. Saturday lunch was a fried meal. Baked beans an' sausages from a tin, mushrooms, bacon an' fritters."

"What are fritters, babes?"

"Chips really, just cut as a disc, like a very thick crisp. Tea on a Saturday was a saveloy, a smoked sausage. Again, fried, I think in butter an' put in a bun. Sunday lunch was always a roast, often beef that had been cooked to within an inch of its life. Brown an' shrunken like old shoe leather pulled out of a bog. Sunday tea was a salad, iceberg lettuce an' tomato with some sort of rolled meat with egg in the middle. Boxed trifle, you made from various sachets, an' a kind of blancmange my mother made from jelly an' evaporated milk beaten together. And there was Bird's Appeal, orange powder that came in a packet, you mixed it with water an' it made orange juice." She sat back in her chair, thoughts clearly on her family. "I loved it all, but now it all seems so basic."

Jack thought about his company's archives. "I think it wasn't until the nineties that food began to really change in this country, that's when the company I work for got into it anyway."

Ann nodded. "The eighties started it; I would say an' it picked up momentum in the nineties."

"Yep, mobile phones, big hair, lime green leg warmers and padded shoulders."

They talked more, every now and then someone remembering another thing from their childhood with a name that would not come to mind. In the end there were so many, they turned to the internet before they went crazy. A flood of names and images, adverts they could sing the words to, things they'd taken for granted and then forgotten. But one mystery remained unanswered, the elusive fourth flavour of ice magic, toffee, fudge, banana or…?

Chapter 8

Pat the horse…

"Come in, everything is ready," Ann pecked Becca on the cheek. "Are the boys not coming?"

"Yes, Jack's running Ben into town to collect something. They're probably caught up in traffic."

"In that case I'll put the kettle on while we wait."

"Great, I could do with a cuppa."

Becca hadn't been in Ann's flat in the daytime and so it was a change to see it in daylight rather than candle and lamp light. It was still cosy, even now, in the dull October half-light, it remained airy and bright. She hadn't noticed the water colours before or the photographs. Two caught her eye.

"Your son?"

"Yes, James, he looks so much like his father now."

"Very handsome."

Ann had talked of her husband and Becca knew he'd died two years ago. He'd been a part of the reason why she'd moved, there had been another reason, but Ann had stopped herself from talking about it and so Becca hadn't pushed. "Is this your husband?" Becca asked as she examined another photo.

"Yes, that is him," Ann smiled. "Andrew was a good man, I loved him very much. It was very hard when he died, dark times."

"How did you cope?"

"Not very well, I must admit. I tried to keep busy, not to rush into clearing the house. All very sensible an' considered, forehead up, that sort of thing. James was a great support." She stopped, and looked at Becca considering her next sentence. "I might as well tell you…"

"You don't have to."

"I think I want to. Confession is good for the soul."

"Something like that, I think it depends on who you're telling."

"It was over a year since Andrew had died. A friend, a male friend," she added pointedly, "and I became close. He was very supportive, there was no ulterior motive an' no pressure. Perhaps that is why it happened; it became an affair. He was what I needed, a comforting, listening friend an' I was what he needed, non-critical attention. It doesn't justify our actions, but perhaps explains them. But in a small village there are few secrets an' plenty of gossips. He was married. The village was outraged. Everyone thought it was their business. His wife milked it for all it was worth an' how very typical it was of her. Some of my friends turned out to be nothing of the sort. It was a shock to realise people I thought I knew, were strangers, an' not the friends I thought them to be. As for the affair, it helped me to move on, hope for the future. For him it brought home how unhappy he was in his marriage, how far from a normal relationship it was. Something similar to how you described your relationship with your mother. I thought the passage of time would allow things to calm down. It did not, but I was not about to be forced out of my home by gossips and hypocrites. Call me stubborn, but in the end, I got sick of making allowances for them. Eventually, we both moved from the village, but in different directions. I stayed with my son for a few weeks and almost two years after Andrew's death I decided I had to take life by the horns and see what was out there. I bought this flat, moved in and broke my leg. I tried not to be paranoid about bad karma. Do you think badly of me?"

"Oh, my god no," Becca could see how much the past still hurt and wondered if Ann had yet come to terms with it. Perhaps they had more in common than either was ready to admit. "If anything, I admire you even more."

Ann hugged her. On cue the kettle started to whistle. "I had better sort that before it blows up. No automatic shut off."

The dynamic duo returned, dry cleaning collected and ready for the evening's performance. Ann gave them all an apron and organised them around the central island of her kitchen.

"This is some of the core values of hygge, preparing a meal together, taking the time to make it from scratch an' enjoying it together. Remember if it goes wrong, it does not matter. That is not why we are here. Enjoy the experience an' the togetherness, that will find its way into your fingers an' into the food.

Lesson One.

"Very well lady an' gentlemen. Quiche."

"Babes, I thought we were doing something simple, like flapjack and you're straight into quiche?"

"Do not worry Ben, just pat the horse."

"Is that a technical term?"

"She means take a deep breath." Becca looked at Ann. "Do you mean that?"

"I do. It's not at all difficult."

"Babes, that's easy for you to say."

"Just follow the recipe an' you will be fine."

"If you say so, still think flapjack would have been easier."

"Now, now Benjamin don't panic," Jack grinned.

"Hang on there, buster," Ben held up a hand. "Only my nan gets to call me that."

"Only your nan. Who just took you to collect your laundry?" Jack wagged a spoon at him.

"When we first met you were young and beautiful and worthy of my attention. Now you're just like the rest of my furniture, sagging and past your prime. It's enough of a reward that I allow you to remain, let alone address me in more familial terms."

"Sagging?"

"What can I say, true beauty is eternal," he took the spoon and looked at his reflection, dabbing the corner of an eye. "Still no crow's feet, perfection. I'm not made for kitchen labour and this is hard labour."

"Just pat the horse Ben," Becca looked at him. "It's pastry, not rock buns. Are you a drag queen or a drama queen?"

"Babes I can play any role, but I'm no Nigella."

Dramatics aside, Ann explained what they were going to do and took them quickly through rubbing in.

"Babes, this is more like a bowl of Psoriasis; I'm covered in it."

She showed them how to add just enough cold water to pull it together.

"All that and I've ended up with a bowl of cellulite."

And then having rescued Ben's efforts, explained the need to let the pastry rest in the fridge before rolling out.

"To quote my close personal friend and business partner, Miss Pesto, how come mine's all floppy." He looked pointedly at Jack's. "And his needs beating down with a rolling pin?" Ben prodded his pastry.

"Now who's sagging," Jack said smugly.

"You did put it in the fridge? Ann asked.

"When was this?"

"Half an hour ago, just before we made the filling," Ann explained.

"May be I did, and maybe I didn't," Ben ignored Jack's I told you so grin.

"He didn't," Jack said flatly.

Becca lifted her flan tin. "Ta-dah. Gentlemen I present to you, one pastry case."

"Yep, mine's done," Jack winked at her and lifted his. "How's yours doing Ben-ja-min?"

Ben straightened and folded his arms. He eyed Jack imperiously. "Come the revolution, pretty boy, you die first."

It didn't take much to sort Ben out, again, and get on with the rest of the recipe. Once blind baked the filling was poured in and the quiches left to cook. Nothing burned, nothing exploded and the kitchen wasn't a disaster. In the end they all had something more than edible.

"I don't know what you two were fussing about," Ben said, admiring his handy work. "Piece of cake."

"It's quiche," they chorused.

"Same thing, it all comes in slices. Pat the donkey already."

Lesson Two

"Now that you can all make pastry…"

"Some of us."

"I thought we'd make…

"Flapjack?"

"No, a tart."

"And why, might I ask, are you all looking at me?"

Lesson Three.

"Flapjack?"

"Scones, Ben, today it's scones."

"Is it Sc-oa-n?"

"Nope, it's sc-o-n."

"Babes you say potato and I say po-tar-to."

"Forget all that stuff. The real issue here is, jam first and then cream, or cream and then jam?"

Lesson Four.

"Victoria sponge."

"Babes, I'm sure you meant to say flapjack."

"Ben, again, if you follow the recipe, it is simple."

"So is flapjack."

Lesson Five.

"An easy one,"

"At last, babes, you know you want to say it fl…fla… come on you can do it."

"You're going to use sponge, fruit, homemade custard and cream, a good old fashioned…"

"I'll not be trifled with."

"Isn't that a Stanley Baxter line?"

"Maybe it is and maybe it isn't."

Lesson Six.

"Yes Ben, we are making flapjack."

There was a raised eyebrow. "Is this a trick?"

***

The moon was out, a crescent of cold light, a distant eye watching the mayhem below. The streets were again home to the legions of the dammed this night. Shapes and apparitions moved from one doorway to the next in search of their prey. She moved away from the window and looked at the clock. Its hands lit by flickering candlelight that cast dancing shapes on its face and across the walls. A wolf howled and screams filled the street outside. Terrified feet thundered by on the pavement, she looked back to the window, the movement made one of her eyeballs drop to the floor. "Damn, that's going to be a problem."

There was a rasping sound at the door. It didn't register in her hearing for some time, the sound tentative and searching, long nails seeking a way in. Her hallway was in darkness, shadows made hiding places that gaped as she passed. The sounds from the street were now muffled and distant. She moved slowly, her foot dragged and her rotting hand struggled with the handle. The latch turned and the door slowly opened.

"Babes, you look like shit."

"Coming from the bride of Frankenstein I'd say that's rich. Where's Jack?"

"Strange, he was there a minute ago." Ben looked about, the stitches on his neck stretching as he turned. "Gone." He looked back at Becca. "What are you anyway?"

Becca affected a vacant stare, her mouth dropped open and she began to shuffle. Hands outstretched, stooped and limping she shuffled down the hallway and turning awkwardly, came back to him, a low moaning welling up from the pit of her stomach.

Ben tapped a black nailed finger on his chin. "No, I'm not seeing it."

"Oh, come on. The empty stare, the pitiful groaning, the clumsy walk."

"Babes, what's new."

Becca was about to give him a nudge when someone's laundry came swooping down the stairs, howling and wailing for all the lost souls of the world.

"Here he comes. Where did you go?"

"I had hem issues," Jack lifted up the edge of his sheet.

"Hem issues?"

"It's a ghost thing, you wouldn't understand." He gave them both the usual hello hug. "Are we ready then?"

"I'll just get my bag. Forgot I'd bought this."

"Babes, red, nice colour, very appropriate."

Becca pulled the door closed behind her. "Would one of you walk behind me, bits keep dropping off and I wouldn't want to lose anything important."

Outside, Jack looked up and down the road. "I thought I saw the taxi pull up."

They all looked about, trying to spot a set of headlights. A coven of assorted witches cackled past.

"It's a long road, they can't always see the numbers easily," Ben started walking. "Wait here, I'll check up the road."

"I'll look down here." Jack started walking.

Wasn't this how most horror films went, someone left on their own, even when it was obvious there was no way that should happen.

Becca sat on the wall as a member of the living dead shuffled over the road towards her.

"Hey, Good one," zombie man said, pointing out the costume. "You're the only other zombie I've seen and definitely the only one carrying a red handbag."

"Yours too, the costume that is. The youth of today have no respect for the recently re-animated. I thought about a grey purse to match my skin tone, but then decided a bit of colour was called for, red blood and all."

"No zombie should be without one. I'd have brought mine, if I'd had one. Look at them, it's all superheroes and princesses. Where are all the vampires and swamp beasts? I thought at least, there'd be more zombies, we're pretty cool at the moment?"

"So did I." Becca looked around. "Maybe we're just a dying breed."

"Shouldn't that be undying," zombie man said.

"Funny, I'll have to remember that one." She wondered how she could get it into a conversation with the bride of Frankenstein and a ghost. "Is one of these yours?" she pointed at the marauding masses of horror.

He sat on the wall near her. "That one over there, the one with the sword through his head."

"Nice,"

"Is yours out there too?"

"No, I ate mine, old zombie habits and all."

"It's a tough one. Every zombie parent's dilemma."

"Sam," he called. "Sam," he got up. "Sorry, I'm going to have to go and get him. I said not too far. I might as well have been talking to myself."

"The sword's probably affecting his hearing."

"More than likely. See you again some time." He dashed after his charge.

"Trick or treat." A small devil held a bucket of sweets out to her.

She made a moaning sound and held out empty hands.

The devil pronged her with its plastic fork and ran off down the street just as a sheet game gliding towards her.

"Are you making friends?" Jack said in his best dad's voice.

"No sweets, so no interest," she explained. "When I was young, it was, the sky is blue, the grass is green, have you got a penny for Halloween, certainly no sweets. My Aunty Irene taught me that one, mind you, it was old fashioned then."

"There we are," Jack pointed. "The bride summons, she must have found the taxi. Come on pick up your eyeball, we've a party to get to."

"Jack will you do me a favour?"

"Of course."

"When we get there, will you ask me if I'm dying for a drink?"

"Why?"

"Because then I can say, shouldn't that be undying."

"I don't get it."

Becca rolled one of her eyes in exasperation.

Jack picked it up and handed it back. "You should have glued that on."

Chapter 9

Me, Myself and I…

It was late November before she knew it. The clocks had long gone back and as the month ploughed on to its finish, it seemed to be dark all the time. Going to work and coming home was a gloomy affair. She left the station and eager to be out of the cold, hurried to the supermarket. She'd tried doing one big shop for the week, but that had provided food she rarely felt like eating when the time came. She then moved to buying what she wanted on the way home. This seemed to work and of late she'd been good. Porridge for breakfast, soup for lunch and salad for tea. She had it in her head she'd get a head start before Christmas hit her waistline and build up a bit of collateral weight loss before she set about eating, what seemed like, half her body weight.

Basket over one arm, she drifted up and down the aisles. She quite liked this on a Friday night. It was strangely relaxing, there was none of the rush the week seemed to cast over her daily shop. But salad was not exactly convincing her tonight. It felt like a night for something warm and comforting, something hygge. The bathroom scales had been smiling at her of late and she didn't want to break the momentum she'd built up. But salad had its limits and after two weeks of nothing but, she sneaked past them. With an act of pure will she avoided the cake, biscuit and chocolate aisles, knowing full well all those little packets would be calling out to her.

Please eat us, you need us. You've earned the pleasure of stuffing us into your mouth. Don't worry about it, just enjoy our fat laden goodness.

The salad just looked at her,

Go on then, pick us, don't pick us, we really couldn't give a shit.

The Christmas lights weren't on yet. But all the shops had been announcing the approach of the festivities for weeks, the best Christmas ever. They said that every year and Becca wondered how many people found it all just one big let-down. So far, she'd ignored the pull to start the buying frenzy the celebration had become. When it was December she'd start and not before. Calorie light carrier bag in hand, she made her way to the quieter streets, leaving behind the lights and the sound of tyres on wet roads. The people thinned and her pace slowed. There was window shopping of another kind on offer, well window viewing, okay window nosing. It was the time of night when people were still busy with the whole getting in from work thing, the time before they all closed the curtains, or drew a blind to shut out the world beyond. Becca wasn't bold enough to look right in through the lit display cases of lounge windows. She did a looking forward, eye straining right or left, to get a glimpse into people's lives. Interesting wallpaper, lamps, huge tellies, a snapshot of a kiss, an argument, kids eating their tea in front of the box. All there, all framed and lit for a slow-walking passer-by trying to look like she wasn't looking.

Once inside and the front door shut against the chill damp air, she checked her mailbox and looked at the tall window that lit the communal entrance and stairs; Becca missed the sun. The collection had been cleared away. It had served its purpose. The spot it had taken over for so long had looked bare, very bare, so she'd continued to put a vase of flowers there, just as a reminder. She checked her post. Flat six was still empty, the mailbox remaining unopened and she still had to meet early bird.

Once in through her front door, she put down her bag and placed the keys on the stand. The peace and stillness were lovely. Not a sound, just her and it was just her. It felt odd knowing the others were away. Jack was visiting his mum and brother, a kind of early Christmas. Ann was in Denmark visiting her brother with her son, James and the rest of her family and Ben was sleeping at his club; in an attempt to keep up with the extra Christmas shows.

"All money in the bank Babes, twenty more years of this, before gravity has its way, and then I'm done."

She took off her coat, Ben's voice fading into the soft light as she walked down the hallway to the kitchen and put the kettle on. She was missing them all, how different her flat would have looked if they'd not come along. Ben helping her to unpack, Ann sorting out her hygge. There was something of all of them from ideas to gifts. Jack had got her into photography and they'd been out a couple of times taking pictures. She'd framed several from their outings and a couple of scenic ones. Ben gave his approval, as he was in most of them and Ann had borrowed Becca's idea and hung some photos from their cooking lessons in her kitchen. She said they were a good way of being mindful, reminders of happy times. Becca now went out once a week, straight after work, with a small group of her colleagues. She'd been reluctant at first, not wanting to mix work with pleasure, but something Ben had said ages ago had quietly germinated in the back of her mind. It was as she'd thought, conversations often went back to work, but even that served a valuable purpose. As Ben had said, with his pack of drag work mates, or was it house of drag queens, it was a way for everybody to let off steam, have a moan, give support, share ideas and laugh at silly things that had happened. So, with that in mind, she'd accepted an offer and not looked back. It had brought her team closer together and helped them to understand each other. As a result, they worked better together and the banter stopped work from being the only focus of the day. Now a part of that, Becca realised what she'd been missing.

She made tea and took two biscuits into the front room and sat on her chair. She didn't turn on the lights, just one lamp, now a favourite. It added a warm glow to the peace and stillness. Having no plans for the weekend, the first time in months, she realised she enjoyed time on her own and missed the opportunities it offered. It was a luxury, but only because she knew she had a choice, it wasn't indefinite. Next week, she would be able to pop and see Jack, or Ben, or Ann, or even go down to Patricia's for a chat and some company. If she didn't have that, would the stillness become emptiness, would the luxury become loneliness?

The fish, sweetcorn and peas didn't hit the spot, she didn't feel full or satisfied. She made herself wait none the less. Having read somewhere that it took time for your brain to register your stomach was full. Her brain eventually did this, but her hibernation genes were saying she should be putting on fat for the winter. She resisted for as long as she could and flicked on the telly. Press, press, press, she thumbed her way through the channels. Some self-obsessed people in swimsuits prattling on about something important only to them. Press. An advert with an overly smiley, over-dubbed man informing her that it was important to get rid of all bacteria, she assumed he meant the good ones as well. Press. Some people in a kitchen generally being miserable and screaming at each other about the importance of family. Press. A nature program, talking about the importance of the environment, while something hairy ripped the shreds out of something feathery. Press. Someone not particularly old telling someone else not particularly old that it was important to provide for her loved ones once she'd gone. Press. Someone's gran being patronized about how important it was to release the equity in her home and spend it all before she was dead. Press. The news, however, did talk about something important and made all the other stuff look vacuous.

After so much rubbish, it didn't take much effort to justify the opening of the treat cupboard and view all the junk stored there. There should have been moths and mould, she'd not been in it for some time. Of course, the sugar level, in such a confined space, wouldn't allow any such sign of decay. She pondered the contents, what was she in the mood for, chocolate, chewy sweets or biscuits? The cup of tea she'd made meant that five biscuits disappeared one after the other in a delicious blur. The chewy sweets got it next. Tomorrow she'd be good again (of course she wouldn't it was the weekend). The sweets didn't quite hit the spot and then she remembered the tub of ice cream. A rummage past frozen peas and sweetcorn uncovered the tub of ice-cold satisfaction. Peeling the lid off she was pleasantly surprised to find it was still a quarter full. She even manged to let it sit for a while to go softer. It tasted better. A spoon and for once a good film, helped the tub of double chocolate pecan love-handles to disappear. No guilt. Woolly socks and the comfort of a throw stopped her from seeing the end of the film. She woke on the sofa with a stiff back. On the telly some pain in the neck was trying to sell her jewellery. With a groan and grunts, someone far older should have been making, Becca got up, folded the throw, switched off the telly and slouched to bed.

Saturday was cold grey and miserable and didn't tempt her to leave the flat. She had enough in so she wouldn't starve. Some of the things she'd bought in her one attempt at a weekly shop, way back in the summer, were still in her freezer. If she got desperate, she'd check them out and then probably chuck them out.

The wind continued to blow and the sound of rain outside kept her inside. By three it had started to get dark again and other than showering and getting into fresh pyjamas Becca had done nothing. She filled the evening with dinner and watched a film. She awoke, a shooting pain in her back and instantly thought, in that half-awake moment, she was having a heart attack. She was relieved to find the remote was the cause and yanked it from under her. She sat up stiffly and rubbed the sore spot. Now wide awake, bed didn't seem like an option even though it was one in the morning. Her stomach said cereal. Often waking up in the middle of the night she got cravings, always for the same thing, a bowl of cereal. She would have got up, but the front door slammed and there was a clatter of noise which made her jump. Her body froze as her ears strained for some clue as to who it might be, but all she could hear was the pumping of her heart in her ears as it rose out of her chest and into her throat. Was someone breaking in? She found herself half poised above the sofa, listening for her own door. There was a commotion of some sorts and then an all mighty clatter, followed by a range of expletives and an overuse of the words bloody buggering hell. The voice was unmistakable and the relief it brought priceless. She got up and headed for the door.

"Patricia."

"Becca."

"You scared the life out of me.

"Sorry my darling, this confounded bag gave way. Look at the mess."

"Here, I'll help."

It was only when the mess of baking tins and plastic tubs was gathered and the broken things swept away that Becca thought to ask the obvious.

"Do you live here?"

"Yes, and so do you it seems. All this time and we didn't know, my darling, I couldn't be more pleased."

Early bird, up at dawn to open the café and back late after clearing away, cleaning and maybe baking for the next day. But this must be late even for her.

"Why so late?"

"That confounded coffee machine," Patricia rubbed at her wrist painfully.

"Are you alright?"

"I slipped on the mess it spewed out, hurt my wrist."

"Here, let me have a look."

"It's fine," Patricia dismissed and went to pick her things up. Something clicked and her legs wobbled from the sudden pain.

After several hours in A&E Patricia's wrist had been attended to. Not a fracture, but badly bruised. It was strapped up and they thanked the overworked staff before catching a taxi back home.

"This is just typical," Patricia looked at her wrist. "How the hell am I going to run a café. I should be there now opening up for Sunday."

"I can help," Becca offered. "I've nothing on for today. I'm at work tomorrow, but I can come after and help with cleaning and stuff."

"Bless you my darling, today's one of my busiest."

They redirected the taxi and went straight to the café. Patricia struggled on, refusing to sit while Becca worked. After a while Becca's ears filtered out the regular array of expletives, made worse by pain and a lack of any sleep. Sheer stubborn denial got Patricia through the morning, while novelty helped Becca sail through it. She enjoyed it and it saved her from another day of plunging the depths of the freezer and films she'd seen too many times before. It was mid-day before she realised, she'd not eaten. That should even out Friday's calories, she thought, as she wiped down a table and walked back to the counter where Patricia was muttering her way through one handed sandwich making. Her wrist was playing up, it should have been resting and even the most obstinate of wills couldn't ignore the pain. They got through lunch with Becca forcefully taking on more of what needed to be done and Patricia increasingly being forced to direct rather than do. By the time Patricia decided the best of the day's business was over and shut the café early, Becca was flagging too. She'd had three hours sleep in the last twenty-four and been on her feet more than she was in any week at work.

"You are a treasure, my darling" Patricia handed her some money from the till.

"No, absolutely not."

"I insist, I couldn't have done this today."

"No," Becca was adamant.

"Very well," Patricia accepted the favour.

"What will you do tomorrow?" Becca asked.

"Well, that dratted thing will need replacing, it's barely got through the day. I'm absolutely buggered with this," she gave her wrist a sour look. "The café will just have to close; Mondays are quiet and perhaps, by Tuesday, I'll be able to manage."

There was no way that was going to work, and it was clear Patricia knew that do, but wouldn't admit defeat. "I'll help. I won't be able to do Monday or Tuesday, but I'm owed hours so I'll take Wednesday off."

"Out of the question."

Patricia said it with such force, Becca knew better than to argue.

Patricia sighed. "My darling, that time is for you to enjoy, its nearly Christmas after all. It's not for keeping this sad old place going. If I can't managed, I can't manage. It's a simple as that." She looked at the café and seemed quite defeated. "Is it worth it I wonder?"

"Now that's just tiredness talking. You need to rest and let that wrist of yours heal. You'll feel differently given enough time."

Becca made sure Patricia was settled and had what she needed before descending the stairs to her own flat. She flopped down on the sofa with the kind of tired satisfaction only a day of physical activity could offer. A familiar knock at the door woke her at eleven.

"Hey babes, it's late, saw your light on," Ben greeted. "You look shattered."

Becca stifled a yawn. "Come in, do you want a drink?"

"I'll make it. Babes, you sit. What's up?"

Becca related the events of the weekend.

"And you say she's sprained it?"

"Bruised, the bone."

"Can she manage the café?"

"No, she'll have to close. Though knowing how stubborn she can be, it'll take something else going wrong to force her to rest. I said I could take some time off to help her, but she was having none of it. And arguing would have been a lost cause."

"Hmm, I might be able to work a little drag queen magic here. Some of the girls know their way around a café, waiting on tables has kept the wolf from many a drag door."

"Really," Becca brightened at the idea. "She'll probably want to pay them."

"Well, some of them could do with the extra cash this time of the year, but will probably end up doing it for free. For all their faults and questionable hair lines, they've got hearts of gold plate."

"She might take some convincing."

"Oh, leave that to me. I have powers and if they fail, I'll set Pasta on her."

***

Early December flew by, with the air of excitement that always preceded Christmas. Twinkling lights, turned dark rainy nights into kaleidoscopes of colour and magic reflected on wet pavements. The café stayed open with Patricia sat behind the till, directing her queendom and enjoying the company of Tonya and Straight Up's alter egos, Sam and Jonathan. She basked in the attention and loved the witty banter the boys brought with them. She began referring to them as her darling boys. Becca helped after work, Ben made several appearances in a starring role, Jack returned and got in on the act, and the new coffee machine behaved, quietly biding its time for when Patricia and it were alone.

"My darling boys, I can't tell you how much I've enjoyed having the both of you here."

"Funny enough so have we." Sam put down the tray, the café was empty, time for a sit down. "It's been quiet today."

"I expect most people are rushing about doing their Christmas shopping," Patricia looked to the window. "I can't be doing with all of that nonsense, a lot of money and panic, far too commercial. If they had any sense they'd be sat in here. It would be a much better use of their time."

Jonathan stuck his head out of the tiny kitchen. "The fridge is almost empty, love. We need a restock." He wiped his hands and leaned against the door frame. "We could go in the mornin'," he looked at Sam.

"Not too early," Sam warned.

"That fridge is huge," Jonathan shook a finger in the direction of the kitchen, "but it doesn't take long to empty."

"My darling," Patricia began, "it's nothing compared to the one I got trapped in."

"Trapped?" Sam asked, trying to imagine one inside the other.

"This one was a walk-in fridge; it was room sized. The foundations had given way slightly along one of its sides so there was a slight tilt and the door would never stay open because of this. I was at university and ended up working at a very grand, but faded hotel waiting on tables. I was warned about the door, being advised to tell someone I was off to the fridge. Sometime later, several tables were short of those little wrapped portions of butter, so I hurried to the fridge to get some. Everything was huge catering packs; we would often sit three hundred people at breakfast."

"How many?"

"It does sound a lot doesn't it. Well, in my haste I forgot to tell anyone. We all knew, if you pushed the fridge door fully back it would take about twenty seconds to close. Enough time to nip in and dash out again. This time I struggled to get the box open, I wasn't going to be beaten. Of course, the door shut and I had no way of getting out, as well as sagging foundations the fridge only had a working handle on one side. I was in for what seemed like a lifetime until my tables started complaining about the lack of service and someone guessed and came looking."

"I just can't imagine you waiting on," Sam said. "You sound too posh."

"How did you manage to serve that many people?" Jonathan asked. "When this place is busy, we end up runnin' about like it's curtain call and we've no wigs."

"There were various tricks of the trade, you might say. All the metal teapots were set out, lids open, tea bags in on a huge countertop. When it came time to serving, we'd pick them up three pots to a hand and someone worked the geyser. As careful as we were, you always got scalded, though we never spilt a pot on diners and six full tea pots were extremely heavy. Manoeuvring them through the cramped dining hall was an art. I remember we were always complimented on the toast."

"How come?"

"It was always hot at the table. And I'm sure you can appreciate that's rather an accomplishment."

"It's hard enough gettin' one round out," Jonathan said, "never mind toast for, you said three hundred a sittin'?"

"Yes, we used to unpack the sliced loaves before anyone came in, toast one side, in enormous grills and then piled them in huge half-baked stacks. When we needed it, we'd quickly toast the other side. The bread was so dreadfully thin it heated the whole thing and we rushed it out like ants. The only problem was that the pasty white bread would sweat in the half-baked stacks and you'd often get several that stuck together."

"How did you sort that?"

"We didn't, there was no time. They went in the bin. A criminal waste these days, but back then health and safety was a pale shadow of the beast it's become."

"What about all of the other meals," Sam asked. "There must have been a huge kitchen staff to cook for that many punters?"

"Believe it or not, the kitchen staff were only in for half the day. They cooked breakfast and we would carry out six plates at a time on metal handled stackers. You didn't get to pick and choose, you got what was brought to the table and let me tell you people appreciated it. Lunch was also made and served, but dinner was part-cooked and assembled on the plates. The plates were then put it these huge steamer cabinets and left to cook until it was time to serve them."

"What," Jonathan pulled a face. "The whole meal on the plate, just sittin' there."

"That sounds revolting, didn't it turn to mush?"

"It worked surprisingly well. The diners usually had a choice of two meals. Meat of some kind with vegetables and gravy, or fish with potatoes and peas. The fish, didn't fare too well at all, the batter would be very pasty, having sat in the steam for hours, but the meat was fine."

"But what if someone didn't want gravy?" Sam asked. "If it's already on, there's no getting it off."

"That was the trick. It didn't happen very often, but occasionally someone would ask for a meal without. So, we would take the plate to the hot water geyser, the one we filled the tea pots with, and wash everything under it. It took a little practise to get it right. The gravy-free food would then go on paper towels before being re-plated."

Jonathan and Sam looked at her in disbelief.

"It's all truth, my darling boys, the world was a very different place then. Better in some ways and far worse in others."

Jonathan wiped the last of the tables. It was six and he needed to get across town, clean himself up, put on his face and be ready for the first of the night's performances. He looked at the clock on the wall, okay for time and then something made him look at his own watch. The clock on the wall had stopped at least half an hour ago.

"Got to go love, I'm late and I'm not in the mood for Tina's toe tappin' time keepin' tantrums."

"Alright my darling," Patricia briefly looked up from her recipes and cash.

He spun and took a step in one hurried move and collided with Sam and the bucket he was carrying. The plastic container buckled and threw up over them.

Sam stood there, dripping. "Why don't you ever look where you're going? She's just like this on stage, stupid tart. All spinning heals and fat hips."

"I'm soaked too," Jonathan pointed at himself. "Look at me, you useless bugger, sneakin' around like a creepin'...fat hips, fat hips."

"It's only water," Patricia broke in. "Stand still, take your jeans off. Don't look at me like that. Off with them. No, leave your shoes where they are. Get a cloth while I put these in the wash."

"I've got to be at the club," Jonathan protested.

"A quick wash and into the drier. Half an hour and we'll get you a taxi. Trousers." Patricia held out an expectant hand. "Don't be coy, I've seen it all before."

With exchanged scowls and a degree of self-conscious modesty they did as they were told and handed the soaking articles to Patricia.

"Come on," Jonathan snapped. "Get a cloth."

Sam gave him a look. "What did your last slave die of?"

"Multiple orgasm, so shift yourself."

Patricia was true to her word and the jeans were both washed and dried in no time. Jonathan hurried into his and went to grab his things. "You know, I think I've lost weight." He began to strut up and down the café experimentally. "They're normally so tight out of the wash." He looked at his reflection in the windows. "I 'ave," he grinned.

Sam folded his arms. "Get my jeans off."

***

Ann's return was perfectly timed. The last week before Christmas pulled Sam and Jonathan back to the club and their own commitments. Ben didn't use any kitchen appliances beyond a microwave and Jack and Becca had no choice but to commit to their own employers Christmas rush. Jonathan had been the cook and didn't mind Patricia's guidance. Ann took over and could only tolerate the interference.

"Patricia, I know how to make a scone. I have been baking for the past four decades."

"Well, in that case you've been doing it wrong for the last forty years."

"Then, go ahead," Ann stepped aside patiently, this was going to be a tough camel to swallow. "Show me how it's done properly."

Patricia shot her a look like a bulldog swallowing a wasp, she knew she'd manoeuvred herself right into a position. Of course, she was so stubborn she tried and did nothing more than produce a one-handed mess that made her wrist ache. "Oh, this is impossible," she grumbled.

"Then if you will let me get on with my second-rate scones, you will at least have something to sell."

Patricia said nothing and grudgingly moved aside. Ann cleared the mess, scrapped the mixture and started again. Ten minutes before opening time Ann had finished all the other things on the list and Patricia, unable to sit doing nothing, got on with jobs doable with one hand. She sat down by her till, frankly she was shattered, but wouldn't let Ann see that. A plate with a hot buttered scone was pushed in front of her.

"Peace offering," Ann said and went back to the small kitchen. She watched, just out of sight, as Patricia regarded the scone and then looked around to make sure no one was watching. She picked up a piece and sniffed it, as if testing some new and unfamiliar food. She took an experimental bite.

Ann appeared a little while later, unlocked the door and turned the little sign to open. "Oh," she said innocently. "You ate it all. Was it acceptable?"

"Quite," Patricia said stiffly.

"Then, I am glad to hear it," Ann smiled to herself and took the plate back to the kitchen

"I still say you should have used raisins."

The coffee machine hissed.

"Oh, don't you jolly well start," Patricia muttered.

The next few days passed with an armed peace. Both fired warning shots and occasionally they clashed. Patricia couldn't help telling Ann how to do things, it was her café after all, but the delivery was blunt and to the point. Ann wasn't one to give up easily, though at times her resolve was sorely tested.

Patricia was in a particularly grumpy mood this day and Ann's patience was running low. They'd avoided each other, either on purpose or by some unconscious instinct. The same instinct that stopped antelope wandering into crocodile filled lakes, and in turn crocodiles from wandering into the hippo's territory. It worked until the café became busy at lunch time, there was less space and less time to calm down.

"Really Ann, table five," Patricia appeared at the kitchen door. "I thought I'd explained how long they've been waiting."

"Clock clear. I'm just finishing it now."

"Ten minutes ago, would have been better. If this wretched wrist wasn't playing up, I'd do the things myself."

Ann cut the sandwich and began to tidy with deliberate and considered control. "I thought you said they were waiting?"

"It's ready then is it? I'd given up hope."

"Right," Ann got as close to snapping as her Danish genes would allow her. "My mother would say, eat some bread. I'm tempted to be less polite and tell you exactly what you can do with your hope and the bread."

"Your mother seems to say all kinds of strange things, if that's anything to go by. Mine was not one for silly sayings, she spoke her mind without sugar coating it."

"Yes, and you have clearly continued the practice. Have you once stopped to consider how your words affect others? It might suit you to shoot from the hip and to speak your mind, but other people have feelings that need some consideration, no matter how small that might be. I've tolerated a lot from people with opinions based on limited experience and an equally limited emotional maturity. And while I'm on the subject…"

The torrent continued to wash over Patricia like a wave and for once she was lost for words. It brought her up short. To have someone speak to her in the same blunt manner was a first. She was left with no choice, but to pick up the two plates, despite her wrist and leave the kitchen.

Ann sighed, with all the weariness of that argument and all the others that had gone before it. She disliked such outbursts, knowing they rarely, if ever, resolved anything. She felt foolish and tired and the feelings brought back too many memories. A tear found its way out. She wiped at it irritably.

"I'm an obstinate, bad tempered old woman," Patricia said, her tone calm and self-effacing as she came to stand by Ann. "My mouth is too big and inclined to speak without my brain's permission." She came closer and gently took Ann's hand. "You have done nothing to deserve my frustration, can you forgive me?"

Ann patted her arm and then got out a paper hanky and blew her nose. "It's Andrew's birthday today," she attempted to explain.

"You have no reason to justify yourself, I'm an old cow and should have been put out to pasture years ago. I moo too much and frankly shit on anything that irritates me."

Ann laughed and blew her nose again. "It's been well over two years now. I thought I had reached a point where I could cope with losing Andrew. I'm tired, I suppose an' clearly haven't moved on as far as I thought. I still miss him an' sometimes it's as if no time has passed since he died."

"My darling, I don't think you ever get over it, you simply learn to live with it."

"It caught me off guard."

"Tiredness and being nagged by a harridan can do that."

"Have you lost someone important to you?" Ann asked.

"A long time ago. But that is a story for another time. He's still with me, put in a place where I now only remember the good parts. You'll get there when you're ready."

Ann suddenly remembered. "The customers?"

"They left. I think our argument frightened them off. I've turned the sign to closed. There are two plates of sandwiches waiting out there and I've managed to make a pot of tea. If it doesn't sound too condescending and if you can bear to talk to me, I do have ears and can be a good listener. Would you allow me to make amends?"

Admitting a degree of vulnerability to each other proved to be a turning point in their relationship. It meant they began talking and in getting to know each other they began to understand and then accept each other's quirks and foibles. Understanding the reason behind each other's habits, or faults took away their sting. And of course, as they talked, they got to know each other better and to trust one another.

***

Patricia turned the little sign to closed and flopped down onto a chair. She was red faced and fanned herself with a t-towel. "I don't mind admitting, I'm shattered."

"It's been busy," Ann put a cup of tea in front of her.

"Thank you my darling. I think I might be getting too old for this."

"It's nothing to do with age, tighten your buttocks."

"If only I could."

"I meant pull yourself together. You are not at that point yet. However, you might have reached a point where the energy you put into the café isn't payed back in terms of enjoyment, or satisfaction, or just good old-fashioned money."

"I'm not so sure about age. Look at me. You on the other hand, have looked after yourself. Indeed, you look as good at the end of the day as you do when you start it. You don't appear to have broken a sweat. I look like I've been tag wrestling."

"Well," Ann began diplomatically. Normally she wouldn't have ventured into this kind of territory, but this land was occupied by Patricia who tended to speak her mind and appreciated it when others did the same. "You tend to start the day looking dishevelled, so it is no great surprise to find you looking the same at the end of it. It sometimes looks like you have just rolled out of bed."

"That, my darling, is because I usually do. I can't be bothered. I lost interest and gravity seems to be in full command of all my wobbly bits. They've gone from ample and perky to sandbags."

"Then perhaps it's time you did something about it."

"I can't be pestered, the effort involved isn't worth the men it attracts."

"Don't do it for anyone else, do it for you. A few simple things will make the world of difference. Underwear, makeup an' a comb can work wonders. Just ask the boys. If they can do it, so can you."

Patricia dabbed her forehead with the t-towel, Ann said nothing more and sipped her tea. There was the faint sound of cogs moving. Patricia took a drink of her tea, and stared into its depths. Eventually she put it down and let out a long sigh of resignation. "Oh, very well then, you've persuaded me."

"I haven't said anything new."

"Your silence speaks volumes. I suppose," Patricia looked down at herself, "it would be nice to see a few less valleys and mountains when I peer out across the sliding landscape of my body." She turned to face Ann properly. "Have I thanked you for all of your help these past few weeks?"

"No."

"Then, I shall say thank you now and ask for further help. Will we be able to get support pants in my size?"

Chapter 10

Christmas…

Jack walked down the stairs to find a house of drag queens waiting for him in the entrance hall. Hair, teeth, eyes and curves. All in glorious technicolour and magnified illusion.

"Ladies," he greeted with a smile.

"Looking finnnnne honey," Chocolate De Clar purred.

"Don't do anything we wouldn't," Tonya Tickle Tongue chirped.

"Yep, and that's the problem," Jack countered. "Too much scope."

A union of hands lifted to a collective gasp of drag outrage.

"Ouch, he's got claws," Pasta Pesto approved.

"'Ave you been trainin' 'er?" Lady Straight Up asked.

Tina pulled out a hanky and dabbed an eye, sniffing with all the melodrama of a black and white movie. "My baby is all grown up."

"Flying the coop, and you all barren and dried up," Mount Rushmore said casually.

"Under all that paddin' there's just two dried up, sad, old prunes," Straight Up sighed.

"Ooo, you northern cow."

"See you tomorrow, babes," Tina called back as she was pushed out of the door.

Jack watched them leave, it was like a gang of Christmas trees had upped-sticks and were off for a night on the town, tinsel, baubles and all. The door slammed and the entrance hall suddenly fell silent. He knocked on Becca's door.

"Hello you. Come on in," Becca greeted, as Jack gave her his usual hello hug. "I can always tell when Ben and his girls are going out. Sounds like a clog factory clocking off?"

"Yep. You been in long?"

"No, just got back in. I was out with that group from work. Christmas drink. It was nice. You okay?"

"Fine," he evaded.

Becca waited until they were in the kitchen and the kettle was on. "So, what's wrong. Fine in your repertoire, usually means don't ask."

He sat down on one of the counter chairs. "Single again."

"Your decision?"

"Laura's."

"Did she say that to your face?"

"Via a text."

"What."

Jack shrugged. "Short and to the point. I didn't bother replying."

"Never liked her anyway. Those eyes brows, what was that about, she always looked permanently surprised."

Jack laughed. Becca thought, this of course was when she should have given him a hug, but hang ups still attached, she offered him tea and heart-felt sympathy. "How are you feeling?"

"Not especially surprised," he stirred himself. "Anyway, it's Christmas Eve…"

"Do you want to talk about it?"

"Nope, I'm good, honestly."

"Come on then, I've a DVD and mince pies. We're the only ones, Ann and Patricia are out too."

"Out, on the town?"

"Despite the sparring, I think they really do like each other. Enough to go to the cinema and then for something to eat."

"Good for them," Jack sat down. "So, what are we watching?"

They'd spent plenty of time working their way through Jack's top ten of sci-fi films, Becca's must-see zombie movies and Ben's gay all-time greats. Now they were working their way through the best Christmas films of all time, at least that's what most of the cases had printed on them.

"Same as Patricia and Ann. You said you'd not seen it and it doesn't get any more Christmassy than this."

"The Bishop's Wife?" Jack looked at the case.

"That's the one. Watch and enjoy," she pressed play and snuggled down into the cushions, good company, a mince pie and the film.

Becca woke, there was a definite feeling in the air. The kind of silence outside that only happens on Christmas morning. She pictured millions of happy faces opening presents, too excited for breakfast. For now, the streets were deserted, but soon enough kids would be out on their new bikes, scooters and other things on wheels. As a kid, she wanted to be dressed, with breakfast out of the way, before she would open any presents; she didn't want to be interrupted once they were opened. Her sister was forced to go along with this, one of many chasmic differences that would open between them. Would she and her husband be at their mother's, or just calling in before going to his family? Was she bothered? She sat up testing out the thought. No, she could honestly say she wasn't. This was her first Christmas in this flat, the first time she'd woken up alone, one way or another on Christmas day. But she didn't feel lonely, soon they'd all be at Ann's. This was a nice quiet start to a new kind of Christmas day; one she'd chosen and could relax into and enjoy without the barbs or the waiting to see what she'd do wrong. She took a deep breath, drawing in the peace, got out of bed, opened the curtains and looked out onto Christmas morning. Crisp and bright, lovely she thought. Feeling lifted, she put on her dressing gown and headed for the lounge. She switched on the tree lights and looked at the presents underneath, all carefully wrapped and ready to go upstairs. The whole day to come and time enough now to enjoy the anticipation. Right, kitchen, coffee on and special fruit bread for breakfast.

After breakfast, she showered and dressed and then opened the presents she'd got from people at work. She'd also opened a tin of chocolates, another reminder of Christmas as a child, the smell that greeted you when the lid first came off, chocolate and wrappers. She had always been allowed to eat some chocolate every Christmas morning, normally that wouldn't be on the cards, but special day and special dispensation. She'd continued the practice and wasn't about to stop now. There was a knock at the door, followed by a clearing of throats and some singing, deep voiced manly singing.

"Morning babes."

Ben and Jack stood, Santa hats on, sporting Christmas jumpers which they duly modelled for her.

"What can I say, they're awful. Here's mine," she pulled on the hem to better show the reindeer face. "It's indescribable."

"We brought Christmas cheer," Jack said holding up three glasses and a bottle of fizz."

"Shouldn't we go up and see if Patricia and Ann need any help," Becca looked up the stairs.

Both shook their heads slowly.

"Babes, we popped in…"

"Being the gentlemen, we are," Jack added.

"To see if they needed any help."

"They don't," Jack said.

"Seriously babes, they don't. They're in their element debating the Christmas dinner. The best we can do is toast their health.

Christmas dinner was a triumph. Everything, from the turkey to the sprouts with chestnuts and bacon to the roast potatoes, couldn't have been better. They watched The Queen's speech, Patricia insisted and then full as they were made room for Christmas pudding with brandy sauce. Then, like millions of other households they sat unable to move and watched a load of repeats on the telly. Even the two tins of chocolates remained unopened.

Ann had suggested they opened presents that night, just so the day's excitement was stretched out a little long.

A supper of left-overs, which no one really needed, but ate anyway, was everything it should be and the rest of the evening eased by with festive programmes, a board game and chocolates that had been begging to be opened all day long. By the time the late-night comedy was on, Patricia was dozing quietly, Ann was talking to family on the computer and the other three were roughly in the same places they'd been in since the Queen.

"Can't believe it's all over for another year," Becca thought back over the day. "All that preparation and fuss and it's done in a whirlwind of a few hours."

Ben patted his stomach. "Tina won't be pleased about this."

"You've got a week," Jack said. "You can come running with me."

"Not on your young straight life. Grapefruit and porridge for the next seven days. Before I forget, I've got you all tickets for the show, come to the back door and George will let you in."

"Looking forward to it," Jack said.

"It'll be great."

"Who's great," Patricia stirred groggily.

"It's okay you can go back to sleep, babes."

"I wasn't asleep, just resting my eyes."

***

Big George let them in and showed them to a private booth with a good view of the small stage. The place was heaving and they all watched as the tall, heavy built man in a dress and feather boa made his way back through the crowd.

"That's what I like to see, a guy not afraid to show his feminine side." Jack looked towards the bar. "I should have asked him to carry me, getting through that lot is going to be interesting. What do you all want to drink?"

"Comin' through, pardon me. Ladies pardon me. Ladies, shift," the last sword cut a path and with a polite smile and several thank yous Lady Straight Up reached the table with a bottle and glasses. "Now then my lovelies, compliments of the house,"

"Thank you," Becca hardly recognised Jonathan, the transformation was so complete it was hard to see him under the illusion. "You look fabulous."

"Ta love, not lookin' bad yourself." She surveyed them all. "You all brush up well. Lady Patricia lookin' fierce. Sam sends his love; he'll come and see you once he's been on."

"My darling boy, you are a vision. If I had legs like that."

"Love, if you had legs like these, I'd send you back through that lot. There's far too much testosterone and all-you-can-eat bras down there. Take my advice make this one last. I'll bring you another, just give me a wave." She picked up the bottle and looked at the label. "You're lucky it's the good stuff, not the cheap plonk that lot are washin' their tonsils in. Right, have a lovely night, first act's on soon." She turned back towards the bar. "Wish me luck."

Becca hadn't been too sure what to expect, she'd watched Drag Race of course, but this was gritty reality, as Ben had put it. Each queen had their own spot complete with dancers and props and a determination to be the star of the evening. There were jokes, banter, cutting comments addressed at the audience and they all sung, no lip syncing. Each looked fabulous, there was no other word for it. An ultra-illusion of femininity, exaggerated for glamour and humour dominating the stage and demanding full attention. The artistry was practised and professional, the performances a spectacle. Tina topped the bill and showed why she held that position, working the crowd with practised ease that belied the true skill delivering it. The evening built to the assembled finale and the countdown to New Year. As the hour struck, the sea of people broke into islands of hugs and hopes.

Chapter 11

A text…

Becca had got out of the wrong side of bed on Monday and not managed any other route since. She didn't know what was nagging at her. Maybe it was just January, cold, wet and dark, with no Christmas sparkle to ward off the gloom. She wasn't prone to depression, but like so many people, seemed to get the winter blues. Going to work in the dark and coming home in it was bad enough in November, but January added an extra degree of groan to it. She knew by February, when the nights had noticeably pulled out that her mood would lift, but right now that seemed a long way off.

She left the station behind and walked to the shops. Work had been crap all week; too much to do and no time to do it. Her mood didn't improve when she arrived at the supermarket to find there were no baskets. She muttered and went in search of one. She picked up biscuits and then happened to walk past a display, the very same biscuits advertised as gluten free. Weren't they anyway? They were oats. She checked the label on both, both had the same ingredients. So, what was the difference, other than a small label and the price being nearly double. Out of petty irritation she put both packets back. It was official, she was on one and became even more bad-tempered when she went to the self-checkout. Bar codes, on the front, on the back, on the side, hidden under a flap. Where else? On the back of someone's head? Why couldn't they put them in the same place?

She was halfway home before she realised her heals were leaving dents in the paving slabs. She felt a wry smile touch her lips, what a grump and why couldn't she walk that fast when she wanted to. Instead of turning left, she carried on and went around the block, she needed some fresh air. When she got back her phone went off. She glanced at the front as she got her keys out. Her sister's name glared at her, at first, she thought she'd read it wrongly. But her stomach told her she hadn't. What did she want? Her sister was eight years older, but acted more like the gap between them was eighty. Victoria was more likely to send a letter than a text. Becca was tempted to read the message right there and then, wanting to get it open and its contents out of the way, but she made herself wait until she was inside. It was just a text, but it churned her stomach.

Once inside and somewhere no one would accidentally see her reaction, she read the text.

Rebecca, it's your sister,

Mam is in hospital. As I'm her only regular visitor I discovered her on the floor at home. I think she's had some kind of heart attack and is now in hospital. It's come out of the blue and has been a shock for me. She is comfortable, but hasn't asked to see you and I think it best, for all concerned, if you didn't come. I still thought it right that you should know, I didn't want that hanging over my head; I'll contact you if anything changes. Reply to this, so I know I have the correct number and I'm not wasting my time.

The bottom had fallen out of Becca's stomach. She put the phone down and sat. Calm down, she picked up the phone and re-read the message. Her feelings everywhere from hurt, to guilt to anger. What the hell did you do with a text like that? The childish part of her wanted to ignore the command at the end. Her gut reaction was to text she was coming down, that she would catch a train that night if there was one. She picked up the phone and texted her intentions. The reply came an hour later, she'd lost count of how many times she'd checked the phone in that time. Checked it was on, checked the sound was working, checked she hadn't missed the reply's arrival. She was about to phone and actually talk when the phone went. The text simply said.

As I said, she's comfortable, there is no need to come down. I will text you if anything changes.

Some part of her was relieved, she was already bracing herself for the inevitable jibes, comments accusations and ultimate arguments. But she also felt some sort of duty that she should be there. That this should be the time when everything was put aside. She picked up the phone and said,

I'm coming down.

This time the reply was almost instant.

No.

The world suddenly seemed full of obstacles. A part of her wanted to find Jack, or Ben and talk to them. Maybe not the best idea, she'd probably get emotional and make a fool of herself. She would deal with this, it was her way, the one she'd learnt from a young age.

She couldn't settle to anything, the phone seemed to be forever on the edge of her vision as she tried to find a way to deal with this. Her head went into overdrive, internal conversations with itself. She'd go down anyway. Her sister wouldn't be happy at all. Would she be allowed in to see her mother? What would she say?

What would her mother say? She'd not wanted to see her. Would her presence make things worse? Questions and possible courses of action crammed themselves into her head. She'd finally make a decision and get a moments peace, only for her mind to start up again and bring her to an entirely different end point. She went round in circles, her head increasingly full of noise and indecision. Whatever she did it seemed like it would be the wrong choice.

She heard laughter in the entrance hall and familiar voices. She heard Ben's feet take the stairs and then a knock at the door. It was only then she realised she'd hadn't even put a light on.

Jack's smile, slid off his face when he saw her. "What's up?" he didn't wait to be asked in and with the door shut gave her a hug. It was a while before the tension in her began to ease and he led her to the kitchen. "Sit down, we'll talk if you want to."

He started making tea and allowed her to sit there, waiting for when she was ready.

"You know I've not seen my mother and sister for quite a while."

Jack nodded. "Yep, I remember you telling me. It hasn't been easy."

"That's one way of putting it." She let out a long sigh, the type that finally signalled a welcome pause in thoughts, and the chance to attempt to make sense from what she was thinking. "I sent my new address to both, but got nothing back and to be honest I didn't expect to, or really want to. Then I got that letter about the will and today, this came." She picked up her phone, brought up the message and handed it to him. She watched as he read it, his expression even.

"Wow," his tone was dry. "That's a lot to take on board." He handed the phone back. "How do you feel?"

"Too many things to unravel. I don't know what to do."

"I'm not surprised. Have you replied?"

"Yes. Take a look at the rest." She watched his expression as he read it.

"No wonder you don't know what to do for the best."

"No. I've thought and rethought a thousand times and done nothing, but go round in circles."

"That's understandable. They might only be texts, but there's a lot of heavy-duty words in there."

"My emotions are all over the place. One minute I want to shout the next I could cry. It's ridiculous. What if I make the wrong choice and end up with regrets?"

"It's a lot to take on board, with no warning no run up, just bang, this is what has happened and this is what your sister wants. The text seems to be more about her than anyone else."

"You're right, it's just like her, but like my mother too."

"So, this is what you're going to do for now," Jack said. "You're coming up to mine to eat," Becca began to argue. "No, you need to eat, if nothing else my cooking will give you something to think about. Believe me it'll clear your mind."

Becca half laughed.

"After that, you can see how you feel and perhaps what you need. Your sister made her needs clear."

He was right, getting out of her flat, eating and being in someone else's company stopped her head eating itself alive with indecision. It was enough to break the cycle she'd have spiralled in all night. Jack offered one piece of advice only.

"All things aside, guilt, expectations, orders, the past, the future. You should do what's right for you and there may not be an answer for that yet?"

It gave her permission to think about herself, if she'd thought those exact same words, she'd have said it was selfish. But he was right. "I'm going to sleep on it. I can't go down there tonight, I'd have nowhere to stay for starters."

"Good decision. If you need anything, you know to ask, right?"

"Thanks, I will. Just getting out of my flat and out of my head has made the world of difference."

She slept fitfully and dreamed. No, it wasn't a dream, it was more a memory she'd forgotten. She'd walked home from secondary school with a friend. It was summer and hot; they'd taken their time. They'd chatted, bought sweets from a newsagents. The walk home had taken longer, but she hadn't been thinking about the time, or that it would be a problem. When she'd got in her mother had gone ballistic.

Where have you been? Have you any idea what time it is? You stupid selfish girl.

She'd apologised. But didn't know what all the fuss was, when she looked at the clock it was fifteen minutes later than her usual time. Was it that bad?

We were worried

Her dad had said calmly. She'd apologised again and decided it was best to go to her room and stay out of the way. But when she'd come down for tea, her mother had started again and this went on all night. Becca couldn't remember how many times she'd said she was sorry, but this only seemed to make things worse. Finally, her dad had said it was time to stop and of course that had been treated with a whole new level of anger from her mother. They'd argued, her dad had gone into the lounge. Her mother had come back into the kitchen, finger pointed in Becca's face.

It would have served you right if something had have happened to you. If some pervert had got his hands on you. It'd have been your fault.

It had been the only time Becca's father had ever got truly angry. It had surprised her mother.

Too far.

He'd shouted as he stormed in.

You always go too far. Enough, she's still a kid for god's sake. You can't say those things to a kid, what kind of a person, a mother are you?

Her mother's face had swelled with rage. But her dad had shouted back even louder,

Enough.

Her mother had stormed upstairs, the door slamming. Her dad had hugged her and she'd cried. Afterwards, Becca's dad had barely been acknowledged by her mother. She was spoken to with grudging functional sentences. This had lasted for weeks. Her sister had blamed her for the atmosphere that filled the house.

She woke from the dream, the same sickly feeling in her stomach, the air of unease now pervading her new home. Things never got back to normal after that. Something had changed. Her father had perhaps meant, enough, in more ways than one. Her mother held onto grudges, never let them die, fuelled them regularly and when possible got even, no matter how long it took. Of course, to get even her mother had to tip the balance, getting even always meant more. It hadn't ended with her father's death it had only been redirected, refocused and that had only stopped when Becca had finally walked away.

The next morning, she rang work to say she wouldn't be in. Trying to juggle that, when she didn't need to, and all of this was silly. She ate breakfast and went out for a walk in the park. It would keep her head clear. She'd been walking for about twenty minutes, not really taking notice of what was around her, or where she was going. All she realised was that at some point her mind had stopped trying to process the situation and occupied itself with the simple act of walking. She felt better for it.

Back home, she phoned Victoria and wouldn't settle for anything other than a full explanation of what had happened. Her siter was not happy, said she hadn't the time, but Becca had insisted and then threatened to come down. By the end of the conversation Victoria had said enough to convince Becca their mother would be out of hospital in a few days. Her sister's initial diagnosing of a heart attack, had been properly diagnosed as a mild stroke. The only thing Victoria had been accurate about was her mother's wish that Becca stay away.

She doesn't want to see you; she's said it more than once.

That was her reply. As short and blunt as that. Had she really expected a different answer? There had been so many times when Becca had thought things might be different, that they might be able to move forward. But it had always been her giving in, meeting her mother and her sister more than halfway. She would have settled for eighty percent, twenty percent. But no, she would give in, wait for the comments and the recriminations to stop. If her mother was ill, Becca's presence would only make things worse, that was certain. She would do as she was asked and stay away. The attached guilt would have to be dealt with, but then she had done that for most of her life, in one way or another. She put the phone down and walked to the window. She'd complained about work being busy, now she would be glad of it. The phone went again and Becca picked it up, this time it was a text from Jack.

Remember, I'm a few steps away if you need to talk. x

She tried to remind herself that talking to people was the sensible thing to do, but she could feel herself going into some kind of survival mode, falling back on instinct and old tried and tested habits. Those told her she was used to dealing with everything herself, that it went against the grain to lean on others. To allow them in and see her vulnerable, or tell her she was a burden. It was easier to keep it to herself. This kind of situation brought out the best and the worst of her. The best, in that she would instantly support others, the worst in that she would push away any such help for herself.

That night, she fell asleep straight away, her brain had exhausted itself, but at two-thirty she awoke. What was it about waking up in the middle of the night that made everything seem so much worse? She tossed and turned trying to get back to sleep, ultimately giving up, she lay there, her mind wandering through childhood memories and clashes as a teenager and then as an adult. All the conversations. All the times she had done her duty as a daughter and still found herself the focus of criticism. Things she had done to be thoughtful, that had been twisted into problems. The flowers she'd sent on her mother's birthday, delivered to the excommunicated next-door neighbours. No thanks for them just blame for the humiliation her mother had endured collecting them. The birthday card sent early, to ensure its safe arrival, just before Becca had gone on holiday. Which resulted in a cross examination of her knowledge of family dates and anger that Becca didn't even know her mother's birthday, her special day. The list was a vast catalogue of petty incidents, but the sum of its parts added up to a lifetime of accusations. Charges that even when explained were seen as a deliberate attempt to avoid blame. Individually they were small barbs, irritations, but collectively they ended with the straw that broke the camel's back. One burden too many. She'd been worn away by a constant drip of acid and only just escaped when she realised how much it affected her. When she lived nearby, she would ring every day, each time not knowing whether she would be greeted with hello, or an accusation her mother had spent the day winding herself up over. She would visit at a weekend, not sure if it would be a trip to the supermarket, or a ride through a list of complaints focused on every friend or relative her mother was still talking too. She began to dread phoning; she began to dread the weekends. Victoria lived closer and visited every day. Perhaps this had protected her from her mother's imagination. Not given her enough time to wind herself up over something said in innocence, or perhaps Victoria was her mother's daughter and too alike to find fault in. Becca was compared to her father, the quiet, self-contained man who had failed in his duties as a husband and provider. The man who had learned not to argue.

Becca sat up, breaking the chain of thought. She got out of bed, headed to the kitchen and made herself a bowl of cereal. Her go to comfort food at this time of night. Bowl in hand, she crunched her way around the flat, the photographs of Jack and Ben, of Ann and Patricia and their various outings and escapes reminded her of the positive things in her life. Each one a step out of the spiral and back to a sense of worth. Her phone rang.

"Victoria, is everything okay?" Becca knew it couldn't be, but could think of no other way to start a conversation.

"Rebecca, mam passed away an hour ago…"

Victoria's voice was impassive. Her words faded into the fog of Becca's emotions.

"Rebecca, are you there?"

"Err, How, I mean what happened. It was just a stroke, a mild stroke."

"She had another, there was a clot, they were going to treat it, she was fine," Victoria paused.

Becca couldn't be sure if Victoria was upset, her voice was just flat, maybe it was shock. "Are you okay?"

"I'm fine," the nature of the answer said otherwise, it also said don't ask me again. "We were on our way there for evening visiting. The phone went." There was a long pause.

"I'll get the train down tomorrow," Becca said.

"No," the word was sharp. "It wouldn't be helpful. It would only make the whole situation harder. I'll have enough to sort."

"I could help."

"I think we can both agree," she was getting snappy, "the time for that has long since gone." There was another pause, Victoria calming herself. "I'll send details of a hotel you can stay at when the funeral has been organised."

"I can stay at mothers; if I'm there I might be able to help," Becca tried again.

"I hardly think that's appropriate. And there's only the one key. Look, I've got to go. I'll call with arrangements later in the week."

The phone went dead. Becca found her way to the sofa. Her mother was dead. She tried the words out, how did she feel? Surreal was the only word that came to mind. What was wrong with her? She didn't feel sad, just empty. Something was gone that had always been there. At the end, had her mother missed her, wanted her there? Should she have gone to the hospital, tried to see her. There was guilt, a finger pointing to her cowardice, but anything else, sat in the shadows, faint whispered accusations, as distant as the relationship that was now at an end. Did she feel relieved? Was she a bad person for feeling this way? She sat in the dark searching for answers.

***

The train sped south, the countryside a blur, the time crawling by as she wished each minute over. Two weeks had come and gone without Becca's participation, she'd been there and not, outwardly a functioning version of herself, inwardly her feelings a confused tangle that drew most of her attention. She had gone to work, eaten, stared at the telly and slept. Sleep that filled itself with the confusion of her emotions, dreams and memories, her brain's attempts to make sense of it all.

She'd distanced herself; she knew that. It was easier to be self-contained, prepared for what was to come. Jack, Ben Ann and even Patricia had accepted it in the end. Help was only such when it was accepted. Each had offered to go with her, Ben had insisted, it had been too much and she had snapped at him. He'd apologised, she'd been embarrassed and then avoided him. She would apologise, talk to him when this was over, when she could function properly, had the energy. She needed all the effort she had to get through the next few days. She didn't want to make things worse. Hoped she would say the right things and if pushed wouldn't snap, wouldn't let out her hurt and anger and guilt. A dig, a jibe would earn the speaker a roasting. She couldn't fully trust herself to remain civil and that's what she feared the most it seemed. It wasn't what others might say it was how she would respond, what she might say. If she started, she might not be able to stop. It would all come out, like lava, burning anything and everything in its way. She couldn't let that happen, couldn't speak ill of the dead.

Outside it was a sunny day, there were patches of snow drops and the first of the daffodils were out. They flashed by in blurs of colour. How many times on days like this, had she sat at work, glanced out of the window and wished she was out to enjoy the weather. Now, she would have been only too happy at work, the sun only a reminder of the other things she could be doing. Even a stressful day at work, followed by an overcrowded train ride and a night in with nothing to do, would seem like bliss. The next time she grumbled about it, she would remind herself of this moment and be thankful of the mundane.

There was no one there to meet her. She found a taxi; the driver was chatty. When she told him, she was down for a funeral, He said he was sorry and spoke only to point out the crematorium as they passed, minutes before he dropped her at the hotel. Victoria had booked her in for one night only. It was meant to be a short visit, clearly. At least she'd be able to walk to the service that afternoon and then get away under her own steam. The next two hours added invisible minutes to their existence and so the time crawled by. The detached calm Becca had felt now turned itself into a sickly feeling that took the bottom out of her stomach. She kept going to the loo, it was nerves only, she didn't need to.

She set off early; she couldn't sit any longer and didn't want to be late. It would be better to arrive early and stay out of the way once she knew exactly where the building and the entrance were. The hotel was on a roundabout and all of five minutes' walk from the cemetery and the crematorium. The grounds were well cared for and sheltered by trees. Another funeral was underway and those attending her mother's, were stood waiting at the front of the building under a covered area. One in and one out, she thought as she drew closer. There weren't a lot of people there. She stopped short of joining them and hovered unnoticed, she hoped, a reasonable distance away.

Someone called her name and she pretended not to hear it. The second attempt to attract her attention was closer and Becca was forced to turn and look. It was Aunty Irene, her mother's sister.

"Is that our Rebecca?" the tone sounded confused. "Why aren't you in the car?"

Becca didn't understand and it showed on her face.

"The car that brings the next of kin, you know with your sister, following the hearse."

"I- I didn't know, I-"

"Hmmm," Irene frowned knowingly. "Wasn't asked. That would be two of us then. I understand me not being allowed, but you, you're one of her daughters. It's not right, even if you didn't get along. Oh, there I go. Give your aunty a hug."

Aunty Irene smelt of Lily of the Valley. She'd used it all her life and Becca always associated her with the scent, familiar and welcome.

Aunty Irene held her at arm's length. "Let me look at you. It's been too long."

Becca felt like she was being scanned, her mind read by a seventy-year-old radar that had lost none of its power.

"Don't you go feeling guilty now. You should have left earlier, escaped. I don't know how you put up with it. Your mam was good at winding herself up and finding someone to blame for it. I got it when we were kids, your dad got it when she married him and you got it when he died. I think your sister's currently working her way through a similar list, it's a shame. Don't let her put you on it." She took hold of Becca's hand and gave it a pat. "How are you coping?"

Becca felt a certain amount of relief. She hadn't expected to find an ally of any kind. "I don't know Aunty Irene. I feel like an enemy soldier on the wrong side of the border. I'm not sure who's going to shoot first and from which direction."

"Well, it won't be me. Your mam and I put up with each other because we were sisters. We didn't especially like each other and put a lot of wasted energy into keeping a relationship going because it was expected of us, because that's what you did. Family was family and appearances were appearances. I knew her longer and better than most, so you'll not get any wagging finger accusations from me. There's plenty who could have come today and chose not to. You're here because she was your mam, but it doesn't mean you had to like her, or put up with the way she treated you. Things are different now, keeping up appearances isn't important anymore. You did the right thing when you left."

"I wish I could believe it."

"You should. It's the truth. Let me ask you this. If a friend treated you the same way your mam did what would you do?"

"Give them a chance to stop."

"And if they didn't?"

"Stop being a friend, walk away."

"Exactly. It's no different with family."

For some reason Becca had never thought of it in that way. Never allowed herself too. Hearing it from someone else was different. The words weren't tied up in a confusion of emotions, there was no baggage attached. Just words, clear and simple. They cut their way through the guilt, someone telling her what she couldn't say for herself.

Aunty Irene was studying her again and then she looked away. "Here it is." They waited respectfully as the car drew up, the chief mourners got out of the following car, the coffin was taken from the hearse and carried into the chapel. Victoria did look her way and Becca tried not to draw any conclusions from that briefest of looks. Aunty Irene nudged her. "Come on, give me your arm and we'll walk in together. I'll lean on you and you lean on me."

She didn't sit at the front, where Victoria and her family sat, the chief mourners. It didn't seem right to join them, not her place. Instead she sat with Aunty Irene, who had a hanky ready, just in case. The coffin sat there with flowers on top, the curtains drawn back until the final goodbye. Her sister sat upright, hardly moving, looking straight ahead. Was she holding back her tears? Becca felt oddly distant, it didn't feel real. Should she be feeling something right now? Ten years ago, she'd sat on the front row of her father's funeral, her place beside her mother, Victoria on the other side. She had cried then; her emotions had needed no guidance.

Now, the vicar spoke, her name was mentioned, much of what he said was unfamiliar, a eulogy for someone she didn't know. They sang a hymn and then some more words, church words spoken countless times at the end of so many lives, a comfort to some. Then music and the low hum of a motor, Victoria began to cry, Aunty Irene blew her nose. Becca watched the curtains close; her mother was gone.

Victoria hadn't lingered to accept condolences; she'd gone straight to the car. She'd glanced in Becca's direction, but that was all. Becca noticed the next group of mourners stood waiting at the front of the building. How many more times would the curtains close that day? Aunty Irene offered her a lift, but Becca said she would walk. She didn't want to arrive early, to be the first. It was only half an hour to her mother's and she wanted some time to herself, time to make some sense of her feelings before dealing with her sister's.

This was the street of her childhood, this was the street where they rode their bikes, played at being horses. This was the street where Daniel Stirk had fallen and cut his head. The gash had seemed huge, it stuck in her mind as some great red rift. There'd been so much blood and panicking parents and then the ambulance. This was the street with the haunted house, the one with the untended garden where the grass was taller than she, the one where the curtains were always shut. They used to dare each other to go into the garden jungle, to go up the drive, to go up to the door, to knock. This was the street where her best doll, Samantha, had married Joe Felling's action man. It hadn't lasted long, there were no children and it was a messy divorce. Samantha had married Big Ted a few days later. This was the street where she and her best friend, Jessica, sold lemonade and rose perfume they'd made from petals pinched out of people's gardens. Where they made mud pies, read magazines, sucked on Push Pops, swapped Pogs and stickers, platted bracelets out of that plastic stuff, swapped Tamagotchi's, braided hair and painted each other's nails. This was the street where she'd fell and ruined her trousers. The trousers her mother had told her to change before she went out to play. She hadn't and then put a hole in them as she fell. Her mother had been incensed, good trousers ruined, she'd been sent to her room, slippers thrown after her. She'd cried all through the day from the regular threats of,

Wait 'till I tell your father.

Her father's response was,

How are you love? How's your knee?

Her mother had then raged at him for undermining her. She'd fallen back on the all too often used phrases,

You never support me.

The truth was Becca's father had supported her mother from the day they married, it had been his duty, a duty expected, a duty fulfilled, but never acknowledged.

The street seemed smaller, less wide. It had shrunk, or maybe it hadn't, there were more cars now, but no children playing outside. One of the big trees had been taken down and so the road was no longer fully lined by them. Few of the people she knew still lived here. Then she reached her house, no her mother's house. Memories of swinging on the gate and hiding in the hedge to spy at passers-by. Of dolls' tea parties on the step. She hadn't been back to this house for some time. She assumed her sister had chosen to hold the wake here to save any mess at her own house.

This was her childhood house, but she felt like an intruder. How much had it changed since she'd last visited? She'd still felt some connection to it then, would she now? She was stood, hand on the gate not really wanting to go in, thinking it would be so easy to walk on down the road and catch a taxi back to the hotel. But no, go in, show your face, don't run away, then you can look back and say you didn't wimp out. She almost knocked on the door, but instead grabbed the handle and pushed. The hallway was little changed, things were where she remembered them. She could hear quiet voices in the lounge and kitchen. Her stomach was churning, but she knew her expression gave nothing of that away. She'd learnt overtime to keep her outward demeanour serene. No matter how fast her legs were paddling. She was praised for it at work, admired even, cool, calm and collected. A private person. Her sister called it moody. No one appeared and her eyes drew her up the stairs to her old room, her feet followed.

She gently nudged the door open, hoping it wouldn't make a sound; the feeling that she was intruding wouldn't be cowed. The room had remained unchanged when she'd originally moved out, but lived nearby and still visited. Now it had been emptied, her lingering presence removed. Excommunicated and expunged, she couldn't help smiling at the irony of her own thoughts. The room had not been repurposed, just cleansed. She imagined herself finding one of her old crayons and writing in large letters, on one of the walls, Becca was 'ere. She did a turn around the small room, making sure her shoes made as little noise as possible and looked out of the window. Over-the-road's garden was a lot neater now than it had been. The big willow tree was gone. She'd often sat under its trailing branches with a friend, hidden by the leafy curtains. Further down she could see Daniel Stirk's house. She wondered how he was, how his head was. Up to the right Joe Felling's house, had his action man moved on, gotten over Samantha? Straight over was Jessica's old house. What was she doing now?

She took a last look at the room, it didn't feel like hers anymore, had all of her old stuff been binned? It was nothing more than that, old stuff, she hadn't taken it when she could, she didn't need it now. Looking down the stairs, the drop didn't seem so far, a bit like the shrinking road outside. There was still a vase on the windowsill halfway down. She had slid down the stairs on a tray once. Broken a vase as she sped to the bottom. That had not gone down well and it was a miracle she'd not broken more. There was no tray to hand this time so she walked down, wondering how she'd had the nerve to slide in the first place, she must have flown like a bobsleigh.

"Hello Becca love," her Aunty Irene appeared from the kitchen. "Thought for a minute you weren't coming." She walked down and gave her a hug. "Come and get a cup of tea in the living room." She dipped her voice. "It's all that's on offer mind."

She sat while her aunty insisted on getting her a cuppa. Before the crematorium, she hadn't seen her in ten years and then it had been a quick hello at her father's funeral, with her mother stood looking straight ahead. Becca would have loved to talk with her, but it had been awkward.

"There aren't many here," Becca looked at the few people quietly chatting in small huddles.

"I don't think your sister intended to do anything after. We always had a wake, it was a chance for everyone to talk, lay the past to rest as it were. Old fashioned, but there's a lot of sense in the old ways, I think they call it closure now."

"I thought there would be a few friends. She can't have fallen out with everyone."

"Your mam was not one for maintaining relationships, or going back to ones she'd decided were over. She'd start off fine with folk. Invites, outings and such like and then there would be a falling out, always the other party's fault. Friends from her work, friends from your father's work and relatives too. Some were allowed back in, but one by one they all got shut out."

Now that her aunty had mentioned it, she remembered people being around, coming and going to tea, trips out and then it would stop. She had been close to Aunty Irene and used to ride her bike round to her house on a Sunday morning. Aunty Irene would bake and Becca would get a selection of goodies on a plate and a drink of tea. They'd chat, do 'jobs' in the garden, or her Aunt's greenhouse. Then for a reason she wasn't told, her mother informed her she wasn't to go to Aunty Irene's on a Sunday. It would have been when she was about fourteen. At that age she hadn't been in a position to question it, or understand that her mother's choice didn't have to be hers. Now she sat talking to her aunty, she felt a bond, something she couldn't quite put a finger one, something often referred to as blood ties, amongst other things. She felt regret for the time lost and would make sure she now remained in touch with Aunty Irene.

"Why do you think she fell out with people so much?"

"We can all be a bit daft, I'm no angel. Taking umbrage over silly things that aren't important. But your mother just couldn't seem to stop herself. She was very good at labelling people, even after just one conversation, sometimes even before she'd met them. That was her mind made up and it wouldn't be changed. She would also chew on things folks said and seemed to come up with stuff that hadn't happened. Reasons to fall out with them, things to accuse them off. Maybe it was insecurity. And she was always a bit of a closed book, you never fully knew what she was thinking, very private at times, stand offish people used to say. On a good day, you couldn't ask for better company and when appearances mattered, she was all things to everyone, but those times seemed to get less. We fell out plenty of times, some of it was my fault. But it just got too much and when she hung up on me, yet again, I said that was the last time."

They chatted away as if the intervening years had only been days. She was introduced to the few relatives there, it was pleasant listening to their stories, memories she shared, others she hadn't been aware of. She'd been sat talking for at least an hour when she caught a glimpse of her sister, perhaps checking on who was still in the lounge. She felt she had to go and say hello, make some sort of token gesture, it would be expected.

"Good luck, love," her Aunty Irene said.

Becca paused in the hallway; she could hear Victoria speaking in the kitchen. She looked up the stairs again and decided she needed the loo, nerves.

"I just want this over with," Victoria said to her husband. She was perched, chewing at a nail she'd caught that morning.

"Not long now," he tried.

"Why don't they just go, I didn't want anyone to come back. They invited themselves. I'd have made sandwiches. There's nothing in to give them. How's it going to look?"

"They've had tea and had their little chats, shared memories and all that. It's the done-thing, love. They're all from an age when that's what you did no matter what. Even if you didn't like the deceased."

"What's that supposed to mean."

"Nothing. Sit down I'll make you a drink."

"I can't sit. I just want this over."

"I'll give them ten more minutes and then thank them for coming and send them on their way. Then we can go home."

Victoria looked at her watch, with some relief. "Is she still in there?"

Her husband just looked at her.

"You know who I mean, Rebecca."

"Last time I looked. And before you say it, I'm not looking again. Ten minutes and then this is done."

Victoria looked at her watch again. They stood and waited, falling into the silence that accompanied the counting of seconds. Victoria's husband thinking about what was on the telly that night, Victoria chewing.

"And she was stood there with that woman." The words came out louder than she wanted.

Her husband looked at her.

She took a breath, long enough to turn down the emotional volume. "I'll bet they had plenty to say and you can bet, once they finished with mam, they'll have started on me."

"Now don't go winding yourself up."

"I'm not winding myself up."

He looked at her again.

She stubbornly took another breath. "It's typical. She swans in and they're all over her. I'm the one who organises the funeral and hardly a hello to my face from any of them. I'm the one that stayed, did the shopping, cleaned, took her to the doctors. Do I get any recognition? Not a..."

Becca took the last few steps into the kitchen; she hadn't meant to listen. "Perhaps if you went in and talked to them. And it was you who didn't answer my letters, you who told me to stay away."

"I didn't say that."

Becca looked at her. "I've a recent text on my phone that says otherwise."

Victoria's husband, gave her an awkward smile and made his excuses.

Becca broke the silence that remained after his departure, even though it felt as if she'd given in, lost the non-verbal battle. "How are you feeling?"

"What kind of a question is that? How do you think I'm feeling? Our mam has just died. I'm exhausted, the stress of," her voice was becoming strained, "of everything. The hospital, time off work, this place, the registrar, the funeral directors, calling relatives." She listed it all, one finger at a time, not stopping to draw breath until she'd got it all out. "As if I didn't have enough to do."

Becca had expected her to say she felt terrible, upset, numb, but not exhausted. "I would have helped."

"Oh, of course. You say that now it's all done. That's so typical of you. You turn up and straight away you're talking to her, that woman. What did she have to say?"

"That woman?"

"Mam's sister, Irene. I noticed you shoulder to shoulder. Thick as thieves," Victoria had got up from the kitchen table and was actually pointing a finger at her, the same way her mother used to, staring over the tip of it, pinning her accusations on her target.

Becca looked at the finger until Victoria lowered it. "I hadn't seen Aunty Irene in a long time. We had a lot of catching up to do. She had a few things to get off her chest, nothing that wasn't true."

"I'll bet," Victoria spoke with satisfaction, her suspicions confirmed. "And how long was it before you got onto me." She went to stand behind the chair.

"You were mentioned once," Becca said simply, she wouldn't lie.

Victoria was either disappointed, or simply didn't believe her. Either way she moved onto the next thing on her list. "I saw you coming up the road, heard you come in," again the statement was expressed as an accusation. "And heard you upstairs. Your things are all gone you know." Victoria was clearly watching for a response, a sign that she'd hit a target. "Out for the bin men."

Becca had suspected as much. It was only stuff she'd told herself, but a part of her would've liked something as a keep sake. There was no point biting. "What will you do with this place?" She didn't care, she was making conversation to stop the lava flow building at the back of her mind.

"I think that's for me to decide, when I'm ready."

"I thought that was implicit in the question." Becca couldn't keep the irritation out of her voice this time. "Don't worry, I'm not sniffing out inheritance. I know I'm out of the will and don't need the money anyway."

Victoria's face flushed; the finger was itching to attack again. "This was our family home; I should have guessed it would mean nothing more than money to you."

"That's not what I said, how on earth did you…" Becca broke off. Her mother did that, took what you'd just said and completely reworded it and threw it back. It never failed to catch Becca out, left her incredulous as to how something could be twisted right there in front of her. Afterwards Becca would sit repeating her own words, almost beginning to doubt herself. This time she was better equipped. "Don't put words into my mouth, Victoria."

There was something in Becca's tone that made Victoria grip the back of the chair. "I'm surprised you came here. I thought you'd be only too eager to get back on the train and leave again."

"You seem to be the one eager for me to go. The whole event feels like an inconvenience to you."

Victoria bristled and dared to come out from behind the chair. She took a step forward to point the finger right in Becca's face. "Don't tell me how I feel. You have no idea. You ran away and left me to deal with her. All the responsibility. It was always like that, you and dad disappearing off, while I did what was expected," there was suddenly emotion in her voice.

"Perhaps you should calm down," Becca feared they'd get to this point. That yet again, one of them would say too much, go too far.

"I am calm," the words were shrill and loud. Victoria glanced at the door, now aware her raised voice would have carried.

The conversations in the other room had certainly stopped. Becca found herself explaining, defending their dad again. "Dad kept out of mother's way because she was happier when he did, when he was around all she did was snipe at him. I quickly learnt to keep myself to myself as well. She preferred your company; you were more like her. I was more like dad, we were quiet together." Becca said it without accusation, it was just how it was, she thought it was the norm. But it was the wrong thing to say and Victoria was her mother's daughter; the reaction should have been expected.

"You were always his favourite. I didn't get a look in. Straight to your defence, but never mine. It was you that broke them, broke everything. That time you came back late from school. I'll never forget that. You won't have given it another thought. But I was older, I could see what it did. They were never right with each other after that. That was you." Her voice was rising, her emotions building and whatever she'd been using to keep them at bay had spent its strength. Emotion, exhaustion, stress now spoke for her. "I was the one she trained," Victoria stabbed a finger at her chest, her voice almost manic. "The one that was going to look after her in her old age. That's what my job was always going to be. I can trust you Victoria," she mimicked. "You won't disappoint me. Next door's daughter let her down, you wouldn't do that. Not like your father has and not like your sister will. Without you there'll be no one to look after me when I'm old."

Victoria had fired. The big guns had spent their ammo and Becca was still standing, well over the border, but unhurt. "That about sums it up; no one except for you. If I was dad's you were hers." Becca was surprised at how calm she felt, the lava had cooled.

"And it ended up that way, didn't it?" Victoria wasn't finished.

Becca wasn't going to apologise, certainly not explain again. "The question is more like; did I jump or was I pushed?"

"You chose to leave," Victor snapped.

"I think both of you made it very hard for me to stay." Becca's voice remained even. "If nothing else, I gave you the pleasure of being right." She stopped herself from saying more. How many times had they been here? At odds arguing around in circles. "Look, this is getting us nowhere. Surely, as sisters we can find some common ground, something we can agree on and part on better terms."

"Sisters?" Victoria had given up any pretence of calm, any cares she would be overheard. Becca knew now it was all coming out. She had to do damaged, make Becca feel as bad as she did. "Our only connection is we have the same parents and nothing more than that."

It was blunt, but it was true. "Why did you ask me here, Victoria?"

Victoria stepped back, suddenly exhausted it seemed. She wiped awkwardly at her nose, there were no tears. She gradually pulled herself together, Becca could see each stage, like some cannon hot from battle, dulling from incandescent white to yellow, orange, to red and then dull throbbing scarlet. Still it was sometime before she could speak. It started with a humourless laugh.

Becca was still in enemy territory, hadn't seen the assassin, it was too late.

Victoria looked her sister straight in the eye, anger spent, cold indifference filled the vacuum. "Honestly. I have no idea."

The journey home didn't really register, she was too lost in her thoughts to take much note of the passage of stations. On the journey down she'd imagined the relief of the return, but she hadn't allowed for the regret, guilt and her sister's final volley. It wasn't the words, it was the delivery, the look in Victoria's eyes. Her sister blamed her, all these years she'd carried that with her. Believed their parent's marriage had ended because she'd come home late. Becca wouldn't carry that back. That was not her doing. It was one event and maybe it was that final straw again, but that camel had been struggling for years, possibly from the start, or shortly after it. How did people fall out of love? Why did some stay together? No choice? Appearances? Fear? Too many possible reasons.

Becca ran through the conversation again, told herself she could have handled it so much better, had she pushed her sister? At least she hadn't gone there, delivered the same kind of final blow, not embarrassed herself, added to the regrets. She was chewing. Had her jaw been moving? Thankfully there weren't enough passengers to notice. No man with a mop of floppy hair to grin at her. She'd thought she would be leaving so much behind, bringing closure to that part of her life and moving forward without it all. She'd looked at her travel bag with a sense of irony; how much extra baggage was she trailing back with her?

Leaving the station, she considered a visit to the supermarket, but couldn't be pestered. There'd probably be something in the freezer and if there wasn't, she didn't really care, she just wanted to be in. She'd not slept well for several nights now and was tired. She just wanted to get in, shut the door and be somewhere familiar. The place would be quiet, everyone would be at work, or out at this time of the day.

Front door, her door, shut. She dropped everything and walked to the kitchen, hoping there was at least one biscuit to go with a cup of tea. There wasn't and the milk smelt suspect. She turned with weary resignation, picked up her coat, should have gone to the supermarket after all. She opened her door to find Ann stood, frozen in the intention of knocking. The next thing she knew Ann was hugging her and she was crying.

Chapter 12

Hospital run…

"How long do we leave her?" Jack looked at Ben, hoping for more insight than he could bring to bear on the problem.

"Babes, if she were a drag queen I'd say about a day, just enough time for them to wallow in self-pity, but stay clear of righteous indignation. Deserted in their hour of need, by the people they thought were their true friends, but turned out to be heartless individuals, entirely focused on their own selfish needs. With a queen, if you hear the same torch songs being played over and over, it's time to step in. With Becca, I don't know?"

"I suppose we've done what we can. Called in, checked up on her, made offers and then tried not to pressure. But then if all four of us have done that, she's probably seen more of us than in a normal week."

"It's been two weeks, two weeks of I'm fine. I just need a bit of time to get my head right, maybe we drag her out this weekend, whether she wants to or not. Sometimes it takes a little nudge to remind you the rest of the world's still out there." Ben looked at the clock and got up. "I'm microwaving rice if you want to stay for tea?"

"Yep, sounds good," Jack said absently.

Ben headed for the kitchen. Deep down at some intuitive level, they both knew Becca was okay, not at risk, or anything like that. But there was a time, and he knew this all too well, when you needed someone else to snap you out of it. Having the time to put your head right was one thing, but at some point, it turned into dwelling and on from there. He looked in the freezer. Picked up two boxes, both claiming to be delicious and authentic. He'd never yet managed to get one out of its little tray and on to his plate looking like the picture on the front of the box. His usually ended up looking like cat sick or at best a melted and traumatised version of the box picture. With practiced skill, gained only by repetition, they were unboxed, poked with a knife and humming away in seconds. Now for the hard bit. How to make it look a bit more presentable. He arranged lettuce and tomatoes on a plate, if only he could apply salad as well as he did eye shadow.

"Smells good." Jack leaned in the doorway.

"It's a start, if I cut out the box lid and slot it into your specs, it might also look good."

"It'll be fine. I'm here for the company not a free meal."

"Who said it was free?"

"Funny."

"Babes, I could show you a few punters who'd say otherwise."

"I'll bet, everyone's a critic. If something looks easy it's usually because the person doing it is very good. You made it look easy on New Year's Eve, but when I sat back and actually watched you and thought about all the things you were doing, or what I guessed you were doing…"

"You mean in the gaps between the funny bits."

"Yep, there was a lot of space, so I had plenty of time to think about it. You were juggling a lot of plates. Walking on heels for a start. There was so much you could have dropped, but you didn't.

It was smooth, skilled, effortless. You made it look easy and some people don't stop to think anything other than that."

"It's just an act, if you've enough mouth and nerve," Ben deflected the compliment.

"Accept the compliment, Ben. I couldn't do it."

Ben was never good at taking compliments, he'd avoid, or deflect praise. It made him feel self-conscious. He didn't know why, probably something about not needing someone else's approval. It wasn't a quality he liked; his parents certainly hadn't taught him that. It was after all the equivalent of throwing the compliment back in the person's face. Jack had picked him up on it several times.

"You need to get better at taking a compliment," Jack read his thoughts.

He was about to deflect again, to make a joke of it, but he knew Jack well enough to know when he was taking the proverbial and when he was being honest. "You're right. I'm too used to self-defence, on the stage it's easier to throw back shade than leave yourself vulnerable, it's become a habit."

"Yep, but I reckon if it's coming from a friend it's usually well meant."

"Jack, babes, don't take this the wrong way, but…"

"Why do I get the feeling something ominous is coming," Jack knew that if Ben used his name, something honest was coming his way, words from Benjamin. There was Tina, Ben and Benjamin. Jack and Becca had come to the conclusion independently and then shared it and laughed at the coincidence. Tina said what she wanted; Ben was a much-diluted version of her. Benjamin was the real deal, shields down, phasers to stun.

"Do you remember that talk we had in the milky coffee café, I called you a Hettie and we got into the whole stereotype, gay, straight thing."

"Yep, we only just scraped the surface of that one. I'd say it was the first day I started to get to know you. The first day you dropped your guard and considered the possibility that I could actual be a friend."

Ben looked at him, Jack held his gaze. That was one of the things he liked about him, he was the only straight man he knew who had the confidence to do that. Women did a lot of eye contact; it was supposed to signify understanding if a woman did it. If a man held eye contact it was supposed to be read as a challenge or sexual interest. "You're probably right. I think we'd been getting the measure of each other, and I was still testing boundaries. I didn't say this then because it didn't seem right, but it's stuck in my mind ever since. I wanted to explain myself, because I think I insulted you when it wasn't deserved."

"It's okay, I didn't take offence. It was more about contradictions, or another form of inequality in the face of the battle for equality. And anyway, you apologised for it at the time. You didn't need to then and you still don't."

"That's good, but I still want to say this."

"Okay."

"When I came out, it still wasn't a safe bet. It hadn't become trendy and was nowhere near common place. You still risked your job, family and friends. I got used to keeping the enemy, all straight men, at bay. I, we, my fellow gays stereotyped straight men just as much as we were labelled. For every faggot, puff, bender insult thrown our way, we had a list just as long of labels to throw back. I had no straight male friends to put that right. I saw my dad as the only exception to that, because he was my dad and his support was always there, I thought he was the exception. It never occurred to me that there could actually be some straight man out there who saw the person and could look beyond a label. You were the first, or the first I allowed in long enough to change that view."

"And I'm glad you did."

"So am I. It's made me realise quite a lot. Things I've held onto that have made me almost as bad as the straight men I was so angry with. Don't get me wrong this isn't absolution for all men, there's plenty of knuckle draggers out there."

"Not just men, women too."

"They can be worse, we've had a few in the club. But anyway, I just wanted to say," he pulled a face trying to sum his thoughts up. "Thanks, I suppose. Thanks for not judging, thanks for being a mate."

Jack got up, "Bring it in," he gestured and hugged Ben.

Ben should have been prepared; this is what Jack did. He made it look easy, no sub context, just a hug of support a thank you. It said more again about Jack's level of confidence. For him it was a plate he'd always found harder to juggle. Hugging another gay man, was simple, he felt in command of any subtext. He knew the rules and could deal with the recipient's hang ups. For him a straight man was a different set of results altogether. Rules he'd not had the opportunity to learn and perhaps realise that those rules had changed as men in general had been allowed, by society, to have emotions, to show them and express love in all its forms. As a man, and a gay man, he was trying to catch up. "How come you're okay with gay, when so many aren't?"

"You're going for the big questions tonight."

"We can talk about sport and cars if you'd like," Ben suggested. "I did swat up when I first got to know you, so that we'd have something to speak about."

"Sport and cars?"

"It was all I could think that might interest a straight man, or my outdated view of one."

"It's not outdated, but its limited. I can talk cars, but sport, never been bothered. I used to mountain bike and now I run and go to the gym, but that's as far as it gets. Football, rugby, tennis, never got interested. Dare say you've handled more balls than me."

Ben laughed more from surprise than anything else. "Babes you're a constant source of surprises, but you've not answered my question."

"You should be able to guess the answer. My brother, I suppose."

"I know about your brother. I know how much you mean to each other. But you said you were fifteen when he told you. Old enough to have opinions and prejudices. Your dad sounds like he would have said enough to sway any opinion. But you didn't absorb it. You were your own man, even then. Not bad for a fifteen-year-old."

"Then I'm not sure. It's just the way I am. I'll take the compliment though."

"You should," Ben offered him a wry smile.

"So, when did you realise you were gay? Anthony said he knew when he was fourteen, but suspected he was different from a lot earlier."

"Sounds familiar. Suspected I was different about ten maybe eleven, had crushes on lads my age when I was in my teens, didn't put a name to it until I was sixteen. October two thousand and one," he paused to count on from his birthday. "I was walking to sixth-form and for whatever reason it hit me. I'm gay, how do I move forward with this. Parents made it easy and I gradually told friends and the rest of the family. Publicly I kept it quiet, at first, acceptance still had a way to go, things have moved on a pace since then."

The microwave pinged. Jack collected cutlery and Ben left the rice in the trays and put them on the plate. "Imagine the plastic's not there." He showed him the box. "Imagine it looks like the food in the picture."

"It's certainly hot," Jack breathed through the mouthful of sauce, trying desperately to drag air through it before his teeth turned to glass.

"I use that thing," Ben gestured at the microwave, "every day and I still can't get to grips with it. But better lava than listeria. The hugging thing. How does that work?"

"What do you mean?"

"You said I make my act look easy. You make the hugging thing look easy."

Jack shrugged. "Again, I never really thought about it."

"That's probably the answer in a nutshell. I over-think it."

"Becca's the same. She said she worries it'll be taken the wrong way. I just do it. Parents did it, brother did it. Come to think of it the whole family were huggers. It was just what you did. I grew up doing it and the habit's just there. I'm not great with words, so a hug tends to be my fall back."

"It's a good default setting," Ben agreed. "You do it a lot, so it comes naturally."

"I guess if I thought about it, I'd falter and it would then be awkward. I do it for the right reasons, if people have a problem, me, the hug, we're gone in seconds. And the problem's theirs."

"You said you didn't think you were good with words," Ben had been surprised by the statement.

"I can get a bit tongue tied, I'm better writing it down, than speaking live. Probably why art, graphic design suits me. It's all there on paper, I can think about it as I go along, at my own pace. Add to it, alter, correct it, make it better."

"It's odd," Ben was used to putting thought into word quickly. "You said I make performing look easy. I'd say I have to work at it. I'd say you speak well, come across as confident, you say you have to work at that."

Jack nodded.

"We're none of us what we seem. It's all layers. Some of it we keep to ourselves, some of it we put out on display, probably the bits we're most confident with, good at. It can make us appear confident, in control. What's that thing about a swan, you know, all grace and elegance above water, but underneath it's paddling like mad?"

"Becca said the same. I think that's true of most people."

***

She'd continued to keep her distance from people; she didn't want to impose the way she was feeling on everyone. At work she could put up a front, pretend that all was well. With Ben and Jack, Patricia and Ann it was different, they would see right through her. Her mother's death had affected her more than she thought it would. The last conversation with her sister was still on her mind and her winter blues hadn't ran their course. They were heading to March and she still felt flat, not sad, just detached. Her enthusiasm for anything was non-existent and she hadn't been sleeping. That perhaps, more than anything, had taken its toll. Put it all together and she knew she was beginning to struggle. She didn't want Ben, Jack, Patricia or Ann seeing her like this. She felt like a weight was sat on her chest and hanging off her face, everything was an effort, like she was carrying some huge beast on her back, some grey shapeless thing. It worried her that it would stay, that come March she wouldn't have shaken it off.

Other things had crept into her thoughts, somethings her Aunty Irene had said about her mother.

She was very good at labelling people. A bit of a closed book. Very private at times. Standoffish.

Similar had been said about her. Was she like her mother? Would she get worse? Push people away, like now, distancing herself from her friends. The thought chilled her and she searched her memories for evidence to back it up, or disprove it. If she had similar traits, she'd stamp on them, bury them so deep they could have no effect. The concerns seemed real, magnified by the way she was thinking. She wanted to lock the door and not show her face until she had this sorted.

***

It was still dark and she turned over, determined to get back to sleep, that's when she noticed the figure, a shadow against the lesser darkness behind it. She sat up, not at all phased by the fact that someone was sitting where she usually flung her clothes. Somehow the meagre light from the window made the figure familiar.

You should take more care of your clothes, throwing them on a chair like that. Mind you it's not very comfortable. One of them trendy, overpriced things of yours I've no doubt.

Becca went straight to defensive; she knew that kind of comment would lead to others. Others her mother had stored up or brewed since their last conversation. "They'll go in the wash tomorrow and I've had the chair for years." she found herself explaining, another habit she thought she'd left behind.

More money than sense, that's your problem.

"They're clothes, that's all."

You never did appreciate what you were given. Those trousers you ruined, stupid bike. I said it was too big for you at the time, but your dad wouldn't listen. She has to learn things for herself.

Find her own way. He was too easy on you. You were always his favourite.

"I had to be someone's,"

There you go again, you're like a broken record, on and on. I can't say anything without you taking it the wrong way, always on the defensive, just like our Irene. Can't say anything.

"You say too much, whatever's in your head has to come out and we all just have to take it, no matter what. I'm surprised Aunty Irene put up with it."

She always had plenty to say for herself, you got like that. No respect. Never agreed with me.

"Because you were the one criticising, complaining about things that didn't matter. I was trying to put stuff into perspective, help you to see another side, so that we didn't fall out."

That's an easy excuse. You never supported me.

"I did lots for you and I wasn't going to blindly agree with everything, I spent a lot of time keeping my mouth shut, until you got so unreasonable."

That's your dad speaking.

"Better to be like him than you."

Don't you kid yourself, you're more like me than you think.

Those words more than any others found their mark. "I'm nothing like you."

Like a little sponge. It was the same when you started going to Irene's. I could hear her voice in everything you said after you'd been there.

"So that's why I wasn't allowed to go round anymore."

She was poisoning you against me.

"She was doing nothing of the kind. That was you winding yourself up, imagining stuff."

And what's that supposed to mean?

"You know, you did it often enough."

I have no idea what you're talking about.

"That's the problem. It was never you, always other people, Aunty Irene, dad, me, but never Victoria."

Don't' start criticising her. She's a proper daughter.

"And what does that make me?"

An accident.

Becca woke with a start, she sat up, heart beating, her eyes adapting to the gloom. Her clothes lay there undisturbed. She brushed her cheek. It was wet.

***

She recognised Ben's knock and considered pretending to be out. But then she thought of her mother's habits and went to the door. He was almost fully made up, enormous wig on a polystyrene head tucked under his arm.

"Oprah," he explained. "Babes, I'd hug you, but this took too long to put on and I'd leave half of it clagged to you. I can't come in, taxi waiting outside. Pesto's covering for me tomorrow night and Jack has got a film and food. So, you're expected at his for seven thirty." Ben held up a hand. "You're coming. We need to see you properly and you need to get out. I've kicked in bigger doors than this, so there'll be no point pretending you're out."

Becca smiled, why was she feeling tearful.

The taxi horn went again, Ben took her hand and gave it a squeeze. If your light's on when I come back, put the kettle on, but don't stay up on my account."

The taxi horn went again, a longer blast this time.

"I'm coming," he shouted. "I swear if he blows that thing again, I'll shove it so far up his arse he'll need a Jack Russell to find it." He squeezed her hand again. "Got to go, love you lots."

Becca watched him go. He'd not given her chance to speak, to come up with an excuse. That had been the plan she guessed.

She was dusting, anything to keep her mind occupied. The hall table seemed to collect more dust than anything in the flat, that and the coffee table in the lounge. She'd finish this and then give the bathroom a clean, was it too late to start hoovering? Hang on, was it dust first then hoover, or hoover first then dust? She heard Jack come in, bound up the stairs and shut his door. But shortly after, she heard him come out and head further up. No one else was in. It was a while before she heard him again, even for him, it sounded hurried. Then he was back in his flat and almost immediately out again. He stopped in the entrance hall and she heard him phoning for a taxi to the hospital. It was at that point that she opened her door.

"Jack, are you alright?"

He hesitated, possibly weighing up what answer to give. "Ben's in hospital?"

"What happened?"

"I'm not sure. I got a text asking for normal clothes. Something happened at the club."

Becca had the image of him in drag, had something bad happened out on the street. "I'll get my coat."

The taxi moved through the traffic, just the radio playing quietly, they were both distracted and the conversation had dwindled. Becca was trying not to imagine the worst. Ben's story about Brian being beaten up had come to mind. She'd dismissed it, Jack had said at the club, not necessarily outside. She'd been out on the town enough times to know what it could be like. The hen parties and the stags, tanked to the gills. Fights, name calling, heckling. There were good drunks, they had a good time and didn't bother anyone apart from being noisy. And there were bad drunks, throwing up in the gutter, rolling on the floor, screaming and yelling in the street, the list went on. To them any feature that stood out was a target, gender, race, sexuality, even your dress sense could earn you a mouthful from some tosser who didn't know when they'd had enough. Ben would have been a clear target, he'd mentioned before he'd sometimes got stick, but he wouldn't let the street trolls get to him, like the online trolls they were more than sad. Had someone thrown an insult? Had he answered back? Had it gone on further from there?

"You're chewing," Jack smiled.

"Worried, I've got him beaten up black and blue."

"We'll see when we get there. I texted for more information and called, but he's not answering. I know it's difficult, but it could be something else altogether. Fell off his heels and gone cartwheeling into a wall. He said once that Lady Straight Up came a cropper tripping over a bin, well his words were, she'd gone wig over tits carrying boxes and fell in a bin with the rest of the rubbish." Jack shrugged; he was making light of things. But Becca could see he was worried too.

The journey seemed to take an age, the more you wanted something to pass the longer it took. Jack kept checking his phone, he was waiting for a ward number. The traffic lights seemed to be against them, everyone stopping them, the red-light glowering. The town was busy and sheer volume was slowing their progress. He could have slipped, Becca told herself, those heels, some of them were monumental. At last, the taxi dropped them off, Jack payed him and they headed for the lights of the visitor entrance. Jack texted again; Ben could be anywhere in the huge complex. Finally, he got an answer. A&E. They were on the wrong side entirely. It took a bit of time to get their bearings and walk through the corridors. Hospitals had an atmosphere and a smell all of their own. She hadn't been in many, thankfully, just routine things for sick relatives. She'd only ever been in once herself, twelve or was it thirteen, with suspected appendicitis, it hadn't been the case and by the next morning she was tucking into sausages waiting to be collected.

She trailed along after Jack, he seemed to know where he was going and was stepping out to get there. The longer it took the more her stomach tied itself in knots and the more her imagination ran on ahead. At last they reached A&E, any longer and Becca would have broken into a sprint. If there'd been a queue at reception, she'd have leaped over it.

They were directed to seats along with an array of people either waiting for others or waiting to be seen. They sat and waited, waited and sat. Unable to think of anything worth saying. The clock didn't seem to be moving and as much as Becca tried not to look at it, her eyes kept finding it. Each time she was disappointed by how little the pointers had moved since her last look. Jack seemed to be dozing, or at least had his eyes closed, head resting back against the wall and a poster that said,

What a Catch.

Then he moved his head and she could see the strap line below, the first word was Chlamydia, maybe not so apt. Someone stumbled in through the main doors, noisy and on the arm of a policewoman, staff came out to help. All eyes moved to the disturbance, some in surprise, some in unease and some in irritation. It was quickly dealt with.

"Shouldn't be allowed," someone said.

"They shouldn't have to put up with that," replied her friend. "It's not right, poor loves, they're here to help."

Becca's eyes found another poster. It read,

We're here to help, don't abuse us.

It seemed ridiculous that a poster like that was needed to protect people who went out of their way to help, to save lives. It also seemed ridiculous that in some cases the poster was the only thing there to protect the staff.

The waiting area moved on through time, its own pace separate to the rest of the world outside. The chairs emptied and were re-occupied. Everyone cycling through bouts of activity and bouts of abject boredom. Becca moved with it, settling into a flat line of calm.

Jack stretched and sat forward on his chair and asked if she wanted a drink. With a reassuring smile and a pat on the knee, he put his stiff legs in to action and went off in search of coffee. She read the posters again, looked at the clock, glanced at people. Everyone was too close to people watch, here such a lengthy observation would be intrusive, staring. But her glances caught enough to make her think how infinitely varied humans were, even in this relatively small, but busy space. All different, some on their phones, some talking quietly, some staring into space, others thumbing through magazines, one trying to keep a small child entertained. All different, waiting for one reason or another. But all trying to keep their minds off why they were here. It occurred to Becca, she had thought of nothing other than Ben; her thoughts had been forced out of their detached spiral and now focused on him. She hoped he was okay, that all the silly thoughts she'd had were wrong. She looked at the clock again and then over to reception and then at two familiar faces.

"Look who I found," Jack said with relief. He was holding a carrier bag, with Tina in it, and supporting Ben with the other arm. Ben was holding his left arm, the sling still too much a novelty to trust, the pain all too fresh in his mind. His was limping quite badly, but beyond that there were no bruises or cuts. In those fleeting seconds, relief flooded through Becca like a wave, washing away her knotted stomach and the worry. She all but leapt to her feet and had to stop herself from hugging him.

"Oh, thank god you're okay. We were so worried; we thought the worst." She looked him up and down for other injuries. "How are you? What happened? Does it hurt?"

Jack steered them both to the doors, Becca almost side stepping in an attempt to protect Ben and clear the way ahead. She managed to wait until they'd manoeuvred him into the taxi before expecting answers.

"I fell off the stage."

"What, during a performance."

"No, thank the gay gods. We'd finished for the night; everyone had gone and I was tidying up and I just fell off the stage."

Becca sensed there was more to it than that and Jack was looking at him, his expression somewhere between suspicion and a smile.

"So, what happened for you to fall off the stage?" Jack asked. "It's pretty big. Come on, you're not telling the whole story here."

Ben rolled his eyes. "Dancing. Before you both start. I was dancing. We'll leave it at that. One turn too many and my wings didn't have any wind beneath them." He flashed each a look. "Any laughter and I get out and walk, is that quite clear."

Getting him up the steps to the front door took a little planning and by the time they were in, it was obvious a climb to his flat wasn't on the cards.

"You can stay at mine," Becca suggested. "There's no way you're getting to yours any time soon. Did you hurt both legs?"

"Both?" Ben was momentarily confused.

"Bruised one, sprained the other," Jack answered for him.

"Then there's no way you're climbing," Becca made the decision for him and bustled him into her flat while Jack went to collect Ben's lists of necessities. It was some time before he returned.

"You need all of this?" Jack lifted two carrier bags.

"The bare essentials," Ben defended.

"I'd call a toothbrush and a change of pants the bare essentials."

"Babes, and that is why I'm a star," he lifted his chin and affected an air of grandeur. "And you, well, if you didn't have your fading looks."

"I'll put these in the spare room," he called through to Becca. She popped her head out of the kitchen door. Okay. You want a drink?"

"Yep, and then I'll leave Gloria Swanson here with you."

The next three weeks, felt like a series of scenes from the movies Ben had introduced her too. He completed her education of gay icons with screenings of films that included All About Eve and Now Voyager, Sunset Boulevard, Mame, Hello Dolly, Calamity Jane, Nine to Five, the Wizard of Oz, Mommie Dearest, Cabaret and Beaches. Her spare room regularly became a scene from Now Voyager and All About Eve.

She was glad to have him around and after two weeks she realised he'd been the distraction she needed. She'd been forced to focus her attention on him, which meant any chewing and dwelling lost their hold. They spent a lot of time talking and bit by bit she recounted events of the funeral and he listened and made no judgement when she revisited things she'd said or wished she'd said.

Becca started baking, working through a list of things she wanted to have a go at. The list had sat untouched since Ann's cookery lessons. Now it wasn't just her who would have to eat the end product. She got carried away until Ben had hobbled into the bathroom one morning and let out a horrified scream. She'd thought he'd fallen into the bath, instead he'd stood on the scales. After that she continued to bake, but took her creations into work, where they were gratefully received.

Jack didn't need an excuse to visit, but if he couldn't think of one, Ben was an obvious fall back. Ann and Patricia called in regularly, again Ben was an easy excuse. He of course enjoyed the attention and fussing and Becca had more visitors than she would normally need. She began to feel better, the flat detached feeling lifted as spring began to assert its hold on the world outside. The low she'd experienced was gradually left behind by a climb of banks, plateaus and occasional dips. However, convoluted the journey; talk, company, activity and time did their job.

"Hi honey, I'm home," she called as she shut the door. She put away her things as Ben popped his head out the kitchen door.

"Hello dear, good day at the office?"

"I see you have that pretty little blue number on I like."

"What this old thing?" He fluttered the apron he'd found in the kitchen drawer. "Dinner'll be ready in half an hour, honey. Now you go and sit yourself down and I'll bring you a nice cup of tea, your slippers, pipe and the newspaper are all there for you."

Becca began to laugh. "I know I said I wanted a taste of domestic bliss, but that's quite enough."

"Babes, I was just warming to my part. I made soup."

"You made soup," she emphasized made.

"Babes, I opened the tin, I found the pan, I'm going to heat the soup. The only thing I didn't do, was make stock and add vegetables."

"That's all soup is. If you know that, you can make soup."

"It was a wild guess. You know the closest I get to cooking is baking Tina's face. Go on sit down, I'll bring you that tea."

Becca sat in the chair by the window. It was nice to come home to someone, but she also missed that short period of absolute silence when she first closed the door behind her.

"There you go, babes, one mug of tea." Ben hobbled in, his attention on the mug. "And two biscuits," he pulled them out of the apron pocket.

"You remembered, you're a treasure."

"Babes, it's starting to get like we're some old married couple. It's always two biscuits, I know you don't like fatty bacon, you like your electric blanket on half an hour before you go to bed, you have porridge in the morning with blueberries and honey, green peppers make you belch, you don't like fresh cream and will only eat potatoes when they're disguised as chips or roasties. I know you hate adverts, don't watch the soaps and can fold your tongue."

Becca started her list on her fingers. "You get ill if you eat prawns, have a love hate relationship with garlic, are in love with Joan Collins, shave your bits so the tape doesn't stick, do face exercises in the morning, don't sleep with a pillow, because it can give you wrinkles and will only eat cream cheese if its disguised as a carrot cake."

"Does this mean we're engaged?"

Becca held up her hand. "No diamond, so we can't be."

Ben sipped his tea. "Do you see yourself ever getting married?"

Becca thought. "Not sure. Relationship, yes. Married maybe. The whole wedding thing has got out of hand. Too much showing off and too much money. Save it, go on a great holiday together, put down a deposit on a house. The day should be special without having to throw money at it."

"Babes, seriously, is there no one on the radar? You never mention anyone. And neither of us got a valentine's card."

"I see you and Jack more than anyone. And the three of us have gone too far down the friends route for me to even register you as anything other than family. There's a couple of guys at work, but both are taken. To be honest, what with moving, new job, new flat, getting settled, meeting all of you and then the funeral and a whole load of guilt sorting, there hasn't been the time. I was too busy and then too flat and at the minute, I just want to get my head back in order and get you sorted."

"You seem like you're well on the way.

"I'm fine. I feel loads better. There are still mornings when the guilt sneaks in and pulls me down, but those days get further apart. What about you? Marriage I mean. Any admirers at the club?"

"Mr Right hasn't bought a ticket yet. He'll come along when I'm ready to be found. Right now, I don't want any long-term complications. So long as there are people around me I care about, and care about me, I'm good. I've always felt I'll not end up a drag spinster, someone will come along."

"And they will. If you're open to the possibility. One of the women at work is convinced she'll never meet anyone. That if she did, they'd want her for all the wrong reasons."

"That sounds more like she's putting obstacles in the way."

"She is, but talk it through with her and she won't have it. She just says I know I won't meet anyone and never have kids."

"She can tell the future then? What's her thoughts on next week's lottery? Babes, if you could run that by her."

"She'd also say she never has any luck. She's actually a nice person, but just so negative about herself. We've chatted lots about that sort of thing and no matter what I say, she won't be moved even an inch."

"What about kids?" Ben asked.

"I'm not the mothering type. It seems to shock a lot of people when I say that, but I'm not."

"Not even with the right guy."

"Well, never say never." Becca shrugged. "I wasn't exactly brought up with a positive idea of motherhood."

"How are you feeling about all that. Your mother's passing, I mean. I don't like to keep nagging on about it, but I like to check in."

"It's fine. I've learnt talking about it is the right thing to do. If I keep it all to myself it doesn't get any better."

"And has it got better."

"Bit by bit. I didn't really notice it slipping away, that flat detached feeling. But like the hands of a clock, you don't see them moving and then you're distracted and when you look back, they've moved. You get on with your life and suddenly realise things are better. A little each day and the next time you think about it, those little bits have added up to a real improvement."

"I'm glad, babes. We were worried for a while."

"Everyone has their moments, some a lot worse than others and in the big scheme of things it was far from the end of the world."

"True, babes, but it's all relative and once emotions get into it, things can turn upside down. One minute you're fine the next you don't recognise yourself. And if you start losing sleep it's amazing how quick you can sink."

"Tell me about it."

"Look at us," Ben gestured, "like two old spinsters sat by the fire sipping tea."

"Jack's the only one doing something about it. At least he's out there looking for Ms Right."

"It's not got him far yet," Ben reminded her. "That beach phone girl was Ms Right Now. He's seeing someone else now, isn't he?"

"It's still on, he's not saying much about it to me," She looked at Ben.

He pulled a face. "Bits about her, but that's all. I'd heard so little, I was starting to wonder if it was still on."

Becca shook her head. "I ask him how things are, but he rarely says much. Could be there's nothing to say. I get the feeling its fizzling out. I'm not even sure how long they've been seeing each other."

"A month at the outside. Certainly not two. They might not have got to the talking or parting stage. Babes, sex is good for about two months and then after that, once you've done it every which way, if there's no spark, no common ground it can only go one way. It's difficult to hold a conversation while someone's tongue is in your gob. When they stop shoving it in that's when you realise there's nothing to talk about."

"Talking from experience," Becca assumed.

"Babes I'd say we've both been there. But I'm not the eternal optimist Jack is. I always say, the more you look for him, the less chance there is of finding Mr Right. Stop looking and he'll come sailing along one day when you're not expecting it."

"That's got me nowhere, so far."

"Babes, the problem is, there aren't many ships that pass this way."

"So, do we start looking," Becca considered the idea.

"I'm more the wait and see type, or the wait and don't see. Either way I can't spare the time right now, especially not at the moment," he looked at his arm.

***

If she'd learnt one thing from the past weeks it had to be that talking was a good thing. A trouble shared was a trouble halved and that could make all the difference in the world. If her parents had been talkers; she might have developed the habit naturally. She talked to her aunty every week now. Ann had become her sounding board along with Ben and on occasion Patricia. Jack spoke to Ben about somethings and sometimes to her, but neither seemed to be his main sounding board. He might not need one, or think he had to keep things to himself and get on with it. Then she remembered Anthony, they were close, his brother was an obvious sounding board. It hadn't occurred to her, but then it wouldn't, would it. Maybe she'd angle their next conversation round to relationships and more specifically how his was going.

The thought hovered at the back of her mind that week, waiting for an appropriate time when she could broach the subject. And typically, the weeks before had been crammed with opportunities. Now that she was seeking them, they were having none of it. Ben was always saying, search for it and you won't find it, it was the same for keys, purses, gloves, lips-sticks and too many small things to list. Start looking for them and you'll never find them. Give up and when you're looking for something else, there they'll be, right under your nose. She thought back to the conversation she'd had with Ben about not enough ships passing their way and about starting to look. She'd also said she wasn't interested and he pretty much the same, but that had been a week ago now and she was beginning to wonder.

In the case of an opportunity to talk with Jack, stop looking worked and the situation presented itself. There he was on the train, this time she winked at hair man when they spotted each other. Thankfully this time she'd not been sat chewing, her nose had been in a book, the novelty of the daily train trip had worn off. The corner of her eye must have picked up on the sudden moment as he'd leaned forward and given her the Jack grin. She gave him a wink and pointed to the free seat next to her.

"Well fancy meeting you here?" she greeted.

"I'm not used to women winking at me on the train," he grinned.

"I only do it to the good-looking ones. And seeing that I couldn't see one this time, I settled for you."

"I'm thankful for small mercies."

"I'm sure you get your fair share."

"Maybe, maybe not. So, girl on the train, how's your day been?"

"Busy, and that's about the best of it. I didn't get time for lunch and right now I could eat a horse."

"I could go a pizza, but just the regular kind, no hooves and things."

"I can compromise. Barbecue?"

"Yep, sounds good to me. I'll come down about seven thirty? And I've got cake." He smiled. "My mum sent me one of her tea loaves through the post."

Becca brightened. "You've never mentioned those before."

"For obvious reasons. I'm selfish when it comes to my mum's tea loaf. But as it's you."

"You might want to re-think that."

"Oh, of course, Benjamin. He'll sulk if he's left out."

"I could lock him in his room."

Becca finished their order and left her door ajar, so Jack could let himself in. She put the phone to charge and started getting plates.

"Hello," Jack's voice announced his arrival. He reached the kitchen, gave her a quick hug and put a tin on the worksurface. "Cake."

"Great. I've strapped Ben to his bed, so we won't have to share."

"Where is he, anyway?"

"On the phone, his dad, I think. Pizza's ordered. Tea?"

"Yep, please." He sat down.

The back of Becca's mind gave her a nudge. Yes, this was a good time to bring it up. Now of course, she felt awkward about it. She wanted her questions to sound natural, but the more she thought about how to do that, the less natural she felt.

"Your chewing," he said with a knowing look. "Everything okay?"

"For a change, yes. We've spent so much time lately talking about me. I've not got round to asking you how things are." Thank goodness for chewing she thought, for once it turned out to be useful.

"Me?"

"Yes, you. Is everything fine with..." Oh this is great Becca thought. She tried to pull the name to mind but, in the end, just offered him an apologetic look. "Thingy, what's her name."

"You mean Ashley," he asked, a smile curling the corners of his mouth.

"See, now that's really bad. But in my defence, you've hardly talked about her."

"There's not exactly a lot to talk about. And to be honest you've had more than enough on your plate and Ben's been a stress head about work and his arm. I wasn't going to add to that."

"You're allowed to talk about stuff as well. I've always thought, the best way to forget your own problems is to hear about someone else's," she stopped herself. "Or good news," she added hopefully.

"Or no news. If I thought it was going anywhere, you two would have been the first to meet her, but it's not. If the sex wasn't amazing, I'd…" it was Jack's turn to stop short. "Sorry, that was more than you needed to hear."

She laughed. "My god that's nothing, you should hear what we talk about at work. I know the ins and outs of too many vaginas."

Jack swallowed his tea before he sprayed it across the room. "It just seems odd talking to you about it," he was trying to puzzle the feeling into words. "It's like you're my sister and talking about sex with your sister is a bit odd. Does that make any sense?"

"Only in that I would never talk sex with mine. I don't think she has sex, or if she does its probably all, put it in there now, faster, harder, you're doing it wrong, try again." She waved the thoughts away. "Anyway, I get what you mean. I just wanted to know you're okay and say that you can always talk to me, no matter what."

"That's good to hear. I will and for now, it's all good."

"You're sure?"

"I'm sure," he smiled.

Becca was happy she'd checked up on him, let him know she cared and found out a bit more about his inner workings as a bonus. She congratulated herself, maybe she was getting better at this talking and not chewing thing. She asked him how his brother was and they talked until the intercom buzzed.

"That'll be the pizzas. I'll go, will you tell Ben?"

Becca went to the main door, collected and paid for the pizza and headed for Ben's room.

"Pizza girl," she called and then pushed the door open. "Honestly, the things I put up with."

They were sat seductively on the bed, wearing two of Ben's wigs.

"Babes if this isn't a set up for a porn vid' I don't know what is."

"Two men on my bed and my mouth's only watering because I'm holding a pizza."

***

Becca sat. At first, she was going to keep her eyes closed, but Ben informed her this wasn't a five-minute slap, so she decided to watch the transformation.

"Do you normally do each other's makeup?" she asked as Ben tested a few products on her hand.

"Not usually, you know your own face and what works. It takes a long time to perfect it. Most queens wouldn't trust anyone else to make them up, especially before a performance. But if you get good at it, they'll seek you out for ideas, queens learn from queens. A bit like daughters from their mothers, or best friends. Occasionally they do each other for a laugh, or if they want a totally different look for a party. We're doing this light, if I put too much on you, it'll age you right up. Right, babes hold still."

"I'm assuming you do this most days." He showed her the bottle.

"Foundation, not necessarily. I usually can't be bothered."

"You should. I'll show you a quick way. Keep it light, natural. Drag make up is exaggerated, but a lot of what we do gets toned down and you see it on women's faces in the street."

That done, he moved onto highlighting and contours. "You'd do this to bring out your best features. I do the same, but also to cut out or knock back the man bits of my face, jaw line and forehead need to be softer."

He continued at a surprising pace with only one hand to work with.

"Do you do all of this every time."

"This and a lot more. If I'm not on stage I tone it down. It looks too clowny away from the lights. Blend, blend, blend." He said dabbing away.

"Fixing powder. Again, you'll do this before you start on your eyes and brows, blah, blah, blah."

By the time he'd done the first stage, Becca could see just how much her face shape had been enhanced. It was amazing, not like anything she'd do, not even for a night out.

He worked on, positioning her head, switching from brush to sponge, clicking open jars and compacts like a machine, explaining what he was doing and getting her to pull all manner of faces. When he'd finished her brows and eyes, she couldn't help stare.

"Oh my god. They look amazing. Oh my god." She kept moving her head from side to side, leaning into the mirror to examine them. "I need you to do this the next time we go out."

"Right, sit up, or we'll never be done."

"How long to do your full stage makeup?"

"With two hands it can take two to three hours if I'm looking for perfection."

Next, he brushed on blusher and focused on her lips. "Like I said, I've kept it simple, so you could do this yourself."

After that, came lashes.

"I'd never think of putting on false eyelashes."

"You don't need to really, you've great lashes, mascara's enough for them. You know it's harder putting these things on someone else. I'm so used to putting my own on. But this is where you're going to have to help, can't do this with one hand."

Lashes done he took the wig, she'd chosen, off the head and handed it to her.

"You'll need to do this." He explained how to position it, hold it and where to place it on her forehead before pulling it on. When she looked up, she clapped her hands like an excited child.

"I love it."

Ben sat down on the bed and allowed her to admire herself from every angle. He remembered the first time he'd truly perfected Tina. He'd felt amazing, the sense of satisfaction had seeped into his very core. Some part of him had been set free, allowed to exist in the real world. Tina had been born and strange as it sounded, even to himself, it hadn't been long before she started to teach him things.

***

All the way through his convalescence, Ben was able to work and was picked up and dropped off by Pesto. Things would have continued as they were if Becca hadn't returned early from work one afternoon to find Ben frozen to the spot on the stairs.

"Oh shit," was all he said and managed an awkward smile.

Becca didn't say anything, settling for folded arms and, "Explain?"

He descended the stairs; the limp had apparently cured completely while she'd been at work that day. "You see, babes," he began tentatively. "It's like this. The arm's genuine, I did fall off the stage. When Jack took you to A&E, he had nothing more to go on than you. And I certainly had no plans, I was too busy knocking back every drug they would give me for the pain. The limp we decided on in the minutes it took him to walk me back to the A&E reception."

"You invented the limp. The one that moved from leg to leg?" Becca wasn't annoyed, but she wasn't going to let him know that, not yet anyway.

"We thought you needed a distraction. We didn't know what to do for the best. It was a hasty thought, tacked on to an unplanned accident." He attempted a casual laugh with an air of light playfulness.

"So, the staying with me wasn't about helping you it was about keeping an eye on me."

"I was your therapy, babes. It gave you a chance to talk, and you weren't exactly doing that were you? You'd all but pushed us out and locked that door. We thought… well, it doesn't matter really, does it. I mean it worked. Didn't it? Babes."

He was clearly sussing her out, it was a novelty seeing Ben cowed and placating. He and Jack were right. All of what Ben had said was true and their plan, however spur of the moment and misguided, had worked. She couldn't hold her expression any longer. "Come here," she said, opening her arms.

She hugged him. "Thankyou. I think."

"Are we forgiven?"

"I haven't decided that yet."

"Ow."

"What was that?"

"Babes, ow, you're crushing my arm."

Chapter 13

It's good to talk…

Ben and Jack showed up at her door a few days after Ben's arm was given the okay.

"We brought this." Jack said, as they revealed what was behind their backs.

"I didn't bin them, just in case," Ben explained.

"We thought it was the right time."

Becca looked at the pictures and the box that had sat unwelcome in her hallway. Things she didn't want to be reminded of, but couldn't throw away. She'd half-regretted giving them to Ben to throw out. Clearly, he'd been aware of that too. "Come in."

"Babes, we thought we'd leave them with you."

"No, I'd rather you came in, I'd like you to see them. I think they've lost whatever pull they had on me. Come in and we'll see."

The box and the picture frames went on the table and now they sat looking at them.

"Well here goes," Becca said, opening the box.

It wasn't very big, just enough for two photo albums. Two albums full of pictures of Becca as a baby, a child and a teenager. Pictures of her in the paddling pool, the first jam tart, the first ice cream. Pictures of her in clothes she wouldn't now be seen dead in, but at the time had been the height of fashion. Toothless grins, gapped tooth grins, awkward smiles, do I have to have my photo taken frowns? Years of family events and holidays. Pictures of Becca with her sister, her dad and her mother. But then they stopped. There wasn't a third album the pictures had stopped about the same time as the argument. Her sister had been right, things had changed then, or more likely reached an end point after a long period of decline.

"I don't remember most of these, it's odd the things you do remember. I've got a memory of looking out of the back of the car as we turned across a set of traffic lights. A memory of looking down from my bedroom window, to the front door, watching my mother talking to a neighbour. Nothing special about them, but they stick. I wonder why them, and not more of this stuff." She turned back through the pages.

"Yep, I can remember being in the bath, I must have been really young," Jack focused on the images. "I remember the boat I was playing with, even a sense of the bathroom and what it looked like, no, what it felt like. And another time buying a screwball ice cream from the ice cream van when it came round." He looked at Ben.

"Bedtime and sneaking a look out of my bedroom window and it still being light outside. Babes, the memory so very clear, the plants the fact that it was summer. That I should have been asleep, again I must have been young. Playing in the beck and building a city of a muddy little island out of house bricks. Like you said nothing important, but clear, even after all this time."

"These photos look like happy memories," Jack said. "I know you said something about them being from a time when things were okay, or you were too young to know differently."

"And looking at them now, some of them are. But as I move through them, to the later stuff, times I can remember, the photos of us smiling seem false. Maybe I didn't want to be reminded that there had been other times, I needed to hold onto the later years. I wanted to distance myself from them, not be reminded of the good times in case I missed them too much. And in the end, it's the bad times that have stayed with me."

"Babes, what about these?" Ben pointed at the picture frames. She turned them over. The one of her and her sister. The one she'd looked at after talking to Ben. It had been as far as she'd got. There were also two wedding photos and two family-photos. My mother didn't want any of this, that's the only reason why I was given it. She was clearing out. These pictures came down off the wall. The happy marriage, and maybe it was to begin with, I don't know. My mother would never talk about those times. The happy family, but I don't remember it as that. Looking at them is like looking at a group of strangers. The other family, that looked like us, but actually liked each other."

"So, how do they make you feel now?" Jack asked.

"Nothing really," Becca said with only the slightest of regrets. "I think I built their presence up into something more than it should have been. When I moved in everything was still pretty raw and I certainly didn't want to be reminded of it." She looked at Ben and squeezed his hand. "I'm glad you didn't throw them out. They're worth keeping. Maybe I'll look back at them sometime in the future and they'll be nothing more than photos. They can go in a cupboard until then."

"So, is it all behind you?"

"I think it is. Parents are gone, there'll always be some guilt there, but I can live with that. There are others who get on with their lives, having put a lot more behind them than a family that didn't get on."

"So, babes," Ben switched to an American ascent. "Do you have closure?"

She put the albums back in the box and stacked the photo frames on top. "Yes, I'd say I do."

***

Becca heard Jack and Ben clatter their way down the stairs. They were off out. It was odd to think that she'd known them only as hair man and high heels and now she couldn't imagine her life without them. Labels had become real people, important people. She's been asked to go, but had politely declined. They were off to see a science fiction film. Jack's lifelong interest had rubbed off on Ben. She had sat through several of Jack's all-time favourites and she'd enjoyed them, but they weren't her thing. And given that Jack had low expectations for what they were going to see, she decided a night in was for her. This plan hadn't lasted long. A second invite found her climbing the stairs to Ann's.

She presented Ann with the thank you flowers, she'd dashed out and bought.

Ann smelt them. "Lovely, a smell of spring. Thankyou I cannot get enough of daffodils at this time of the year." She invited Becca in and took her through to the lounge. "I'm surprised you found these; the season must be coming to an end by now. Next, it will be tulips."

"Becca, my darling," Patricia greeted.

She leant over so Patricia could give her the customary peck on the cheek. "I heard the boys going out."

"They're going for a curry then a film."

Ann came back into the room with tall glasses and a bottle of fizz. "I thought we might start with a bit of this."

"How lovely, what are we celebrating?" Patricia asked.

"Nothing in particular, do we need an excuse?"

"Not at all, mummy held the opinion that fizzy wine was only for celebrations, but she grew up when such things were expensive even if you could get them. Now it's everywhere. Champagne, prosecco, cava."

Ann poured and handed them one each. "Let's celebrate then. To friendship."

As expected, the food was delicious, a warming stew Ann served with huge chunks of her own bread.

"This was one of my mother's favourites, so the recipe is at least as old as me."

"I'm old," Patricia corrected. "You Ann, my darling, are only middle aged."

"You're not old," Becca corrected.

"I'm nearly into my sixties and when mummy reached that age, she was old, she looked it. She was worn out."

Ann nodded. "I think people did look older than their years back then. Then, sixty was old an' seventy was ancient. Now sixty is the new fifty an' seventy is the new sixty. Eighty now seems old an' that will change soon enough."

"Well I still feel old," Patricia was adamant. "I mean, look at me."

"You look nice," Becca meant it. She'd noticed that Patricia had suddenly started to dress better, wore a little makeup and had done something better with her hair. This had started before Christmas when Patricia had hurt her wrist and the café had needed extra hands to run it. The changes were Ann's influence she suspected.

"That is because of your hard living," Ann joked. "You have lived enough lives for all three of us."

"My darling, I think you might be right," Patricia chuckled. "I reached my mid-fifties and wondered where the years had gone. Gravity and time hadn't been kind, I just gave up and thought to hell with it, I'm going to eat what I want and keep away from my reflection. I hate it though, when I have to look in the mirror, I wonder who I'm looking at. Inside I still think I'm twenty-eight."

"Me also," Ann agreed. "That is interesting. I would say I still feel like I'm in my late twenties. It would be nice if I could get the outside to look as young as I feel, but I would never say I am old. That is just a state of mind Patricia and you are not that much older than me."

"Well," Becca began. "I don't think either of you are old. There are some women at work in their forties and they say things like, wait until you get to my age."

"Forties is nothing," Patricia waved a hand. "I, on the other hand creak like an old house. I laugh too much and I pee myself, bend over and break wind, come back up and belch. I swear one of these days I'll meet myself halfway and explode."

The mental image made Ann laugh, and the more Ann laughed the more Patricia couldn't help herself. It wasn't long before Becca was gasping for air and her stomach was aching. It got to the point where they couldn't make a noise; no more air would come out and then Patricia broke wind and they erupted into further hoots of laughter.

"I haven't laughed like that in a long time," Becca said, wiping her eyes and wincing as she went to straighten.

"You have to laugh at it all, or you would sit down and give up," Ann said. "Is it time for pudding or shall we wait until halfway through the film an' have a cake break?"

"I shouldn't be eating it at all," Patricia said patting her tummy. "This is only getting bigger and my new underwear will have its limits. It's so hard to keep the weight off when you get to my age."

"Oh, that starts a lot earlier," Ann said. "I really have to watch my weight. All the things I enjoy just go straight to my hips."

"Straight to my bum," Becca complained.

"If I could direct it," Patricia pointed. "I'd have it go straight to my titties. They used to be so ample, they were my pride and joy. I ensnared many a handsome man with them. Now they're just something I drag along the floor when I get into the shower."

They stared to laugh again.

"Do men talk about all of this stuff?" Becca wondered. "Men in general I mean."

"I would say so," Ann replied. "We are not so different. Society, or perhaps the media, like to pit us against each other."

"But that's how it was." Patricia said. "When I was young, men were men and women were women. They had sex and marriage and children in common. Back in the day, I would have said we're totally different. Men were the hunter gatherers and had to be stoic, silent but strong. Women were the home makers and had to be empathic and emotional. It was all cod's wallop, but we felt obliged to play the parts society gave us. It was always pointed out how different men and women were and what their roles should be. We were all trapped really."

"Times have changed," Ann agreed. "There are some differences between the sexes, of course, but we have more in common than we realise."

Becca thought about Jack and Ben. "I think it is different now. The world's opening up, emotions, wellbeing, equality, gender, sexuality, is all up for debate. It's beginning to equal out and open up. We're starting to realise that everything's not black and white, there are so many shades in between. I suppose we'll be talking about it for a good while yet."

"There is still a lot to put right," Ann said. "A lot of water under the bridge to learn from an', I think, get over and move on from. How long do you rake over the coals of the past before you decide it's time to look forward, to move on?"

"Gemma, cuts my hair," Becca began, "She's my age, maybe a bit older, and has a very odd view of men and women. I was talking about Jack and Ben. She asked if I was seeing one of them.

I explained the situation, but she was having none of it. She said men and women can't ever just be friends. That the sex thing always gets in the way."

"My darling, I'd be only too happy for the sex thing to get in the way. It's been too long since my ladies parts have had a good seeing too."

Ann choked on her drink and the laughter began again. It was a while before they returned to the conversation.

"I would say it depends on the man and the woman." Patricia said at last. "Some will see friendship as totally natural; others will be at it like rabbits, the hole is the goal. I will admit, when I was younger, I was quite desirable and had the sex drive of a combine harvester. Men for me were sex objects, the key to the door of my raging libido."

"You would have been seen as an exception," Ann said. "And possibly a lot worse. Women weren't supposed to be interested in sex and there was a lot of social shame to try and stop them."

"I didn't care."

"You'll have to go further into the countryside with that one." Ann noted the puzzled look. "It's Danish, for I don't believe you."

"My darling, I really didn't care. I was quite foolish and shameless in my youth."

"Then you were a trail blazer. Good for you."

"Contraception," Patricia said, "freed women to some extent. Then the sixties liberated sex from the moderates. Women were allowed to enjoy it, even initiate it. Though it's taken a lot longer for that to be the rule rather than the exception."

***

It was official, her life was finally the way she'd always hoped it would be. She had a job she liked, with a good life work balance. She'd stopped keeping colleagues at arm's length and found that friendship at work, worked. She had a flat she liked in a really nice area. With help it was now a cosy comfortable haven. She had friends, close friends she now thought of as family. People who had altered her preconceptions and taught her to talk instead of chew. They'd given her so much and with no expectations. Without being saccharin, she wanted to thank them for that, start to give back some of what they'd given her.

But how to do it?

Food, was the answer that came to her as she popped another biscuit into her mouth. She'd cook them a meal. Not reheat a meal, or assemble a meal, no, she'd cook one from scratch.

After she'd invited them for Easter dinner, she began to ask herself just what was an Easter dinner? Why had she said it would be homemade? Did anyone know what an Easter dinner was? Could cook it? Make it look homemade and deliver it unnoticed?

Why had she set herself this challenge, was she insane?

First course, main course and of course, a pudding. Fattening Ben up, while he was trapped in her flat, had given her enough practise at baking and preparing desserts to feel confident she could produce a great one. That left the starter and main course. Watching Ina Garten and buying one of Mary Berry's cookery books showed her some short cuts for an easy starter that would look like she'd gone to a lot of trouble. So that just left the main course. The only one she could make from scratch; was tuna surprise and she'd already played that dinner card. Besides, it wouldn't offer her the attention-grabbing table she wanted. Festive dinners usually included a roast of some kind. Chicken, pork, or beef. Beef didn't feel right for Easter and neither did pork. So, it would have to be chicken, maybe it was the yellow chick connection that made chicken seem like a suitable Easter meal. She'd not focus too much on little, yellow, fluffy chicks when she was shoving a pound of stuffing into the body cavity of a farm fresh bird. But chicken sounded good and would be something spectacular to carry in on a platter loaded with roast potatoes. In fact, she saw no problems to this menu other than she'd never cooked a whole chicken and didn't want to poison her guests. It turned out, mercifully, that her new best mates, Ina and Mary had the answers.

Becca decided she would have a trial run of the whole menu. That way she could make her mistakes before she fed them to anyone and get her timings right. She set aside a whole weekend for the shopping, prep and cooking of this feast. All went well. She even found herself pretending to present a cookery program while she did it. Mind banter knowledgeably informing her millions of devout followers how to cook such a meal, and make it look simple. Everything tidy, well timed and presented with a generous helping of witty charm.

In reality things went a little differently. But at least she learnt several things from the test run.

One, it was indeed possible to make a fabulous looking starter from some surprisingly simple ingredients, but that leaving it sitting around on the countertop for several hours wasn't a good idea.

Two, remembering to turn the oven on, actually helped the chicken to cook.

Three, there was a lot of smoke involved in the production of the perfect roast potato.

Four, there's a lot more to gravy than granules.

Five, custard is easy to make and really does taste far better than anything bought.

Six, cream can be overwhipped, leaving you with butter which doesn't go well on a trifle.

Seven, raspberries soaked in sherry are divine and if you eat a lot, they'll give you toilet problems for the next twenty-four hours.

Eight, set the table before you do anything.

Nine, don't drink a whole bottle of prosecco while you're tackling any of the above.

Easter arrived and on Monday so did her guests. She'd made sure the flat looked its best, they all got a little chocolate egg each and a glass of prosecco. She was calm, chatty and had even got changed. Once they were all settled, she went into the kitchen, took a deep breath and began to present her meal. To her surprise and considerable relief, the evening passed without incident, everyone including her had a lovely time.

"Becca, my darling, these starters are delicious. How did you have time to do them?"

"Oh, they're simple really."

"Wow, babes roast chicken I couldn't do that in the microwave and these roast potatoes are fabulous."

"As long as you get the oven right and keep an eye on things it's pretty straight forward."

"Yep, I'd say that was the best trifle I've ever eaten."

"It's just cream, custard and raspberries, anyone can do it."

The deep breath she'd taken was finally let out when Ann unexpectedly came in to help her with coffee.

"Becca you've even made little chocolates."

"Err, oh, Ann. Yes, I got that idea from you. I thought it was very hygge." Becca was doing a strange leaning thing with her hips and arms, trying with little effect, to hide the mess.

"It has all been lovely; you have made us all feel very special." Ann lowered her voice. "Now, can I help you clean some of this up before anyone else sees it."

"Oh, my god, yes please. I don't know where to start."

Chapter 14

A Decision…

"I can't get my leg over that." Patricia looked at the contraption in disbelief. "When I said I wanted an adventure I didn't mean on one of these things."

"Patricia eat some bread an' then stick your finger in the soil."

"You can Danish at me all you like. My short legs will not part far enough to accommodate that thing."

"I will help you, once you are on, it will be as if you've been doing this all your life."

"You may well have, but the only thing I've straddled is a man's…"

"Enough already, here let me help."

"Unhand me madame."

Ann was having none of it and despite Patricia's protestations, she soon had her on the bike. She got on herself and having shuffled Patricia back a bit. Started up the engine with a rev.

"Oh," Patricia said experiencing some sort of epiphany. "Now you're talking."

"Hang on," Ann instructed and with a roar they leapt down the street with Patricia's scream of pleasure echoing off the houses.

Ann had been taught to ride a bike by her father and it had become her chosen form of transport. When she'd met her husband, they toured Europe on bikes. It was only when James had come along that they surrendered the freedom of two wheels for the safety of four. They were about to return to the world of biking when Andrew became ill and the reunion had never come about. It had felt strange getting back on a bike again without her husband to ride with. But now Ann was about making a new life not holding back, Andrew would be with her no matter where she went.

Ann took them down the A1 and off towards the dales. The bike gripped the road and hugged the corners as she'd hoped. It felt like she'd never been away from one. Skills not used for years quickly returned and by the time she steered them through the cathedral town she'd ironed out the bumps in her handling, if not those in the road. Patricia had run out of air and was now letting the wind and the countryside whiz past.

They made a detour to explore a popular attraction created by the wind, the rocks it had carved were a maze of huge and small monuments. They wandered between the boulders and great mounds of stone, both thinking what a marvellous place it would have been for a game of hide and seek. Places to climb and squeeze through, conquer and jump from. The bracken had just started to poke through in places, in full summer it would be waist-high and create a jungle that could be populated by elephants and tigers, offer lost worlds full of dinosaurs, present places to build a den and have a tea party in the sap green shade of the ferns. Ann and Patricia settled for an ice cream and the view, offered by one out-crop across the dales.

"You know I would have loved this pace as small child," Patricia said munching away with relish.

"We almost missed it the first time Andrew and I came this way. It was like discovering a hidden world, back then it didn't get so many visitors an' we continued to come for years. James loved it, as you said, it is a child's playground. We'd pack a picnic an' could easily spend the day here. In the summer the smell of the bracken an' the colour provided by the heather transforms it into a whole other world. You have to come here at least four times a year to get even the smallest glimpse of how much the seasons change it."

"I'm up for that, especially if the tea stall stays open all year."

They glided down the road as it descended into a small town and then left their stomachs behind as Ann applied the power and climbed the long steep bank out. The engine sound described the road and terrain. Turns, drops, banking, accelerating, slowing, gliding. They climbed to the top of the world and onto the bleak beauty of the dales. Small hamlets often hidden in mist and wide-open spaces with no sign of civilisation as far as the eye could see.

They crested a hill and there in the distance a small squat building nestled on the moor side. Ann slowed and they pulled in.

Patricia climbed off with assistance and took off her helmet. She looked about them. "The peace," she said, taking a deep breath.

"It is a special place." Ann agreed. "I always enjoyed that first moment here. The journey, the noise the exhilaration an' then helmet off an' this place fills you with such calm. We should go in before it gets busy. They do the best beans on toast here an' then we can go down into the caves."

Patricia crammed another chunk of scone in her mouth. "I had no idea beans on toast could be so sublime. And this scone, heaven."

"Cherry an' almond. I would have this meal every time we came here. I was worried they might have stopped."

"But you weren't disappointed, my darling. And neither am I. I felt so alive on the bike, once the sheer terror had subsided. Now I can definitely see the attraction. If I could have stretched out my arms it would have felt like flying."

After the caverns they walked a nearby reservoir, a farmhouse that had been abandoned was in the process of being renovated, brought back to life. Ann had always imagined living in it. It was good to see it getting a second chance. From there they followed the main road through the dales and stopped at a small market town, popular with visitors. She drove carefully through the busy square and stopped in the hotel car park.

"Our overnight stop," Ann said, retrieving their small bags from the bike's panniers.

"It looks very nice. I hope they do a good breakfast. I adore a fry up when I've not had to make it myself."

Dinner was steak and ale pie with chips and a nod at vegetables by way of some peas. Pudding was an apple crumble. Ann had suggested it and Patricia had agreed to such a mundane sweet at Ann's insistence. When it came her eyes lit up at the accompaniment.

"Ice cream and custard, sheer heaven."

Food eaten, they took a stroll around the village, now empty of tourists. The pubs were busy so the place didn't feel dead. Ann took them up to the town head and then they turned left.

"Chapel Street. A good solid name, a proper dales name I'd say." Patricia read the sign as they walked past.

"There's an even better one a few minutes' walk away. Moody Sty Lane. We used to stay at a cottage there. This way leads up on the moors above the village, we won't need to go far to get a view."

They followed the street and then as it became a lane, headed past the last of the village buildings and over a stile between stone walls. There was a distinct smell of sheep in the air, not unpleasant, but very country. After a short climb Ann brought them to a halt at a view down over the village and across the dale to the hills some way in the distance. The moon and stars were out in an ink blue sky. An owl called from the nearby grass-wood.

Patricia took another deep breath, storing the sensation away as a reminder. "There are so many stars, the city lights hide them and then you come out here and it's like glitter spilled across the sky. It's so peaceful, I think I could live somewhere like this."

"When I left my village, I considered coming here. I have such fond memories of this place an' thought the peace would be good for me. I stayed a week in the hotel, but came to realise that I needed a busier location, somewhere with more distractions. I wasn't ready to be alone with my thoughts."

"I understand, completely," Patricia said. "Tranquillity is only calming when you're at peace with yourself. Maybe not the place to settle, but certainly a place to visit more often."

"I think so, it's taken me a while to build up the courage to come here again. Its full of memories of Andrew and I wanted to be in a position to enjoy them an' not mourn them."

"Very wise, my darling. And are you enjoying them?"

"Most certainly." Ann looked back to the view. She'd stood here with Andrew many a time and now she could share it with a good friend.

"Do you miss him very much?" Patricia asked.

"I think about him every day, sometimes more than others. I do miss him, but I'm not sad about it anymore. I've learnt to accept it and move on. As shallow as it sounds, the affair helped an' looking back so did all of the trouble it caused. I know that sounds terrible."

"Not a bit," Patricia said. "There is nothing like trouble, or work to refocus the mind, distract an aching heart."

"Are you talking from experience?" Ann asked.

"Different to yours. We weren't married. I was living in Austria. I had a small guest house in a place called Zell am See. Beautiful, we must go. Excellent coffee and cake. He came to stay for a holiday and ended up staying for a lot longer. He was beautiful, but then so was I. We were both beautiful together. I remember his skin was like velvet and porcelain all in one. He played the guitar. We boated on the lake, climbed the mountains drank coffee and looked at the stars. The blue sky, the blue lake and his blue eyes. I couldn't have asked for more. Each day was bliss, the guest house was doing well, he mucked in and helped out, we were quite the team. We had five years and then one morning he didn't come back with the boat and the shopping."

"He left," Ann asked in disbelief.

"No, he drowned. He couldn't swim. I have no idea how it happened. They pulled him out of the lake. He was cold, blue like china. The life and the light had left him. And the light died in me for a time. But like you, each day I moved on, bit by little bit. Now, when I think of him, I see blue skies again."

"Oh, Patricia, I'm so sorry."

"My darling, there is nothing to be sorry about. I had five years. I could have had nothing."

They were quiet for some time. Until Patricia took another deep breath, this time marking a decision finally made. "I'm going to sell the café."

"You've been thinking about it for some time."

"Yes, and this is a reminder that I've still got a life to live. The café has served its purpose and now it's time to hand it on. Time for someone else to give it a new lease of life, and perhaps for me to stop hiding from the rest of mine."

"What will you do?"

"Well, I've never lived a conventional life and I'm jolly well not going to start now. The cafe is the closet to normal my life's ever been. It may take some time to sell of course. It's not exactly a thriving business. But I won't abandon it. When it does go, I want to spend some time in my flat. In the year since I bought it, I've hardly spent any time there. After that, I want to travel again, revisit places from my debauched youth."

"Revisit, not relive," Ann cautioned.

"Oh, my darling, there would be no chance of that. I've not the energy or the need, for that matter. My life has been very full, I intended to have no regrets when I finally gave it all up. And I don't. I tried all things and everything, it was an education."

"Have you ever thought about writing it all down?"

"Gosh, I wouldn't know where to start."

"Then perhaps that's what your travels could be, a revisit an' a chance to retrace yours footsteps, to write about your memories. There must also be new experiences an' new places."

"Well, I'm not sure about the writing part, but certainly new experiences and new places. Will you come with me? I'm not sure I want to do all of it on my own."

"I would like that very much. There are some places I would like to revisit; it would be a pleasure to show them to you."

"And I should like that very much. You know a young man with the blackest of hair and the darkest of eyes once travelled all the way from London to take me to Paris. I had finished university and was visiting friends and he and I became friendly. But I had to return before anything could become of it. A week later he turned up at mummy and daddy's under the guise of visiting relations. He was booked into a hotel, but mummy insisted he stayed with us. Of course, we began a secret and passionate affair. It was all very clandestine and wonderful. I ran away with him to Paris and we spent a year there. He took me to all of the places he knew. Introduced me to the sights and sounds of Paris and its people. It was the start of my second education."

"What did your parents do?"

"Daddy approved of it whole heartedly, and I suspect mummy's invitation was not the innocent offer of hospitality it might first have appeared to be. If my life would make a book, theirs would be a compendium of several. In fact, I think my family would make quite an excellent mini-series."

Ann walked Patricia's little legs off the next day. She took them along a section of the Dales Way to a point where, at some time in the very distant past, a stream had carved a ravine down through the dale's stone. It started as a gap to be squeezed through, but quickly opened up to what would have been a series of waterfalls and boiling chasms sometime after the ice age and the great melt that had shaped the area. They came back via a hamlet and then an impressive climb back onto the dales. The thought of an ice cream carried them down through the grass-woods and back to their start point. Patricia bought ice creams from what she announced was a very handsome young man. The young man in question went very red, but took the attention in good humour.

Only the promise of a large, a very large gin and tonic got her dressed and down into the dining room. Of course, once the menu arrived all thoughts of aching feet were replaced with the promise of liver, bacon and onions. They were further soothed by the medicinal properties of a large and extremely velvety chocolate tart.

The following morning, another breakfast, made tasty by an array of local produce, made the bikes powerful engine a necessity, rather than an indulgence. Ann flew them to their next stop, another larger market town with a castle they spent some time looking round. Though her main objective had been to find a local bakers she and Andrew had always visited. As far as Ann was concerned it made the best pasties and curd tart to be had anywhere.

Patricia agreed entirely about the pasties and differed only in that she settled on a slice of Bakewell tart, which she duly inhaled. They browsed the shops and walked a part of the canal. All too quickly it was time to head back.

"Promise me my darling, we will do more of this."

"Absolutely."

"An one more thing, can we go over the cobbles again?"

Chapter 15

Three go Dating...

"And this is a good idea because?" Jack left the question hanging.

"Well," Becca began, she thought it was an idea, she wouldn't have gone so far as to say it was a good idea. One that hadn't gone away since she'd first mentioned it to Ben ages ago. "You've not found Ms Right and neither of us have found a Mr Right. They're not going to walk down the street and find us."

"Babes, you know what I think, the more you look the less you find."

"You've said that several times now," Becca complained. "I've had no expectations for years and where's that got me? We need to be proactive. Seek and ye shall find."

"Yep, that's exactly what they say about trouble," Jack added.

"Come on you two, show a bit of enthusiasm here."

They both waggled a finger in the air and made a pathetic cheering sound.

"I'm doing this alone then," she looked at them both, hands on hips.

Ben looked at Jack, a resigned look on his face.

Jack shrugged. "Okay," he muttered. "We'll give it a try."

Becca cheered. "There, that wasn't so bad. It'll be great you just wait and see."

Mr Right?

Becca had seen his picture, he'd seen hers, they'd exchanged messages and she was sure he wasn't an axe murderer. They were going to meet for the first time and she'd followed all of the advice, tell a friend and meet in a public place. They'd decided on a restaurant in town. She'd had her hair done, but declined a fake tan special offer, for fear it would fall on the wrong side of sun kissed. She'd seen too many orange women in town and several with tide marks. Most of the girls at the salon were tan fans. They looked fine; the only problem was their hands. Most of them spent a good amount of the day with their hands in water and so had patchy white skin to the wrist. It wasn't a good look. She'd got used to the card machine being covered in fake tan and the cream phone that was now brown.

She had waxed, though his chances of seeing the fruits of that labour were beyond slim. Of course, she'd showered, done her own nails, been made up by Ben. It was more than she would normally bother with, but it did look great. The wind wasn't blowing a gale outside, so she stood a good chance of arriving with her hair intact. There had been several wardrobe trials. Underwear was chosen, she'd not gone down the lines of practical and total comfort, but nor had she gone for sexy. It was a compromise, not that she was expecting anything like that, but best to be prepared and frankly she felt a bit sexy in them. The bra in particular was a favourite, it did this lift and push forward thing and made her boobs look great and at this stage in the game, any confidence boost was a good one. At one point, she was convinced she had nothing to wear, but wouldn't go and buy a new dress, maybe if there was a third date, he'd be worth the expenditure. Now she'd managed to narrow down her choice to two. She checked both thoroughly and then positioned her phone to take shots of her back. All angles examined in detail; she finally decided on one.

Now she was ready, she checked her bag, everything there. She checked herself in the mirror again. Ran through her greeting and the list of talking points she'd fall back on if it got awkward. She looked at her watch, it was going to be a long ten minutes until the taxi. Being busy had kept her mind off the actual prospect of the date. Now the minutes dragged, her imagination had started to kick in and her stomach was gurgling. Gurgling loudly. Oh god, what if he thought she was breaking wind? What if she needed to? Her stomach was hinting at the possibility. It would happen in the middle of a conversation; she'd laugh at something and it would happen. How did you get out of that on a first date? What if he didn't like her? What if she didn't like him? Would the time fly by or drag? Would they run out of things to say? Why had she thought this was a good idea? Stop. She took a deep breath. She was an adult, she was in control, she needed the loo.

If it wasn't going well, they would stop after the main course, shake hands and thank each other for a pleasant evening. This is how adults behaved and she was an adult, an adult with a stomach that wanted to be heard.

Ms Right?

Jack had seen her picture, she'd seen his, they'd exchanged messages and he was sure she wasn't a bunny boiler. They were going to meet for lunch. He got his hair cut, showered, checked his nails, made sure there was no ear or nose hair and made sure everywhere else was in good order. Underwear was chosen, he'd gone for his date pants. They did the lift and push forward thing and if he was being honest, he felt good in them and they gave him a confidence boost, everybody needed that on a first date, didn't they? Not that he was expecting anything like that, but best to be prepared. He picked a good shirt, it fitted really well and smart jeans and a jacket. Was this too casual? Should he wear trousers? He swapped jeans a couple of times and angled himself between two mirrors to check everything was okay. He held a hand in front of his mouth and breathed out and then quickly inhaled. Still smelt of toothpaste. He went and brushed his teeth again just to be certain. Right, hair, clothes, shoes sorted. Cards, in case one decided not to work. Not giving embarrassment a way in through that door. Cash, phone on silent. Should he offer to pay? That was the mine field, some dates had expected it, some were insulted by it. He'd have to suss that one out. Okay, he said to himself, that's me ready. Now just the taxi to wait for. He looked at his watched, ready too early, the next fifteen minutes were going to drag.

Mr Right?

Ben had seen the other guy's picture, he'd seen his, they'd exchanged messages and he was sure he wasn't a gay basher. It happened, straight men luring gays on dates and then beating them up. They were going out for coffee and then maybe lunch. Coffee offered a good exit plan; it didn't last as long as a meal and he could keep the conversation going on his own if need be. He got his hair cut, showered, considered a bit of foundation and then thought no, that might put the other guy off. You never knew how comfortable another gay man was with that sort of thing. These were the times when Ben was glad he didn't shave his eyebrows and sideburns, like other queens. Some of them went on dates looking like surprised aliens. He'd manscaped, he did it as a matter of course, but had taken extra care. Not that he was expecting anything to happen, but if there was a chance, he wasn't going to be caught out with an unruly jungle for the other guy to keep spitting out. He had his best underwear on, it was expensive and he'd not had chance to wear it, he knew his bum looked great in it and it did that lift a push forward thing, not that he needed it, he told himself, but confidence was everything. Tina was good at it, he less so. He knew exactly what he would wear. Smart jeans, shirt and a jacket, several days of trying outfits had got rid of any chance of stress on that front. He filmed himself on the camera and checked every angle. This was as good as it got, piece of cake. Now all he had to do was wait for the taxi. The next hour was going to drag.

***

"So how did it go?" Becca asked them both.

"Fabulous," Ben gestured expressively. "We met for coffee. The minute he walked in I thought wow, he was one of those guys that make the clothes look good not the other way round. And the body underneath it, all the right bumps in all the right places. Of course, I thought I'm out of my league here, but he couldn't keep his hands off me. Eye contact, smiles, the lot. He wasn't arrogant, he was charming, interested, asked all of the right questions and laughed at my jokes. We hit it off straight away. Coffee turned into lunch and we laughed and joked. He even offered to pay, but we split the bill. He gave me a good-bye kiss and my knees felt like they were going to buckle. We swapped numbers and he called me before I had time to get home. He said what a wonderful afternoon it had been and when could he see me again. And then when I got home, I found out I'd won the lottery and that my new face cream had actually worked and I looked ten years younger."

Jack and Becca had by now caught up.

"You're joking then," Becca said, crest fallen.

"Did he even show up?"

"No, no show, no call, nothing. I had coffee and several sugar and fat pills to make up for it and went shopping."

"Have you heard nothing from him?" Jack asked.

Ben shook his head.

Becca squeezed his hand.

Ben looked at Jack. "And what about you?"

"In short, she liked talking about herself, expected me to pay, didn't say thank you when I did and assumed she was on a dead cert to get into my pants. If she'd said thank you," he shrugged. "She'd probably have been right. But I called her a cab and she made her excuses and left."

"My god," Becca groaned.

"However," he said with a grin. "The woman who served us, took pity on me and brought me pudding. We got to talking and swapped numbers. She's called Sarah and seems really nice."

"There you go," Ben gestured expansively. "It's as I always say, the minute you stop looking, pow, they find you. So, babes, how did yours go? Spill the beans?"

Becca looked at the biscuits Jack had carefully arranged on the plate. "Spill the beans, I'd rather eat those." She started before Ben could object. "He was there waiting for me, nicely dressed, looked like the photo. His first words were,"

You look great, that's a really nice dress.

"He got up and pulled out the seat for me, which threw me a bit, I wasn't expecting it."

I've got to admit I was a bit nervous. I hoped you won't be disappointed.

"I was flattered that my opinion mattered and that he was bothered enough to be nervous. I complimented him and said I wasn't at all disappointed."

Let's hope it continues that way.

"He asked me how my day had been as we ordered drinks, and when I felt I'd said enough I asked him about his."

I work for a big car manufacturer. I deal with international sales.

"He made it sound interesting, it involved travel and it sounded like he had a well-paid job, though he didn't make a thing of it. We ordered a starter, it felt comfortable enough not to go straight to a main course and he seemed happy about that too. We got onto talking about the city and some of the changes that have happened lately. He finished his drink and ordered another, it seemed a bit quick and I put it down to nerves. Then we started talking about travel and that kept us going until the starters arrived. The conversation continued and flowed. Mains came and we were getting on really well. I'd relaxed and was starting to throw in a few bits of, this is me information, like it or leave now. None of it phased him in the least and he joked about some of his quirks. Nothing cringe worthy."

"Babes, why do I think there's a but coming?"

"Hang on, who's story is this? We had a few laughs and, to be honest he was quite witty. He laughed at my jokes and I began to feel this had legs, might even manage a second date. We ordered pudding and as it turned out the same thing. That got us talking about favourites and that led us onto music. He said he was a huge Elvis fan. Full album collection, been to Graceland and all of that. I said I read his estate was being well managed and that it was now probably worth more than when he was alive. That clearly was the wrong thing to say,"

I disagree

"He said. Not in the, let me tell you about some information you might not know, kind of way, but in the, how dare you, sort of way." Becca nodded at them both. "Yes, my mouth gaped open too. I just sat there in disbelief as he headed into this rant about, well, all sorts of Elvis related things. If I was polite, I'd have said he was very passionate about it all. But, I'm not and it was just a rant. It killed the conversation, the evening, my appetite. My 'don't make a scene gene' kicked in and I ate my dessert, what a waste, I didn't enjoy a single mouthful. All the time I was just thinking of my escape phrase. Anyway, my embarrassment slowly converted itself into irritation. I wanted to be gone before it distilled down any further into something a bit more flammable. I managed to keep my mouth shut and eat my pudding at the same time. Quite a feat I think looking back. The silence dragged on and maybe it was now obvious that I wasn't happy. By then I must have had a face like thunder. Part of me expected him to say,"

I'm really sorry, I'm over sensitive about that and I shouldn't have taken it out on you.

"Instead, after he'd calmed himself, he said,"

'Is that it, conversation over, you've gone very quiet on me.'

"Are you surprised after that display, talk about over the top," I said.

'You clearly don't understand how important Elvis is to me.'

"Important is one thing," I said, "but that, that was totally uncalled for."

'You know what your problem is, don't you?'

Ben leaned in, "Don't stop there, what did he say?"

"That's the point when I stood up and said. Don't presume to know the first thing about me. I usually meet problems head on, but you are one I'm more than happy to walk away from. I was quite proud of that, usually I think of what I should have said sometime after, when it's too late. I did consider pausing to pay on my way out, but no one was at the till and I thought, stuff it, dinner's on him."

"Babes it would have been, literally, if I'd been there."

"Why didn't you wake one of us when you got in," Jack asked.

"I was just glad to be back home. I got changed and watched a film. The more I thought about it the more I couldn't believe it had really happened. It sounded too absurd to be true. I kept picturing his face, the pained look, the outrage. It struck me as funny and I ended up laughing about it." She picked up a biscuit and bit into it. "Hmm, these are really good. Are we watching a film and can we order pizza? I'm famished."

Jack's unexpected date turned out to be called Sarah, he began taking about her, a good sign. Becca hoped that the relationship had wheels and that it might actually go somewhere. Ben reminded her that Jack had found success by not looking, reaffirming his thoughts that if you stopped, the right person would find you. He used that excuse to take himself out of the dating game, saying in his usual dry and dramatic way, that he preferred meaningless sex with relative strangers. And soon after, he found a source of very good meaningless sex. Really, really, vastly and outstandingly good meaningless sex. It added weight to his theory and Becca began to wonder if she should follow suit. In the end she did what she normally did and that was to not give up. Even when common sense told her it was time.

Date number two wasn't with the man in the photograph, or rather was with the man who was fifteen years older than the photograph. She knew it was him as she walked towards their meeting place, he had seen her before she could turn around. His opening line had been,

A bit of a surprise, I know, but we were getting on so well I thought if we met it wouldn't matter.

Becca had said, "If I was just looking for a friend it might not have mattered, we do have a lot in common, but I'm not looking for a friend and not so sure about a friend who lied about themselves."

He'd come across as a nice man, in their emails. If he'd been someone at work, they would have been friends and who knows, it might have moved on from there. But that wasn't the case and he wasn't being truthful.

Date three was a sniffer. He looked like his photo, they got on, the conversation was fine, but every ten to fifteen seconds he sniffed, and yes, she had started to time this. At first it hadn't registered, but gradually, bit by bit, no matter how hard she tried to ignore it, it began to irritate her. She focused on their conversation, she tried to blot it out, but it just kept happening. Sniff, sniff, sniff. She considered handing him a hanky and saying,

"Do you have a cold?"

Or

"Thought you might need this."

Or

"I notice you're sniffing a lot, are you okay?"

Or

"Sorry, would you mind blowing your nose."

Or

"Please blow your nose."

Or

"For crying out loud will you please blow your bloody nose and stop sniffing."

Of course, even though she rehearsed it in her mind and tried to find the politest words, she didn't say anything. She'd become far too uptight about it. It just grated on her to the point of distraction.

Date four, took her to a very good restaurant, wouldn't let her pay, was handsome, had hair like Jack's, in that the wind kept ruffling it and it kept falling exactly back into place. Her hair, if it hadn't been set to within an inch of its life, would now look like it had been attacked by an egg whisk. He also dressed well, had a very good job, was successful, could hold a conversation and was charm personified. He also had an amazing body, as she later found out. The only problem was he knew it. She met him seven more times after their first date; the food and the sex were really, really, vastly and outstandingly good.

Chapter 16

Unexpected visitor…

Becca put her shopping through her door and followed Ann up the stairs.

"Make yourself comfortable while I put the kettle on," Ann took off her coat and put her own bags away. "That was a success."

"I got everything I'd intended. Normally it works that if I have the money to burn, I don't see anything."

"I hadn't realised that dress was on sale," Ann referred to a summer frock Becca had noticed the minute they'd walked into one shop.

"It was perfect, fitted great and then when I got to the till and she said, oh this is twenty percent off, I felt like I'd won the lottery." Becca settled into a chair; it had been a really nice evening. Ann had met her from work and they'd gone shopping and had a meal. It was a good way to start the weekend.

"What will you do tomorrow?" Ann asked from the kitchen.

"I feel like a lazy day. This week has been busy and I fancy a pyjama morning. I've food in, so I don't need to go out for anything. But I thought I'd go to Patricia's on Sunday. I've missed a couple of weekends. Has she had any offers yet?"

"Nothing she'd seriously consider, I think. But it's early days still an' she's in no rush. She said it could take some time."

"What about you? Have you plans for the weekend?"

"My son's coming for a visit."

"That'll be nice. You didn't say. Will we get the chance to meet James?"

"It was last minute. I only got the text while we were out; he's just going to stay overnight an' then head off the next morning."

"Well, if you have time, I'd love to meet him."

"That's why I asked if you had plans. I thought I'd take him to Patricia's on Sunday for breakfast before he goes. They've chatted on the phone an' he'd like to meet her. Of course, I've told him all about you, Ben an' Jack."

"Had you a time in mind?"

"As soon as she opens."

"Great, I'll either meet you there, or if you knock on your way passed, I'll come with you."

"Good, I'll try an' catch the boys and see if they're around too. It'll be a nice morning."

***

James arrived, all blonde haired and blue eyes, very much like his mother, slim, smart and easy company. Patricia chatted with him as if they'd known each other for years. He and Jack hit it off and Becca liked him from the start. Only Ben seemed uncertain. He was uncharacteristically quiet at the café and when Ann invited them all around for dinner on Monday night, Becca thought he would make his excuses. It seemed that James had decided to stay a little longer and didn't need to rush off quite so quickly. Becca had never seen Ben so uncomfortable and began to worry that he'd had some news, and was keeping it under his hat. Her imagination began its usual trick of trying out various reasons as to what might be wrong. Someone was ill, or had died, the club was in trouble, he'd found out he was ill. She was starting to worry and thought it best, for both their sakes, she found out just what was up. It was a while before Becca got him alone in the kitchen. He was pretending to be busy with dishes and she came back from the bathroom, via the kitchen, to figure out a way of getting him in there too.

"Oh, you're already here. Are you alright?" She kept her voice low and glanced back at the door.

"I'm good."

"Don't believe you. You're too quiet. Talk to me Ben."

Ben put the last plate in the dishwasher and slumped back against the work top. "You're going to think I'm stupid."

"Never."

"It's James," he admitted.

Becca tried not to look at him like he was stupid. "James? Has he said something?"

"He doesn't need to, he just is."

Becca knew she was missing out on something. "You're going to have to fill in some gaps in that sentence. He just is?"

Ben seemed to be in pain, or at least his expression suggested he was, or was about to say something he didn't want to.

"He's lovely."

Becca's couldn't hide her surprise. She knew when Ben was allowing himself to be vulnerable and Benjamin was definitely speaking now, vulnerable and even shy. But she hadn't expected the depth of feeling in those two words.

"See, I knew you'd think I was stupid."

Becca stepped forward and gave him a hug. "Oh, you silly thing. You're not stupid."

"He's just so nice and pleasant and well, lovely."

Becca stepped back to look at him. "You really are smitten, aren't you?"

"Fool that I am."

"He is gay you know."

"I didn't know. He's way out of my league."

"What. Of course, he's not."

"I know he's nowhere near Jack good looking, but I think he's…"

"Lovely," Becca finished for him.

"There's just something about him. Something inside just seems to shine out of him. I'm trying not to look because I could just sit there and stare all night long. I've hardly spoken to him, I can feel myself going red just at the thought. I'd be all tongue tied and he'd think I was stupid."

"Just be yourself."

"Oh, no. I'd say something crass and common and he'd think, what an idiot. Anyway, he'll be gone tomorrow. So, it doesn't matter."

At that point, as if on cue, James walked in. Clearly only expecting one of them to be in the kitchen. "Hi, Becca, I didn't know you were in here."

Good recovery, she thought. "I'm not," she said and quickly left.

If the floor could have opened and swallowed him, Ben would have jumped in readily.

James came over to lean on the countertop next to him. "We've not had time to talk."

"Err, no," Ben managed.

"Are you okay? Mum said you're usually chatty and wondered if something was wrong."

"Headache." The old excuse was all that came to mind. I stand on a stage and think on my feet, he thought and here I am using the headache excuse. "I carry all my stress in my shoulders." He heard himself saying.

"I've got a great cure for that. Here."

Ben found himself being manoeuvred so that James was stood behind him and then his shoulders were being rubbed and his legs literally wanted to sit him on the floor. He could feel his pulse rate shoot up and render his mouth incapable of anything close to coherent speech.

James was chatting and it was some time before Ben remembered he had ears as well as shoulders.

"Mum's busy tomorrow and said you're usually free mornings and afternoons. I was hoping you might show me around."

Ben managed some sort of croaking noise from a throat that had gone dry.

"If you're busy, it's not a problem. I'm dumping myself on you."

He sounded disappointed, but Ben was so caught up in feeling self-conscious he couldn't think what to say. The massage stopped, now James was probably feeling self-conscious, he had this idiot stood in front of him who couldn't even answer a simple question. The more Ben delayed the worse he felt and the more his mouth wouldn't do what he wanted it to.

"Sorry," James mistook Ben's silence. "I can be a bit pushy."

Ben wanted to look him in the face and say you're nothing of the kind, you're the most beautiful man I've ever met, I think your funny and adorable and lovely and I'd sell my best wigs to spend tomorrow with you. Instead he mumbled something unintelligible before leaving.

***

She took the route from the station and passed the small supermarket and then down the avenue and on to the terrace, the shops hadn't opened yet and people were on their way to work. Passed the church with the grey tower, along the side of the green and then onto the road. Large Edwardian houses, many with walled gardens, and Victorian villas as well, expensive. She paused to check the address in the text and looked up into the eyes of a stranger.

"Victoria?" he asked.

"Yes," she assumed this was the man her sister had said would greet her and let her in. He seemed off hand, certainly not welcoming. But then what could she expect, if he was Rebecca's friend, she no doubt would have said things. She should have come later, to avoid strangers, come straight to the flat, had the papers signed, stayed the night and been away as early as possible.

"Ben," he introduced himself. "Do you need help with the bag?"

"I can manage. It isn't heavy, I have no wish to stay longer than necessary."

Too bloody right, Ben thought and smiled, in the way that Tina did when she was forced to be polite, there was a lot of teeth, a bit like a crocodile. He opened the main door and showed her across the entrance hall to Becca's front door. Opening it, he stepped aside to allow her entry.

"You'll have things to do," Victoria walked in. "Don't let me keep you," she said stiffly.

He didn't answer, his brain was applying the brakes, it didn't trust his mouth. He closed the door. Why had she come this early in the afternoon? Cheaper train maybe.

Hearing the door click shut was a relief, she let out a long sigh, she hoped her stomach would settle. This was difficult enough, without having to deal with others. If there had been any way this could be done by post she would have, but she wouldn't trust the service with the documents and so, had no choice, but to make the journey in person. She put down her bag and hung her coat, noticing one of Becca's. She looked at the label and guessed the price tag. Looking at the hallway she appraised the décor, just as she'd thought. She smoothed the front of her skirt and stepped further into the flat.

Victoria noted the photographs on the wall, none were family, all strangers. Two women, another man and the one who had met her. Her eyes settled on a group portrait of some drag queens. "Oh, for goodness sake," she muttered and moved on. She looked into the living room with its attached dining area. Not her taste, too many things to collect dust. She ran a finger absently on a shelf as she examined the objects there. No dust, she probably had a cleaner, Becca was always lazy that way. Victoria stopped in the middle of the room, and looked about her, she sighed again, her stomach had settled somewhat. Just let me get this over with, she picked at a piece of fluff on her sleeve and walked to the kitchen.

***

There was a knock at the door, he didn't recognise it. Surely it wouldn't be that Victoria woman. He braced himself, keep your mouth out of gear, let your brain have it's say. He opened the door.

"James," his voice squeaked and he cleared his throat. Can I help you? was the only thing that came to mind and he wasn't about to say that. He'd made enough of a fool of himself last night. The silence hung between them.

James laughed, possibly at himself, or the situation, or both. "I think the local cats heard that one."

"It was a bit high," he lowered his voice, and his eyebrows and cringed, bloody hell, now I sound like Barry White.

James looked like he was building himself up to something and before Ben decided that inviting him in would actually be a nice thing to do, James started speaking.

"I'm not usually this tongue tied," he said. "But I've altered plans for you and I'm not about to waste the time. So here goes," he took a breath. "I may be about to stick my neck out here, mum would say something like, stick a finger in the soil." He stopped and mentally reset. "Right, what I'm trying to say here is, I really like you Ben. I know we've hardly talked, barely said a word, but there's just something about you. Don't know if it's those brown eyes of yours, or the smile, but the minute I saw you I thought, wow."

"Wow," Ben repeated.

James took a step closer. "Is that a good wow, or a bad wow?"

***

Oh god, she thought to herself as she turned down her road. I usually enjoy this bit, the final leg and then home. She'll be there waiting. I wonder if she's been in every room, assessing the cleaning, the furnishings? Why on earth did I say she could stay? She was going to use a hotel. What made me say you can stay with me? She was walking very fast. So much so, that her shins were beginning to ache. She deliberately slowed her pace. It's only a night, Becca reminded herself. She'll go to bed early and I'll be off to work before she gets up, or maybe she'll just go. She tried to distract herself and thought about Ben. Had James gone down to see him? He'd caught her before she'd left Ann's last night, asking advice, wondering if he was chasing after a lost cause. When she'd told him how much Ben liked him, he'd smiled and the dwindling flicker in him had sparked into life again. She'd felt the warmth from it and become excited for them both. Hopefully Ben hadn't messed it up. James seemed like a good match for him. He brought out the Benjamin in Ben. For a few moments she basked in the warm glow of a possible match and then caught sight of her front window and was reminded of who was waiting there, more smouldering than glowing. She almost paused at the foot of the steps to bolster herself. But instead marched up them, key ready, her sister could be watching and she wasn't about to show any signs of discomfort.

Opening her own door, felt different, normally it was very still in the hallway beyond, but kidding herself or not, she was sure she could sense someone else was in the flat, that her sister was there waiting impatiently for her. She closed the door. Round one, she thought to herself and took off her coat. If she'd had sleeves to roll up she would have.

"Victoria," she called, there was no wobble in her voice, she was at least glad of that.

"In here."

And where is that supposed to be? The kitchen, the living room, the toilet? But then it wouldn't be that, her sister didn't do things like that. She didn't burp, break wind, smile and a host of other functions. One of Jack's sci-fi robots would be more human.

"I'm in your living room."

Right, thought Becca I'll go in the kitchen. "I'm going to make some tea, have you had one, or should I make you one?"

"I've had nothing since I arrived."

She managed to make it sound like an accusation. "Why didn't you help yourself, I said you could."

There was no answer.

Becca could feel her irritation rising already. "Do you want a cup of tea?"

"If you're making one, don't go to any trouble on my part."

Becca filled the kettle and switched it on. She put tea in the pot and got mugs out. She was about to get milk when there was a knock at the door.

She answered it to find Ann stood there.

"I am just going out an' thought I would check you had everything you needed," her voice was lowered.

"I'm fine thanks. I shopped for tea on my way back from work. Do you want to come in and meet her?"

"No, it is fine. I won't intrude. I should be going any way, or I'll be late. Catch you later." Ann gave her hand a quick squeeze and headed for the entrance hall door.

Becca watched her go out and then returned to the kettle.

"There you go, milk no sugar, unless you've changed the way you have it."

"I'm surprised you remember."

Becca was going to respond, but Victoria continued.

"Who was that at the door?"

"One of my neighbours, Ann." Becca explained. "She was just checking if we needed anything."

"More like being nosey, why didn't she come in?"

Everything sounded like a challenge, a question to find a fault and when there wasn't one, like their mother, Victoria would invent one. "She was in a hurry," Becca said simply.

"Too much of a hurry to say hello, hardly friendly."

Becca resisted the urge to defend Ann.

"I see you have a photograph of dad on the mantle."

Here we go, Becca thought. She's probably had a good look round; found somethings she doesn't like and spent the afternoon winding herself up over it. What else would there be? "It's a good one, don't you think?" Keep it light, Becca told herself. It's hours until bedtime.

"He never took a good photograph. I suppose it's as good as any. You don't have one of our mam?"

"No, why would I?"

Victoria didn't reply. Perhaps she read the tone in Becca's voice, or was it that she'd returned the question with one of her own. Victoria didn't touch the tea. But got up and went to some of the other photographs on the wall. "But you have one of Aunty Irene. One of her, but not one of your own mam?"

"I like Aunty Irene," Becca left it at that, it said enough.

"Who are these people?"

"Friends."

"And do they have names?" Victoria snapped, clearly irritated by Becca's continued tone.

"They do, but you're not really interested are you Victoria? Are you trying to make a point or just going off on one like mother used to?"

"I'm trying to make conversation."

"Then you need to practise, this is more like an interrogation." Becca wasn't going to let Victoria get away with her usual behaviour. She'd allowed her mother to behave in this way and she wasn't going to let the same thing happen again. She was about to say as much, but there was another knock.

"How's it going?" Jack kept his voice down.

"We haven't killed each other yet, but the night's young."

"Maybe an early night might be a good idea," he suggested.

"I'd go now, if I wasn't hungry. Are you off out," Becca asked, wishing she was going with him.

"Meeting Sarah. If you need to ring, my phone's staying on, just in case."

Becca smiled. "Thanks. Go on, get yourself gone, don't keep her waiting."

Jack gave her a quick hug. "Take care. Don't forget," he made a phone gesture as he headed for the entrance hall door.

She returned to the glaring eyes of Victoria. "Another of your friends I've no doubt."

"Yes, Jack is off out to meet up with Sarah, his girlfriend, he just called in to see if you were settled."

"A likely story. I suppose he didn't want to come in and meet me. Or are you keeping them away from me, just in case I say something that reveals the real Rebecca to them?"

"What on earth is that supposed to mean?" Becca came to stand right in front of her.

"This new belligerent you. You've changed since you've come here," the accusation was delivered without pretence.

"I have changed, and for the better. I don't have anyone trying to keep me under their thumb."

Again, Victoria chose not to answer, maybe there was no answer.

"You haven't touched your tea," Becca pointed to the mug.

"It was too hot," Victoria got her phone out of her bag and pretended to be interested in it.

Becca sat down and drank her own tea. They sat in cold silence.

The minutes couldn't have crawled any slower, their little iron boots dragging time behind them. Becca, sat in her own flat, feeling like she couldn't move, couldn't put the tv on, couldn't relax, couldn't do anything other than sit and stare out of the window. When it got to quarter to seven, she got up. It was close enough to dinner time to make a start. It was an excuse to go into another room. "I'm going to make a start on tea. I thought I'd do pasta?"

"If you like."

"It was phrased as a question, is that alright for you?"

"I'm not hungry. I'll have some later if I feel like it. But before you do. I have the papers here for you to sign." Victoria rummaged in her bag and brought out a small folder. "We're both named as executors of the will, but I can apply for the grant of probate on my own. That means I won't have to waste time coming backwards and forwards with things for you to sign."

"I still don't understand why you had to bring them. They could have been posted, I would have signed and returned them to you."

"They might have gone missing in the post. The solicitor charged enough for these and will do so again if they get lost. I wasn't about to waste the money. I'm doing all of the work for this. Contacting the charities she's wasting money on, paying the bills, the funeral costs, the extra house insurance. The solicitor's expenses all come out of the profits from the sale of the house, you know. They're not getting the lion's share if I can help it."

"I wouldn't have thought that would be an issue, the house will be worth a lot." Becca was careful not to make her own tone sound accusatory. She wasn't interested in the will, her mother's money or the inheritance she wasn't getting.

"I'm being careful with our money," Victoria emphasised the I'm. "It's bad enough having to pay a solicitor to print out a few forms, I'm not giving them more than I have to."

Victoria might have placed her emphasis on I'm, but Becca heard the 'our'. "Our money?"

"Yes, We're the main beneficiaries."

"Becca was confused. "She took me out of her will."

"No. She threatened to, but in the end she didn't."

"I don't understand?"

"No, I dare say you don't. She should have done it straight away, but she didn't and now the money will still be split between us," Victoria clearly wasn't happy about this.

"Why didn't she go through with it?"

"She'd made the appointment. But dad had their wills drawn up, he of course, wanted you in it. I'm assuming his wishes stuck in her head. She dithered, maybe even felt some sort of guilt over it. I told her not to be ridiculous. When she'd finally made up her mind to get on with it and have her will re-written, she had the stroke and that was it."

"Guilt?" Becca felt uncomfortable, she could cope with being disliked, but not this. "You mean the same type of guilt that made her cry at dad's funeral. Because that wasn't sorrow, that was her feeling sorry for herself, guilt over all the things she'd said and done to him. No one to drive her around, stop her from having to rely on the buses. No one to do all the jobs around the house. The list she used to present him with at a weekend after he'd been at work all week. Right in his hand as he entered the door..." She stopped herself, this is what she'd been afraid of at the funeral.

Victoria had stood up, folded her arms, a barrier against a flood of red-hot lava. "Stop it, stop it. We've had all this before. I don't want to hear it. Just sign the form." She stabbed a finger at it "You've got half of it all. Half for doing nothing."

Had her mother really considered changing her mind? Had dad's wishes still meant anything to her? Or was this another of Victoria's little games. She knew how to find the cracks in Becca's defences, to wind her up even as a child. She looked at Victoria, seeing something of the look of satisfaction from so many times in the past, the look now quickly hidden. And then Victoria's last sentence registered. Half for doing nothing. Was she expected to rise to that? She knew it was far from true, at least until she'd left. "I'll sign your forms and then I'm going to boil pasta."

Becca had just put down the pen when the door went again. Who now? How many more times? she thought, as she headed for the door.

"Patricia."

"I had quiche left over at the café. It will only go to waste. I thought you and your sister, Victoria, would like some." Patricia didn't hover in the doorway. She handed the quiche to Becca and walked in.

Becca hovered in the doorway, quiche in hand.

"My name is Patricia; I understand you are Victoria."

Becca wasn't sure if she should make a run for it with the quiche, or go in and hide in the kitchen.

"Babes, are you going somewhere with that quiche?"

Becca recovered herself quickly.

"Did I make you jump? Babes, it's only Michelle Obama."

"I've just let Patricia in. Are you off to the club?"

He looked down at himself. "What do you think. I was going to pop in and say hello to that sister of yours. But Patricia beat me to it, said you might need a bit of a breather. Is she behaving herself?"

"Which one?"

"Your sister?"

"No more than usual. Where's James?"

"He headed off an hour ago. He's got a meeting tomorrow and some other things to sort, then he's coming back for a couple of days."

"He works for himself, doesn't he?"

"Yes, that's why he was up here in the first place. It was only meant to be an overnight on his way passed. But he altered his plans because of me." Ben smiled.

"Love's young dream," Becca realised she was still stood holding the quiche.

"I wouldn't go as far as love."

"Not yet," Becca said with an expectant smile.

Ben looked at his watch. "Look, babes I've got to go. Ring if you need moral support."

"Keep your fingers crossed, break a leg," she gave him a wry smile as he left and then turned back to her own performance. Round two, she told herself.

She popped her head into the living room.

"Can I offer anyone anything."

"We're fine, my darling," Patricia smiled innocently. "We're getting on like a house on fire."

Victoria looked more like she'd been flash bombed, or had been caught red handed by a member of the Gestapo. Patricia cross examined her for the next hour.

Becca ate her dinner. She could hear Patricia from the kitchen, not well enough to catch every word, but enough to get some idea of how the conversation was going. By conversation, it was more Patricia talking and Victoria interjecting, interjections that became increasingly irritable as time went on. Eventually Patricia came into the kitchen.

"Nice chat?" Becca asked.

"Very pleasant, Victoria has gone to her room. She's tired apparently."

"Was it much of a conversation?"

"I wouldn't exactly call it that," Patricia said. "We started talking about family and friendships. I told her something of mine. It wasn't until some way in that I realised she seemed uncomfortable. I fear; she may have made a few comparisons with current events. It wasn't my intention to do anything of the kind and if I've caused offence you must let me apologise."

"I wouldn't worry. Victoria can put two and two together and come up with five on any subject."

"Well, my darling, if an apology is needed, I'm more than happy to clarify my intentions. I don't want to make things worse between the two of you. My mouth can run away with itself at times."

"I don't think things can get any worse. Or, at least I'm trying not to add to the baggage of my relationship with her. If nothing more, I want to say goodbye to her without being left with another pile of baggage to deal with."

"Very sensible, I would say. Anyway, my darling, you know where I am if you need anything. I'll leave you to your porridge. I'll see myself out."

Becca was about to say it's pasta, but then she looked properly at the plate.

She didn't see any more of her sister that night and frankly was relieved. Victoria had what she wanted. That at least was settled and she wondered if she would see her in the morning before she left for work. The thought occurred to her that this might be the last time she saw her. They had no other reason to stay in touch and a part of her felt sad about that. It was an ending, a parting of the ways, if nothing else it was the last of something that was familiar. At least she now probably had the evening to herself, it had been a long day at work, knowing she was coming home to something else that needed working at and not an evening relaxing, or at least unwinding.

Her initial relief passed; she couldn't help but be drawn back to the revelation of her mother's supposed guilt. She hadn't expected to hear the word used in relation to her mother. She could cope with her mother's low opinion of her, she could use that as a justification for leaving, but someone else's guilt was a different matter entirely, even if it had only been momentary. She had two choices, two ways to go from here. Dwell on the negative, or move forward and look to the future. Common sense pointed her in the obvious direction.

Her sister was up before her, Becca looked at her clock. She must have been up at the crack of dawn. Becca had ten minutes more in bed, before her own alarm went off and she would have to get ready for work. Did she stay in bed or get up? She heard Victoria zip her bag closed. It sounded as if she was leaving. She got up and allowed instinct to guide her actions. Round three? Victoria was putting on her coat.

"I intended not to wake you."

"It's time I was up anyway, you were going without a goodbye," Becca stated the obvious, did she sound disappointed.

"I think enough was said last night."

"We're very different, I suppose and never really had much in common. But that said we are sisters and I didn't want you to leave without at least a goodbye." Becca wasn't really sure she believed that herself, but she was determined to do what she could to leave the door open for her sister.

"I think it's too late for goodbyes, you made that quite clear before mam died. And as for that little sermon your posh friend delivered last night. I would rather have heard that from you than her. At least you could've had the guts to say that to my face rather than have some lacky cast aspersions."

"I've no idea what Patricia said last night. And anything I need to say to you, I can say for myself."

"I doubt that very much."

Rebecca held her tongue, it seemed that Victoria was determined to make it easy for her to say goodbye. Not intentionally, but true to form. Nothing was ever going to change.

"Well," Becca began. "You know where I live, you have my address and phone number."

"Oh, don't worry," Victoria snapped. "I know where to send the cheque, you needn't worry about that."

"That's not what I meant."

"I can think of no other reason to call, or contact you. We're sisters, but not by choice. That was forced upon us. I have casual acquaintances I am closer to than you…"

Becca interrupted, if Victoria was starting one of her speeches, she'd have to continue it on the other side of the door. "I'll get the door for you." She walked past her sister and opened the door. Victoria was caught short and had to think to close her mouth. But as usual, seemed determined to have the last word, a final stab. She walked out of the flat and turned. "Mam was right about you. You were…"

Becca closed the door. Enough.

Chapter 17

Plus, One…

Becca sat watching Ann bake, there was something mesmeric about it, or was it just relaxing. She did it with quiet skill that made it look deceptively easy. It brought back memories of watching her Aunty Irene bake. Coffee cake, jam tarts, fairy cakes. All iced and decorated, all delicious. The smell of baking, her aunty's kitchen, the open door in the summer and the smell of tomatoes ripening in the greenhouse nearby. Her Sunday visits seemed a lifetime ago, but still remained clear in her mind. Sitting here now, was a reminder of good times.

They chatted about this and that. The weather, the news, what was on at the cinema. About Ben and James. Ann talked about her sister in America.

"Speaking of sisters. Have you heard from yours?" Ann ventured.

"No, but I didn't expect to."

"An' how do you feel about that?"

"Fine. It's the way it is. I still find it odd she came down though."

"As you said it could well have been to save paying money to the solicitor, it sounded important to her. But she may have had similar thoughts to you."

"How do you mean?"

"She might have wanted to be certain that it was a time for a parting of the ways."

"I hadn't thought of it like that. You're right though, if I wanted to walk away with a clear conscience, why wouldn't she."

Ann paused in her mixing. "We all have reasons for our actions, no matter how odd they may seem to others. The main thing, however, is that you feel alright about it."

"I think I am." She'd had this conversation in her head, not especially to Ann, but one of those inner talks when she tried to sort out her feelings, tried to make sense of things for her own piece of mind. It was good to be able to really speak to someone about it. "When I finally realised things were never going to change between my mother and me, it took me time to come to terms with that. It's different with my sister. We didn't get on from the start and enough of the kids at school disliked their siblings for it to seem normal. Even after a year of not seeing each other, we went straight to it, arguing as if no time had passed."

"It's interesting that friends may not see each other in months, and pick up from where they left off. Talking as if they have never been parted. It's the same at the opposite end of the scale. Society, if you like, understands that not everyone can get on with each other, and accepts that brothers and sisters might not to get on at all, but..."

"But not so easily understand about mothers and daughters."

"Exactly."

Becca smiled. "Thanks."

"You are welcome," Ann said. "But what for?"

"I'm not sure how I'd have coped if you hadn't come to see me the night I returned from the funeral. There was so much going on in my head. You kept me on an even keel. Even Jack and Ben's little plan did what I needed it too."

"That's talking, for you. It does wonders."

"I think you're right. There's only the money from the will and what to do with it. My mother hadn't meant to leave it to me, time caught up with her before she could change her will."

"Have you had any thoughts on what you might do?"

"I don't want it. I thought about giving it to charities."

Ann stopped and put down the tin she was greasing. "Whatever money your mother has is also half your father's. Would he have wanted you to have some?"

"Victoria said something about that. Dad would have, yes."

"Then perhaps you might bear that in mind while you think about your choices. Best thing is not to rush into anything,"

"I won't, there isn't any reason to."

Ann began spooning cake mix into her pans ready to go in the oven.

Becca noticed four more cooling. "This is a lot of cake, if there's ever such a thing."

"I'm doing them for Patricia, she's been busy. Did you know she has had an offer for the café?"

"Really, that quick. She thought it could take years."

"Apparently, the café has 'retro' appeal. I do think she has been lucky, the right person just happened to come along at the right time. But it's not a done deal."

"Is it a good offer?"

"Well, it's one she is willing to accept."

Becca felt pleased and sorry all at the same time. She loved visiting the café, loved its timeless appeal, but Patricia was the important one here not nostalgia. "More change," Becca said. "I could do with things being boring for a while."

"Ben and James, Jack and Sarah, Patricia and the cafe. There is a lot of it about. But if there is one thing we can guarantee, it's change. I'm not sure who I'm quoting but they said, nothing good ever gets away. We all value this little family of ours far too much to let it go. I think we're stuck with each for the duration."

***

This was it, a night of firsts and lasts. The last time they would eat at Patricia's and the first time they would all be together. Ben and James, Jack and Sarah, Ann and Patricia and Becca, the plus one. The happy spinster, should she bring knitting, have a cat, smell of violets and start talking to her plants? Maybe not yet. Anyway, she felt as if she should make some effort tonight, this would be the first time she'd meet Sarah, she wanted to make a good impression. That awkward balance between not looking like she'd made an effort, but actually had. Then there was the trickier, being friendly, but not overly welcoming to the point of weird. Would Sarah like her? Would she like Sarah? She felt a bit nervous and wondered if the others were too. Either way, it would probably be harder for Sarah meeting everyone in one big group like this.

Patricia and Ann were in the small kitchen arguing, or as Patricia put it constructively discussing. Ben and James hadn't arrived yet; Ben needed to finish his act and then get cleaned up before arriving. Now Jack and Sarah came in, Becca gave smiling eye contact to both in equal measure. Jack gave her his usual hug and Becca made a point of hugging Sarah.

Sarah looked at her with relief. "I'm so glad you did that. I never know whether to hug, kiss, shake hands, bow or rub noses."

Becca laughed, recognising her own dilemmas in someone else. "I'm usually terrible at it. This is probably the first time I've got it right."

"Well done," Jack said. "There's hope for you yet."

Sarah was introduced to Patricia and Ann; it quickly became clear she was going to fit right in. Becca glanced over to Jack, he was looking at her with an expectant look on his face, Becca winked.

Ben and James arrived and there were more hellos and nice-to-meet-yous and heard-so-much-about-yous. Jack seemed relieved that everyone was getting on.

The other tables had been put to the side, so that they could set out one long one in the middle of the café. They sat talking and laughing, exchanging stories, catching Sarah up on tales and making sure Jack didn't get too full of himself. He took the ribbing in good humour and it felt like they'd all known each other for years. Patricia regaled them with stories about the café, the near fire, the police raid, the woman with the farting Chihuahua, the man with the broken belt and the loose change, the aged sisters and the exploding eggs. The stories were entertaining, the food was excellent and pudding earning that special silence that only a good dessert can. It was a fitting meal to end that chapter of the cafe's life and Patricia's time with it. Becca sat looking about the table. Seven very different people, but a family of sorts, no less and she was quite happy to be their plus one.

"My darlings, I can't think of any other people I would rather share this evening with. Without you I think I may have continued the daily routine of this place and lost myself in old age. You have all brought something to my life I thought I'd lost. This isn't an ending, it's a new beginning. Wherever life takes us, may we never truly be parted."

They raised their glasses to words Becca wholeheartedly agreed with.

Chapter 18

Newbie...

Becca was up early. It was odd not hearing Patricia go out at the crack of dawn. She'd heard Jack bound down the stairs for his run, before he bounded back up, only to descend half an hour later, equally boundy, as he headed off to work. She'd heard Ben come in during the wee small hours of the morning, tired feet trying not to clump their way up the stairs. That only left Ann's footsteps to make themselves heard. No more hair man, or high heels, pauses or early bird. They all had proper names now. Becca looked at the clock. She'd almost used up her ten minutes between first and second alarm. It would be going off again and she'd have no choice but to get up and join all of the other humans racing to work.

When their DVD nights continued uninterrupted Becca felt pleasantly reassured that she'd gained a friend in Sarah, but more importantly hadn't lost the close friendship she enjoyed with Jack and Ben. The three sat watching something that had announced itself as the hilarious, laugh out loud, must see, feel good film of the year. The fact that it was only June and that the film had to tell you, it was all of these things, had made them all suspicious before they played it. Watching it offered little more than mutual groans and a plot that had been repeated tenfold in any number of recent comedies. The pizzas they ate, were not a let-down and the half time cake was the highlight of the evening.

Jack yawned and stretched. "That was hilarious then," he pressed the remote.

"Could have been worse," Becca offered.

"Babes, come on, I can raise more laughs than that when the club's empty."

"I was thinking," Jack knew the minute he'd spoken it was a mistake. "Yes, I do that sometimes, so don't bother yourselves. As I was about to say, we've not done a road trip in a long time. How about next weekend we head out?"

"Great."

"As long as we're back by seven. Pasta's covered enough for me lately. I owe her now."

"No problem. We can be back for then, drop you at the club."

"Sounds great," Becca said. "Did you have anywhere in mind?"

"Nope, I thought we could decide that now."

"I've an idea," Ben jumped in. "It fits in with that retro theme we stared a while back. It's somewhere I used to go to as a kid. I've not been for ages, but I think you'll both like it.

The weather was okay for June, warmish, cloudyish, dryish. As they drove south, along what Ben said was called the coast road, Becca realised she'd been in her flat for over a year. That first day, opening the front door for the first time, opening her own door and stepping into the empty flat. Her shoes echoing off the boards and around the white walls. The smell of fresh paint, a fresh start for her. She thought back to her life then; how much it and indeed, she had changed. So much behind her, but more in front.

They parked in a car park that seemed to mark the transition between the newer part of the village and the older part. They walked past a small café at the top and headed down a steep path to the original fishing village. The community that had been there for hundreds of years. With every ten steps they seemed to leave the modern world further behind. For the most part the village had resisted many of the changes that had robbed other places of their character. The cobbled street sloped its way between the mixture of Victorian, Georgian and older houses. There was a museum and gift shops. There was a sweet shop, an art shop, another café, a butchers and two pubs. All felt a part of this living museum. Eventually coming out at a harbour, they sat on benches, a pub to their left and houses behind them, with enviable views out to sea. The tide was out and so the small number of boats either sat or leaned, patiently waiting for its return. Children and dogs played on the beach, the seagulls made their presence heard and the sun was trying to come out. They bought crab sandwiches and something delicious called cobbler cake from a tiny café and sat eating and chatting with the rest of the world going about its business.

"This is great," Becca put down her cup. "And what a view."

"Yep, best seats in the house," Jack agreed.

Ben was looking out to sea. "If you sailed out in that direction," he pointed," Where would you end up?"

Becca followed his line of sight, as if somehow that would help. "Denmark possibly."

"Speaking of Denmark," Jack leaned forward slightly to look across Becca at Ben. "How's things going with James?"

Ben tried to look none comital, but the edges of his lips gave things away. "Really good, almost too good."

"What makes you say that?" Jack asked.

"In the past, when things have been this nice, something's gone wrong and I've ended up watching The Bridges of Madison County."

"Is that bad? Jack asked, not knowing the film.

"Bad enough, though it's a good film," Ben added. "I can't shake the feeling that somewhere along the line he's going to realise it's just me he's dating and get bored."

"Nope," Jack shook his head. "That's not going to happen."

"Babes, I hope so,"

"Believe us, he sees it," Jack added. "He's no fool."

"And what about you?" Becca turned to look at Jack.

"What about me?"

"You and Sarah."

He shrugged. "We're good. I like her, she seems to like me."

"Why wouldn't she?" Becca asked. "There's a lot to like."

"You know what I mean." Jack was getting awkward.

"Well, we all like her, you seem happy together and she says a lot about you."

"You've talked?"

"We have. I think she was checking me out as much as I was checking her out."

Jack looked at her. "And?"

"Sarah was just making sure I wasn't some secret torch bearer. I was making sure she was good enough for you. Once we'd got that out of the way we got on with talking about far more interesting things. She's asked me to be bridesmaid. I've already bought the dress."

"And I've got a hat, a really big one with flowers and feathers."

"How did I end up with friends like you two?" he groaned.

"You get the friends you deserve," Becca gave him a nudge.

"I wasn't joking," Ben was looking at both of them. "I really have got a hat like that."

"So, what about you?" Jack was now looking at Becca.

"I've got all I need, thank you very much."

It was another of those days when everything fell into place. The sort of day that reminded Becca what life was really about. Ben and Jack had gone paddling in the sea and were now trying to soak each other like a pair of ten years-olds. Time to join them. As she stood up, she looked out beyond the beach and the harbour, past the landmark cliff and out to the sea. The sky may have been overcast, but there were no dark clouds on the horizon.

***

"Hi," it was a high energy greeting, the type Becca would give to a very close friend she'd not seen in months. "Hello, you're my first neighbour," still a huge smile and lots of accompanying gestures with one hand, while the other hugged a box. The gestures were a language in themselves and Becca wondered what they would look like with the sound off, Tina would be hard pushed to match them. The new girl shook Becca's hand, but didn't stop to draw breath. "It's so great to meet you. I'm so pleased. Isn't it exciting? I've been up and down these stairs and I'm pooped and I wondered, would I meet any one and what would they be like and now I have and you're so great and I'm so pleased."

It was totally infectious and Becca could feel herself going from groan it's Monday night to yeeha it's Friday. Soon she was grinning and bouncing up and down, and a few seconds later they were giggling, but Becca did manage to stop herself from emulating the little squeals of joy the other emitted like a baby dolphin.

There were hurried footsteps from above and Jack appeared. "Is everything okay, I could hear screaming or something?"

"Hi, neighbour. I'm…" she suddenly looked back to Becca. Finger swirling at the side of her head. "Oh no, listen to me, haven't even said who I am. Jessica, Jess for short, did I say I'm so pleased to meet you. She seemed to teleport up the three stairs to where Jack stood, bemused by the energy ball now moving into flat six.

"I'm Jessica, Jess for short," she shook his hand off.

"Err, yep, I'm Jack. Pleased to meet you."

Then somehow, she was back beside Becca, shaking her hand. "I'm Jessica, Jess for short. So excited." She gave Becca another full-on beaming smile, even brighter than Jack's.

"I'm Becca, its lovely to have someone in the top flat at last."

"I know, such a long way up," she did a quick impression of a rocket going up and down.

"What the hell's going on down here, has someone formed a cat's choir?"

"Oh wow, I love it, another neighbour and you wear wigs, I love wigs."

Ben's eyes did a quick up check, he'd forgot it was on. "Beyoncé. New delivery," he explained.

"It's fantastic, I'm Jessica, Jess for short, that's what everyone calls me."

"And I'm Ben and aren't you just one crackling ball of energy. I'll get my jump leads."

"I'm not normally like this, but this is just so great and you're all so great," she wrinkled up her face and did a little dance. "When I'm settled, you've all got to come round. I do great salad and cocktails."

"Now you're talking, babes. Come on, give me the box, let's get you sorted out. You got any more of these?"

"Loads," Jessica enthused as if it was some brilliant game.

"I'm parked outside."

"Yep, and so is half the road," Jack said. "Which one's yours?"

"Oh, you can't miss it, you'll know it's mine the minute you see it."

Becca and Jack headed for the door. "Yep," Jack muttered to Becca. "It'll be the one hovering two feet off the floor with fireworks coming out of the top.

Chapter 19

Jam by the Stairs…

Blue sky, sunshine. She took the long route back from the station, wanting to make the most of the light and the warmth. A quick stop for milk and then down no railings avenue and on to long terrace. Passed grey tower church, along the side of the little green and then onto her road. Maybe she'd go for a walk in the park once she'd got in and changed. She'd have to fend for herself for the next couple of weeks; Jack was away with work, Sarah was catching up with friends, Ben had taken James and the house of drag queens on a staff holiday, Patricia and Ann would have set off that afternoon to Denmark on a biking tour and Jess had left Becca in charge of her plant collection, while she visited a sister in sunbeam sparkle land. Things had changed, but in a good way and she had changed with them, not totally sorted, but then she'd always considered herself a work in progress.

"Hey,"

The shout came from behind her, still some way off.

"Hey there. Hi, excuse me."

Did she turn? Was it anything to do with her? In the end she thought it best. It was a man and now that she'd stopped, he jogged to catch up. It was a trot, not a sprint, he didn't look threatening. But then in the zombie movies how many times had she shouted at the screen,

Run, he's after you. Don't just stand there.

It was the same thing as the creaking noise in the cellar,

Oh, I know, I'll go and have a look, I'm totally alone and what do you know, the light's not working, but I'll go and check anyway.

Was this when she should run, he was getting close.

He'd slowed. "Hi, this could be really embarrassing, but I think we've met. It's the red bag that I spotted. Are you zombie girl?"

Becca managed to look bemused, and puzzled all at the same time. Then she looked at the purse she was carrying.

"Halloween, sat on the wall, I had to run off after my god son." He was rattling the description off as quickly as he could, either to reassure her he wasn't a stalker, or because he was starting to think he'd got the wrong person.

Strangely, amongst all of the things he'd just said, Becca only really registered god son.

"It was you I talked too wasn't it?" he added hopefully.

"It was, and yes it's the same red purse. Nice to see you back in the world of the living. You found a cure as well."

He was puzzled for only an instant. "Got you, not a zombie anymore. You've stopped eating brains too."

"Totally cured, just the occasional steak these days."

"Bacon sandwiches are my downfall."

"Now you're talking."

Zombie man suddenly realised something. And held out his hand. "No manners," he apologised. "Thom."

"Becca." She shook his hand and then realised she was grinning, but then so was he.

How long had they talked for? She had no idea, she just knew that the conversation had flowed and that all the way through he'd smiled and she'd smiled and bang, the spark had sprung into life. She hadn't wanted to stop talking. He'd asked for her mobile number, which she'd had every intention of giving him. They'd said goodbye and he'd walked through the gate of the house opposite. She'd stopped looking and there he'd been, right under her nose all this time. A colony of butterflies had taken refuge in her stomach and held aloft, she now floated over the road, up the steps and banged into the front door. Best open it first. He had gone in, hadn't he? It wouldn't be fair if he'd seen that.

It felt strange knowing they were all away. The place seemed empty. She closed the door and turned, and there it was, a jar of jam by the stairs.

Please take a few moments to write a review on Amazon. Honest, constructive feedback is very welcome and encourages writers to continue publishing.

Thanks for reading.

Also

You can contact me at

leemeason@icloud.com

Printed in Great Britain
by Amazon